Dear
Secret Pal
you said you li
Books and this one
Looks... interesting?
HaHa, ♡ you

♡ Kristen

Secrets

of the

Model
Dorm

Secrets

of the

Model
Dorm

a novel

Amanda Kerlin
and Phil Oh

ATRIA BOOKS

New York   London   Toronto   Sydney

ATRIA BOOKS

1230 Avenue of the Americas
New York, NY 10020

ISBN-13: 978-0-7432-9826-1
ISBN-10:   0-7432-9826-8

First Atria Books hardcover edition January 2007

10   9   8   7   6   5   4   3   2   1

ATRIA BOOKS is a trademark of Simon & Schuster, Inc.

Manufactured in the United States of America

Designed by Jaime Putorti

For information about special discounts for bulk purchases,
please contact Simon & Schuster Special Sales at
1-800-456-6798 or business@simonandschuster.com.

Prologue

TOM FORD YIPPED FROM INSIDE the bedroom, his tiny claws scratching against the door. His whining was the last thing I wanted to hear after a long day of castings.

"I wouldn't do that if I were you," Kylie said, sloshing around a half-drunk martini.

"Why?" I asked, turning the handle of the bedroom door. Tom Ford bolted from the room, his little legs carrying him as fast as they could. I immediately regretted not heeding her advice: My sixteen-year-old roommate's long, thin model legs were splayed out to each side of her bed. On top of her was a man, pumping away and shouting in a South American accent. Our poor dog, Tom Ford, had been trapped in the bedroom—terrified by their cries of pleasure; he'd been desperate to get out.

The metal frame bunk bed creaked so loudly that they didn't hear me come in. I stood in the doorway, dumbstruck. Not because I'd walked in on my sixteen-year-old roommate getting drilled by her Latin lover. That in and of itself wasn't so shocking. What *did* catch my attention was the fact that she was entirely naked—except for the pair of Dior heels she had strapped to her feet. *My Dior* heels. The guy quickened his pace, and the heels started banging against the bottom of the top bunk. Shit, that can't be good for the shoes. I debated trying to sneak them off without her noticing, but decided that after her fun I'd just give her a little talk about how we *ask* before we borrow people's things.

I closed the door and left them to finish their business.

"I *told* you not to do that," Kylie said, taking a sip of her drink.

On the couch, Lucia was crying again. All six-foot-one of her was laid across the cushions, her face buried in a throw pillow. She peeked her tear-soaked face at me, reached mournfully to the coffee table, and pulled another Kleenex from the box. Tom Ford licked her hand, trying to comfort her, to no avail. After blowing her delicate reddened nose into it, Lucia threw the Kleenex onto the pyramid of other used tissues. She was quiet for about a second, then her skinny body started shaking again as the sobs came. Kylie, who was sitting in pajamas on the chair next to her, looked annoyed. Lucia's crying was distracting her from the television just as her favorite character was getting voted off the Survivor island.

"Shut up, Lucia. . . . Shut up! And watch it—you're getting makeup all over the couch," the redheaded Kylie said in a slurred Australian accent in between chugs of her drink.

I should have asked the Slovak what's wrong, but I probably already knew the answer—she was depressed, so pretty much anything was liable to send her waterworks spurting.

Usually either: a) she was missing her home, family, and cows in Slovakia, b) she missed her photographer ex-boyfriend who had dumped her for a younger model, c) her older married man had canceled a hotel date to spend time with his wife, or d) some interesting combo of the previous three.

Kylie drained her martini glass and hiccuped a bit. She stood up, all wobbly from vodka, and took her empty glass into the kitchen for a refill. She measured out two spoonfuls of Metamucil Orange that she then mixed with straight, chilled vodka to make her specialty—the Metamucil martini. It was a sad fact that Metamucil and vodka were about the only things we had in the kitchen.

I sat down on the armrest, next to the sniffling Slovak, and looked suspiciously at the bedroom door. A couple of the girl's banshee wails crept out, and I feared for the safety of my Diors.

Lucia started to pull herself up a bit, having gotten over whatever was bothering her. Her lip still quivered as she looked in her compact mirror and tried to clean up the mess her tears had made. She was wearing a very revealing Dolce & Gabbana dress her married boyfriend had bought her—it looked like she had been on her way out before falling prey to a case of the weeps.

"Heath Ledger supposed to be at Marquee tonight, Svetlana said," Lucia told me as she applied damage control to her face. "Lucia like Heath."

"Isn't he married, too?"

She didn't seem to hear me.

Soon Lucia was ready to go again. She stood up, smoothed her dress, and looked at herself in the mirror on the wall.

"How's my makeup?"

"Don't worry, you look beautiful, Lucia," I said.

"Really?"

"Really," I answered. She smiled at me. And I wasn't lying—she *was* beautiful. I guess we all were, or at least were considered interesting-looking enough to be offered New York modeling contracts based on nothing but a dream, our complexion, and slender bodies.

"I will get Heath's number," she said as she snatched her fake Prada bag and walked defiantly out the door for the club, where she would never meet any A-list celebs, but instead another sea of

desperate investment bankers with too much money, too much cocaine, and too little sex in their lives.

Just as soon as Lucia left the apartment, Kylie shot past on the
way to the bathroom—she'd had one too many sips of her Metamucil martini. Slamming the door shut, she began puking—a little
more violently than usual. I sighed, took off my flats, walked over to
the bathroom door, and knocked.

"Are you all right, Kylie?" I asked through the door.

"Uh-oh," I heard her say as soon as she stopped heaving.

"What?" I asked.

"Who the hell left their bloody Manolos next to the toilet?" she said.

At this the man emerged from our bedroom, half-dressed, his
dark skin glistening with a postcoital aura. I recognized him from
the party circuit: The latest victim of Christiane's boundless libido
was a Brazilian male model. Inside the bathroom Kylie started barfing again. The Brazilian walked to the door and pointed at it with a
worried look on his face.

"Will she be long?"

NOW ALL THIS MAY SEEM STRANGE, but it was utterly routine
to me at this point. You see, I had lived in the model dorm for almost six months by the time Lucia went on her wild-goose chase
for Heath Ledger, Kylie puked on the $700 heels Svetlana got
from one of her Russian mafia boyfriends, and the hot Brazilian
came out of our bedroom, oblivious to the fact that he'd just had
incredibly loud sex with a sixteen-year-old. It all came with the
territory.

Just arrived from Eastern European countries with names I
sometimes couldn't even pronounce, from cow towns in the Mid-
west, from the rough favelas of Rio, we were all aspiring models,

landing in the dorm with visions of *Vogue* spreads and Fashion Week runways dancing in our heads.

The model dorm was where the Agency stuck the new girls. Girls who were new to modeling, new to the country, or who just weren't making enough money to live anywhere else. For $2,000 a month we had the privilege of sharing a bedroom with three, four, or even five other girls—in bunk beds—in our "very own" one-bedroom apartment in the lifeless Financial District, in far downtown Manhattan. Since none of us were regularly landing well-paying modeling jobs, we couldn't afford to pay rent on our own, so the Agency charged it to our accounts, which meant that any money we earned would go directly back to our Agency before we even had a chance to spend a nickel of it. The money covered the room, no board, a small weekly stipend, and—naturally—unlimited access to the gym several floors below.

We were merely girls, the oldest of us only twenty-two, all of a sudden leading grown-up lives with no supervision—save for the weekly measurements at the Agency. We weren't going to college, but this was our own university—instead of classes on Plato or biochemistry, we had to learn how to walk properly and survive on two calories a day. We were dropped in the middle of the most exciting city in the world, crammed together in a ten-by-twelve-foot bedroom. We made the model dorm our home. This book is the story of that dorm: high treachery, backseat blowjobs, cocaine diets, illicit pregnancies, $1,000 bottles of champagne, wealthy club managers from France, tears, couture fashion, and all.

LIKE MOST YOUNG GIRLS, I occasionally fantasized about strutting down the runway, a supermodel, next to Cindy Crawford, Naomi Campbell, or Christy Turlington. I'd flip through the pages of my mother's fashion magazines, entranced by the beautiful women in their beautiful clothes, a glossy world that seemed to be another planet altogether. But I never thought that a modeling career was in my cards, especially after beginning that sadistic social experience known as junior high. As a result of an early growth spurt, I towered awkwardly over my classmates, teetering down the school's hallways, not quite in control of my limbs. The other kids teased me constantly—especially the popular girls. My school day basically became an exercise in trying to keep as under the radar as I could, which wasn't easy, considering that my lanky body made me instantly recognizable in a crowd. It also didn't help with the boys. It seemed like I was a foot taller than them—I'll leave it to you to imagine how we looked when slow-dancing at school functions.

Then, over the summer between eighth grade and high school, something happened. It was like my body told the rest of me to hurry up already, and things filled out, my knees were no longer quite so knobby, my face seemed to take shape gracefully, and I was ushered into the early stages of womanhood. I was still taller than everybody else, but my first day in high school was a revelation. Boys started staring at me as I passed in the hallways. At first I thought maybe there was something really wrong with me, but I realized quickly that their gawking was a positive thing. The girls were still mean, but now it was because their boyfriends were paying attention to me. It was the good kind of attention.

One day at the beach, the summer after my freshman year, I noticed a man with a camera gazing intently at me. My friends teased me about it, and I blushed red. All of a sudden, they stood up and ran into the surf, laughing shrilly and leaving me alone. I looked through my bangs and saw the man walking toward me. I didn't know whether to run off too, but before I could decide, he was beside me.

"Hi, I'm Greg." He put out his hand, wearing a disarming smile that put me at ease. "I'm a professional photographer. Have you ever thought about being a model?"

Not seriously. But the seed was planted, and soon that was all I was thinking about.

Greg put me in contact with a local agency, and I started doing small-time work, shoots for local department store catalogs, fashion shows at local malls. I started getting used to the nuances and quirks of the industry, and smelled the bigger, glamorous world out there, much more exciting than Saturday-morning trips past the food court on makeshift runways. New York was never far from my mind.

Now that I was a model, almost overnight I went from serving as the butt of my classmates' jokes to being the girl everyone said was pretty and stuck up. Everyone except my parents, that is. Not that they thought I was ugly or anything—far from it—it's just that they didn't want me to get carried away by this dream. They wanted me to be more than just a pretty face, more than just arm candy to some ex-PGA player who had retired to our suburban Virginia town and ran a series of flashy car dealerships off the interstate.

My parents pictured me shuttling off to a well-respected college when I graduated high school, my transcript stocked with A.P. classes and my spirit shot through with a burning passion for the courses in English literature or political science I'd be taking—I can smell the ivy now, just thinking about it. Because for them, that was it—college straight off or a life scooping ice cream at the Dairy Queen, living in a trailer with three kids from two different fathers (one of whom was in jail), scratching lottery tickets all day in hopes of winning it big.

Well, I didn't even finish high school. I had a different idea. I was going to be a model.

1

AS THE PLANE DESCENDED TO JFK, I caught glimpses of the New York City landmarks that were so familiar from the movies—the Brooklyn Bridge, the Empire State Building, Central Park. It was what I now recognize as one of those glorious early September days just after Labor Day, when the humidity has finally broken and everyone decides it's finally safe to return from the Hamptons or venture out of their air-conditioned apartments—as good a day as any to begin my career as a hopeful supermodel in New York.

After the small-town work in Virginia, I had signed on with a boutique agency in Miami and spent time working small swimsuit shoots, a flash of prestige here and there. Miami's like a farm team for the big leagues. While in Florida, a representative of the Agency scouted me. My heart palpitated in the meeting—what was going to

happen? It was short and sweet. They liked my look. I had the potential for big, big things. Would I consider relocating to New York
and signing with the Agency? They'd put me up in their special
apartment for their girls. *Would I consider relocating to New York?* It
seemed like the dumbest question in the world at the time, like asking a man who's been trekking across a desert for five days straight,
"Would you care for a sip of water?"

And so here I was, in the city.

Outside the baggage claim waited a shuttle the Agency had
arranged, and my bags and I were soon zipping toward my future—*as a
model in New York!* Even though I'm generally levelheaded and had
modeled in Miami, the thought made my breath catch for a second.
This was where it all happened, where I could make an actual career. A
tingling started in the back of my neck and crept down to my wiggling
toes. I closed my eyes, sank down in the seat, and wallowed in the feeling for a moment, my imagination taken away by a movie montage of
clichéd ideas—skipping down Fifth Avenue in couture Chanel just
bought from Saks, strolling through Central Park with a handsome man
on an autumn day when all the leaves seemed to be setting the ground
on fire, sipping cocktails at one of New York's hot spots at a table with
the city's glitterati, making the cover of W magazine. . . .

When I opened my eyes, we were on the Brooklyn Bridge.
Through the windows of the speeding vehicle I saw the skyscrapers
in Midtown, their lights twinkling in the evening. They looked close
enough to touch.

The shuttle came to an abrupt halt in front of a building that
looked like all the other ones, except for a stainless-steel sign that
spelled out the building's name above its glass doors, MAISON 46.

The driver turned to me. "Here you go, miss." He jumped out
and pulled my bags into the lobby for me.

On the street, I paused to look around. Turning slowly in one place on the sidewalk, I peered up into the purple night sky. The skyscrapers seemed to rise forever.

The driver came out of the building after bringing in my last bag and saw me standing, frozen to the ground.

"This is not right address?" he asked me with some concern. "The street and number same you gave me."

"No, no, it's right. I was just thinking," I answered, breaking my eyes away from the sliver of sky.

He didn't move, and I realized he was probably looking for a tip. I opened my handbag and saw I had only the crisp hundred-dollar bill my mother had pressed into my hand before sending me off on what she considered to be a foolish girlish whim that I would be returning from in a month, obviously admitting how right she and my father had been the whole time.

The driver saw my hesitation as I looked into my purse and smiled at me. "Don't worry—next time, okay?"

The shuttle careened down the street to its next destination and, after its taillights faded, I turned to what would be my new home. From inside the glass doors, the doorman looked at me, and I decided not to keep my new home waiting.

I pushed open the tall doors and entered into the lobby, which had a dull sheen from the brushed steel that lined the walls. The doorman stood upright at his shiny desk in an impeccable maroon uniform with matching cap. He looked me up and down with an amused expression on his face.

"Apartment 1480?" he asked.

"Yes, but how did you—?" I asked, surprised. Had the Agency left my picture?

"Ms. Johnston, correct?" he cut me off. "The elevators to the fourteenth floor are on the left."

"Don't I need a key?" I asked innocently enough.

He chuckled. "I'm sure the door'll be unlocked, don't you worry. Try to get one of the girls to make you a copy. Good luck."

I STOOD AND LOOKED at the number on the door: 1480. Taking a breath, I turned the knob—it really was unlocked. The door swung slowly open and I had the first look at what was to be my new home. The living room looked as if it had been transplanted directly from some eight-year-old IKEA showroom—once-snappy side tables with their paint now a bit chipped, a stained red sofa bed, along with a few wobbly wooden stools, indicated the Agency's taste in modern design. (And its frugality.) The indoor carpeting was pocked with a few large, suspicious-looking splotches.

The first thing I noticed besides the furniture and dilapidated carpet was Kylie, just as you met her earlier. She lay slumped down on a dingy overstuffed chair, her long legs coming together at the knees, then forking out lazily. She looked about my age—eighteen or so, although everyone's perennially eighteen in the modeling business. With a martini glass teetered dangerously in her hand, she snored a little bit, passed out in front of the television while her idol, Heidi Klum, was auf'ing another wannabe designer. Kylie's mother, herself a martini-sipping television aficionado, had named her daughter after the actress in *Neighbours,* her favorite Australian soap opera. Ironically, it's Kylie Minogue's signature feature, her juicy ass, that our Kylie spent hours squatting and lunging to avoid. Her red hair was meticulously done, and the makeup on her face, with its defined cheekbones and almost perfect symmetry, looked stunning. I found out later that she had been on another series of unsuccessful castings that day. After work she had changed into decidedly unglamorous sweatpants and a ratty T-shirt, which I would come to find was her nightly uniform for getting wasted on her special "regulating" cocktails.

Farther off, in the corner of the apartment, was a rickety computer desk. A girl leaned sideways in the chair, clacking away at the keyboard. She was wearing a pink floral silk robe that hung loosely on her delicate shoulders. It wasn't fastened all the way. Her ponytail bobbed as she typed and puffed on a cigarette, halfheartedly trying to blow the smoke out the window, then ashing in a coffee mug. She didn't even turn when the door opened.

I let the door swing closed behind me and put down my bags. Kylie woke up with a snort. She opened her glassy eyes and peered at me, confused for a second.

"Hi, I'm Heather," I said, smiling, stepping forward to shake her hand when I saw she had woken up fully. Kylie put her glass down and stood up woozily to greet me.

"Oh, hello. I thought they mentioned something about a new girl coming in," she said in a lilting Australian accent. "I'm Kylie—you didn't bring any duty-free, by chance, did you? I think we're out. Except whiskey. I can't stand bourbon, all that bloody sugar, you know, and from corn."

"Oh, no, I didn't. . . . I'm from Virginia, so it was a domestic flight," I said.

"Whatever. I'll go get some downstairs in a few. Anyway, welcome." Now that she was fully awake, she gave me the once-over suspiciously.

Kylie looked me up and down for the first time, then relaxed. I seemed to pass her test—of nondirect competition, I would find out later. Kylie was a shorter (only five-ten) model, better suited for high-fashion print work, and the Agency had told me I was better suited for more commercial work, like catalogs and lad mags like *Maxim* or *FHM*. She seemed relieved I wasn't another girl she was going to have to scrap it out with, and as a token of friendship, she put out her unsteady, gazelle-like arm to offer me a sip of her drink.

"Nip of vodka?" she asked.

Not wanting to be rude, I took the glass from her and had a small sip. I almost spit it right back up, and Kylie laughed.

"They all do that the first time—Metamucil martini, a specialty I've concocted here," she said, snatching the glass from me and taking a drink of her own. "Nothing bloody better to unwind a girl and keep her nice and trim. *Trust* me."

From the corner came an angry yell in Russian, which made me jump. The girl at the computer started hitting the side of the monitor with the flat of her hand, telling it all sorts of most likely not-so-friendly things in her native language. She turned to us and, with no introduction, spoke to me in a horribly broken Russian accent. "You know computer?"

As she turned, her robe slid open, exposing a perfectly rounded breast, just one part of what I could tell was a textbook model body hiding under the pink silk. She was at least six feet tall, with legs that seemed to extend forever. Almost as an afterthought—not out of any sense of decency—she tied the robe back up tightly, drawing it against her defined collarbones. Her hair, tightly bound in a ponytail, was platinum blond. As for her face, it was from the classic mold that fashion types adored among Eastern Europeans—not necessarily the prettiest, but sharp and striking with exaggerated cheekbones, almost severe, like some come-to-flesh version of an expressionist painting.

"The computer?" I asked.

"Fix for Svetlana?" she asked, motioning to the frozen monitor. It took me a second to realize that when she said *Svetlana,* she was referring to herself—it was the best introduction I was going to get.

"I don't know, I can try. . . ."

"Yes, try," she said, eagerly motioning me over and putting out her cigarette in the cup.

On the screen, frozen, was what looked like a chat room, although I couldn't read anything, since it was all in Cyrillic. A picture of two naked women covered in body glitter was at the top.

"Svetlana friends," she said, pointing at the screen.

I punched a few buttons on the keyboard, but nothing happened. The space bar: nothing. Still captured on the screen, as in some time capsule, was God knows what she had been typing just a minute earlier. I went to the last resort of pressing Ctrl-Alt-Del, and the entire screen went blank.

"Oops," I said.

Svetlana saw the blank screen and looked panicked for just a second.

"I'm so sorry; it wasn't supposed to do that; it's just restarting now; just wait a second," I said.

But Svetlana was already listlessly lighting another cigarette and looking out the window, running her hand over her glistening blond hair.

"Svetlana bored," she said. "And Svetlana *hungry.*"

"You? What is your name?"

"Name? I'm Heather. It's nice to . . ."

"Heather, you and Svetlana, we do Double Seven tonight," she interrupted.

"Double Seven?"

"Yes, yes, Double Seven! We have very much fun together! Is very good!" she squealed in her Russian accent, shaking my arm.

I strung together what little I knew of Svetlana at this point—basically centered around her interest in chat rooms filled with pictures of glittery naked women. What was this Double Seven? And why does she want me to do one with her?

"I, uhh, I . . ." I stammered, trying to figure out the logistics of a double seven. "Heather and Svetlana go, yes? Best new club! Free drinks for models. Svetlana model! Heather model! We go!"

With relief, I realized she was talking about Double Seven, a hot new nightclub I had actually seen mentioned on the Page Six website while trying to study up on my adopted hometown.

"Svetlana, Heather's very tired after all the traveling, and I haven't even seen my room yet," I said. Why had I referred to myself in the third-person?

Svetlana looked a bit disappointed, but certainly not deterred.

"Okay, but tomorrow, Svetlana and Heather go for party?" She clutched my arm with her delicate fingers and looked at me with the Slavic equivalent of puppy-dog eyes, and I couldn't refuse her. She kissed me on the cheek and smiled sweetly. At that point, it seemed implausible that we would soon become best friends. Well, not really friends, but whatever.

I went to pick up a bag I had put down in order to fix the computer, and the strap slipped out of my hand. A paperback book on the artist Mark Rothko slid out onto the mottled carpet—I'd picked it up at a local bookstore before I left Virginia. Svetlana picked up the book with a puzzled look, like no printed matter besides glossy fashion magazines had ever crossed the threshold of the dorm.

"He's one of my favorites," I said to my new roommate, pointing to the book. I'd always had an interest in art since I was a child. My dad would take me to the National Gallery of Art in Washington, D.C., and show me all the colorful pastels, and I'd ooh and aah like I was watching a fireworks display. I'd started out loving the French impressionists, but since I now thought of myself as all grown up, had moved on to more edgy artists from the twentieth century. I was excited to be in New York to get a chance to see some of the most famous art in the world firsthand, and maybe even visit some of the galleries I knew were downtown, showing the latest brilliant artists from around the world.

"Have you been to MoMA?" I asked Svetlana. The Museum of Modern Art had opened again in its new building, and I couldn't wait to check it out.

Svetlana looked confused.

"Moomba? That club close long time, Svetlana never gone, but I hear Leonardo and Tobey hang out there, yes," she said, like I'd just outed myself as being hopelessly out of touch. I didn't bother correcting her.

A snore broke the moment—Kylie had passed out again, flopped in the chair. A bead of slobber ran down from her cherry-red lips onto her chin.

Svetlana took a long drag of her cigarette and looked at the Australian with a smug smile on her face. "She never get job looking like that."

The front door opened, and two girls entered, carrying bags from the pharmacy. Svetlana quickly stubbed out her cigarette and nonchalantly sat back down at the computer desk. One of the girls, who looked a bit older—maybe twenty-two—with lustrous brunette hair, still fabulous in old jeans and a hoodie, smiled widely when she saw me. She put down her bag and reached her hand out.

"Hi, I'm Laura, nice to meet you! Welcome to our palace." Laura emptied a box of tampons and three rolls of toilet paper from the plastic bag and looked quickly around the room, sniffing at the cigarette smoke. She seemed at home in that dingy living room.

"I'm Heather," I replied, shaking her slender hand. "Nice to meet you, too."

Laura turned to the girl behind her. She was a wispy, striking blond. She shyly introduced herself to me before scampering into the kitchen.

I wish I could remember her name, but she was out of the dorm in two days, sent back to wherever she had come from, having given it her shot here in New York. To tell you the truth, I can't remember half the girls who lived there—everyone seemed to blur together after a while, in and out, the few successful ones moving on to a swankier (and cheaper) place, while the majority simply were sent back home by the Agency, chewed up and spit out by the fickle beast that was the modeling industry.

Picking up the T.P. from the table, Laura brought it into the bathroom.

"Svetlana, Kylie—you guys need to pay me for the toilet paper," she called as she stashed the rolls under the sink. "I'm the only one who ever gets it, and we're always out. And it's gross—one of you guys needs to clean the toilet. I'm not the one constantly vomiting in here."·

Svetlana, logging back on the computer, pretended not to hear her, while Kylie rolled a quarter-turn in her chair and groaned a bit.

"Have you seen the room?" Laura asked as she came out of the bathroom.

"Not yet, no," I answered.

"Well, here it is, you've got one of the top bunks," she said, walking to a door next to the computer.

Bunks? I thought as she opened the door to the bedroom.

Laura flipped on the light and motioned me in. The bedroom was as shabby as the living room, except about fifty times smaller. Crammed inside were *three* sets of bunk beds. One six-compartment dresser was stuck in between a set of the bunks. Colorful skirts, panties, and jeans flowed out of the half-shut drawers. The space beneath the beds over-flowed with suitcases, other clothes they'd managed to stuff in, and all sorts of heels and boots. With barely any space to turn around between the bunks, the room seemed better suited for midgets than any other potential residents, and the thought of six model-height girls sharing it already made me feel a tad claustrophobic.

"Home sweet home," Laura said. "You'll get used to it. That one's yours." She motioned to an empty mattress on a top bunk to the left. "I bet your room back home was bigger than this, right?"

It had actually been a *lot* bigger—and I had it all to myself.

"I hope you don't have too much stuff," said Laura. I sheepishly realized I had brought about every fashionable—or at least fashion-able in Virginia Beach and Miami—article of clothing I could possibly fit in my suitcases. "The Agency treats us like queens, right?" Laura laughed at this and walked out to tend to some chores.

I took a look around by myself, and climbed up on my bunk. It squeaked loudly as I sat down. Little did I know exactly *how much* mattress-squeaking would be going on in that room.

THAT FIRST NIGHT IN THE MODEL DORM probably goes down in the books as the most peaceful of my stay there. Sure, Svetlana and one other girl I never was even introduced to came stumbling home at five A.M., but at least they were alone and had drank enough to pass out as soon as their heads hit their pillows. Everyone slept soundly that night—everyone except me, that is.

I tossed and turned, couldn't seem to get to sleep. But I'll be honest—my insomnia wasn't because I was chewing over some complex issue, or even just worrying how I'd make out as a model now that I was in New York. It was because I hadn't quite gotten the knack of sleeping with my feet dangling over the end of the bed. The Agency, apparently to save a few dollars, had settled for normal-length twin beds for the bunks, forcing me into all sorts of contortions to fit on the mattress.

Around six in the morning, the sun beginning to creep into the room through the blinds, I walked to go to the bathroom. When I got back, tiptoeing groggily into the room so I wouldn't wake anyone, I almost burst out laughing, except I was too bleary-eyed to muster the energy: Enough dawn light had come in that I saw the other four models, sleeping like angels—and all of their legs hanging awkwardly over the aluminum-pole ends of the bed frames. Just one of the occupational inconveniences of being an aspiring fashion model, I would learn.

2

THE WINDOWS OF THE AGENCY'S OFFICE peered down at me as I stood outside the next day. I felt like maybe they were even judging me, just a little bit, but that was probably my sleeplessness-induced paranoia. So I stood on the street in Soho, the crowds of fashionistas and tourists and artists dashing past me, the occasional Marc Jacobs bag brushing against my leg, its owner hurrying off to what was no doubt some terribly important meeting. *No time like the present,* I thought as I boldly stepped to the entrance and took the elevator to the Agency's floor.

I was coming in to get my marching orders for the next day or two, and to endure what would become my weekly measurements.

Entering the first door, I found a waiting area with fashion magazines tastefully arranged on the coffee table. The decor was modern and sleek. You could say it was your normal everyday upscale wait-ing room, except there was a gigantic window that opened onto the main room of the Agency—you could see and be seen alike. A tall well-dressed man saw me enter and motioned for me to go to the door leading me inside. After buzzing me in, he walked briskly to-ward me with a big smile and kissed me on both cheeks in the French fashion.

"Hi, I'm Luke, one of the bookers here. Lovely to meet you, Heather. You look *fabulous* in that shirt. So skinny!"

"Thanks. . . ." Trying to look as confident as possible, I still blushed, not expecting a compliment on walking in. I could imme-diately tell that Luke was one of those gay guys that every girl dreams of having as a friend—long on compliments, supersweet, and ready to listen.

"Who is that?!" a disembodied female voice shouted from be-hind a particularly thick partition in the office. It wasn't exactly what you'd call friendly. The tiniest of chills ran down my spine. Just for a second.

"Heather's here, Rachel."

"Oh."

And that was all I heard or saw (or *didn't* see, rather) of Rachel that first day. I knew she was the owner of the Agency, a successful ex-model herself. But what I didn't know, and would later learn, was that she was by far the most feared of those in the Agency, a pit bull of a woman in a size-two dress and stilettos, who ruthlessly told even the dangerously skinny girls to shed five pounds the day before a casting, who would dismiss you with just an icy glance. Her fa-vorite phrase when chewing out one of the girls was to start: "Do you think I made it by . . . ?" as in, "Do you think I made it by worrying about trivial things like *eating*? Quit whining." But she got girls jobs.

Luke showed me around the Agency's office. On one wall, I was faced with a mosaic of pouting lips and perfect bone structure from all the comp cards of the girls the Agency represented. Each card had the "signature" picture of the model, along with all her vitals: name, weight, height, waist size, eye color, etc. The opposite wall was plastered with the recent magazine covers and editorials the Agency's girls had appeared in. It was impressive. I wondered if I'd be up there soon, taking my place next to one of the models who had snagged an editorial in *Elle* magazine.

The tour conveniently ended in a corner of the office where I was faced with a scale.

"Honey, time for your first measurements, just to see where we're at!" Luke said gleefully, and the way he used "we" made me feel a bit better about getting examined. Stripping down to my bra and panties, I stepped onto the scale. Luke looked at the number and took a few notes.

"Okay, that's good, good. I think we can do a bit better, though, maybe five pounds to start, shooting for ten, don't you think? You're a gorgeous girl, and we really want to get you out there in perfect shape! Just like when you were fifteen." He said this so sweetly and with such a smile—he actually knew how to tell a girl she needed to lose weight without sending her into a fit of tears—that I immediately wanted to agree. I nodded, thinking about what sort of meager food I could survive on, how much I'd run on the treadmill, and no booze, of course (too many calories).

Using a tape measure, Luke took the rest of my measurements, scribbled notes, then clapped his book shut with a sense of finality.

"Okay, all done! We'll have to have you come in every week for this, just to see how we're doing, okay, sweetie?"

I put my skirt and top back on, and it was done. Pretty painless compared to what some other agencies put girls through, I would later learn. The agency of another model I knew took Polaroids of her in her underwear, then had their weekly meeting where all the bookers assembled around a table, and with a bright red marker circled the "problem areas" on the girl's body. Then her agent sat her down and discussed how to trim off that extra inch of "fat" from her hips. In two days, before the Donna Karan casting. Sounds like fun, huh?

Luke quickly briefed me on what I'd be doing in the coming week—a whole block of "go-sees," test shots, and meetings. Go-sees were meetings the Agency had arranged with booking editors at magazines, managers of ad campaigns, photographers—basically anyone who would possibly pay to take pictures of me or who could possibly *get* someone to. The test shots with photographers were going to build up my portfolio of pictures, creating a precious book that would reflect who I was as a model. And the meetings—the Agency wanted me to come into contact with anyone and everyone who would take even a millisecond to look at me.

Luke handed me an agenda of all these meetings, each day crammed full of times and addresses and a dizzying array of names. He flashed a "go get 'em" grin before taking a swig of Vitamin Water.

And then my first visit was over, just like that.

I took the elevator down to the street and looked up at the windows of the Agency again. They didn't look so menacing this time. Just five pounds. And then another five. Not *too* hard.

THAT NIGHT I WAS WRITING an e-mail to my parents—after hiding a few open windows on Russian chat sites Svetlana had been digging into—when Laura stormed in.

I jumped up as she swung the door open with a clang.

"Those bastards," she murmured, throwing her bag down on the floor. A cell phone and a tube of lipstick tumbled out after the toss. Laura's immaculate face was flushed with anger.

"What? What's wrong?"

Laura's entrance had caused enough of a commotion to break up a conversation between Svetlana and her friend Yelena, another Russian model from the Agency who was slumming it by hanging out in the dorm that evening. She had made it and was earning enough to live in a proper apartment—it was still a share, but an apartment nonetheless, and definitely no bunk beds to be seen. They had been chattering in Russian for nearly an hour about a new Ukrainian girl who'd been brought on by the Agency. I found this out when Svetlana had turned to me, practically out of nowhere, her nostrils flaring, and started in English: "This Ukrainian *kuirva!* You know? Svetlana and Yelena *know,* Heather, she eat much, don't work out, she not last with Agency, Svetlana know. I think she drink too much, too." She took a satisfactory drag from her Marlboro Red. Yelena had nodded, licking her lips at the gossip, and then they had started up their slam session again. Too many blond Eastern Europeans in the Agency = fewer jobs for the two girls. I had been a bit surprised at their cattiness, although it was tame compared to what I was going to see over the next few months.

So when Laura arrived, the poor Ukrainian girl's reputation got a reprieve from her enemies, the Russians turning to look at our roommate's dramatic entrance.

"Wrong?!" Laura motioned around the apartment. "*This* is what's wrong, Heather! You know how much we pay to live in this place, and I make a simple request to the Agency and they just pretend they don't hear. We *live* here, and I don't want to see everyone suffer because they're cheap."

"Well, we don't actually *pay,* I mean. . . ." I tried to reason with her.

"Heather, wake up! We *do* have to pay as soon as we make any money. They keep a nice running tab. You know how we've been using deli napkins for toilet paper?" I *didn't* know; I had just moved in. "Well, we shouldn't argue about who's going to buy it next—the Agency should do a better job of taking care of us. That's not too much to ask."

We all nodded a bit tentatively. Toilet paper. It seemed crazy. But it looked like it had become a crusade for Laura, the sticking point for her argument about how the Agency was mistreating us. The problem was that I sensed that all the girls on contract with them had an abject fear of the Agency, as if at any moment they could take away all legitimacy and approval of us as models and send us packing if we didn't do exactly what they asked. But Laura, faithful Laura, who seemed to actually like the close quarters and camaraderie of the dorm, had finally snapped. She had been complaining to anybody who would listen to her at the Agency—mostly the other models—and it seemed *someone* (hopefully not one of us at the dorm) ratted her out to one of the agents to try to score some brownie points. The result was that Laura had been called in that day for what she thought was a normal check-in and measurements.

Kylie emerged from the bedroom, having been woken in the middle of one of her beauty naps by Laura's tirade. Her eyes were big and puffy, and she instinctively walked to the kitchen for a pick-me-up.

Laura continued, "Somebody's informing." She raised an eyebrow and looked at us all. "I know it's not one of *you* guys, but one of the other girls at the Agency is informing. Rachel called me in today, all secret-like, and said she heard I wasn't happy with how things were going at the dorm, that I was bitching about not having toilet paper. I told her she had heard right. And you know what she said?"

I didn't know, but I guessed that it hadn't been so good. Talks with Rachel often ended in tears, fragile egos entirely ground down under her spiky heels.

"She said to me, all pissed off, 'Do you think I made it by worrying about goddamn toilet paper?! What do you think you're living in, a Howard Johnson?'" Laura stamped her foot down as she said this. "A Howard Johnson, can you believe that? And then she said we weren't getting any free toilet paper, no arguments, and that if I didn't like it, I didn't have to stay here, and that if I didn't like it here, maybe I didn't like the Agency. We've got to do something about the way we're being treated here!"

We all held our breath. She had crossed the Agency. A troublemaker.

"So who's with me?"

For a moment after Laura's declaration of war, everyone stared quietly at the spot on the floor at their feet. Those at the Agency were the gatekeepers to our success, the people who held our modeling fates in their hands, deciding whose comp cards went where, who should be sent to what casting. . . . To anger them, for something as trivial as a roll of Charmin, seemed like pure suicide.

But then Kylie piped up, raising a cocktail that had materialized in her hand. "It *is* just some bloody toilet paper, know what I mean? But we deserve that, human rights and all that rubbish. It means something," the Aussie declared, her hair sprouting wildly about her head after a morning and afternoon of deep snoozing. It was the closest she'd ever get to a UN address.

Yelena snickered a little—just a little—obviously amused by our plight, since *she* didn't have to live in the dorm.

"You need toilet paper? I go buy some for you, you don't have money?" Yelena asked, faking concern.

No one dignified her jab with an answer. Even Svetlana gave her an icy glare.

"You're right, Laura. I have a friend in college, and they said in the dorms there they get as much toilet paper as they want," I said.

Svetlana nodded, her Russian blood starting to boil up at the thought of revolution, perhaps.

"All right, we're in this together—toilet paper, or they're going to have to answer to us," Laura said, victorious, having won our support for now.

"Yeah! Though what exactly are you proposing? How do we get our message across to the Agency?" I asked.

"Hit 'em where it counts—their pocketbook. If we don't go on our castings, it'll make them look bad in the eyes of the casting agents. And if we don't go and aren't booking jobs, how are they going to make any money off us? They can't keep treating us like this, right?" Laura proclaimed.

"Right!" we shouted in unison.

And so the Toilet Paper Insurrection began. Dammit, we were *models,* we deserved our two-ply. Revolutions have been waged over sillier things than toilet paper—just check your history books.

A COUPLE DAYS AFTER THE LAUNCH of the T.P. Insurrection, I found myself flying through Chelsea, up Eighth Avenue in a cab with Svetlana and a club promoter who had just bought us dinner at Japonais. I had made good on my promise to her: We were on our way to a club—Marquee—and my pulse was racing with excitement about what the night would bring.

I hadn't thought much about paper products or revolutions since the insurrection began, but they were certainly on my mind now in the back of the cab. With one hand, Svetlana was holding a wad of toilet paper up to her nose to stop the bleeding and, with the other, she was massaging the well-toned thigh of the promoter through his Gucci slacks. He smiled weakly at her and then went back to looking at the street scene that sped by outside the taxi.

My first full week in New York had been as dizzying as the driver's manic swerving, as the cab took a screeching turn onto Twenty-third Street. The Agency had decided to keep me on contract, ensuring that I wouldn't be sent back to Virginia and an "I told you so" homecoming. As soon as I had my measurements, I had gone on a series of go-sees. I told myself they didn't *really* count as castings and that Laura wouldn't be disappointed in my breaking solidarity. I'd just gotten there—she couldn't expect me to be a martyr, could she?

Not that it mattered, anyway. The T.P. Insurrection had lasted in full force all of maybe fourteen hours—merely one day after our fist-shaking resolution, all of us girls were sneaking out to our appointments. It had become a farce, with everyone pretending everyone else was keeping to the rules, even though we knew *nobody* was. Even Laura vanished with her portfolio in hand every now and then, supposedly to "get some air." So, breaking the spirit, if not the letter, of our pact, I had spent days on go-sees, traipsing into chic magazine buildings and running up and down Fashion Avenue from place to place, all the while carrying my book of photos from my previous work in Virginia and Miami. In between the go-sees I spent time at the studios of various pseudo-famous photographers, getting test shots done to beef up my portfolio, as most of my shots were admittedly from when I was younger and thinner.

The go-sees were all pretty much the same: a brief chat where I put on my best smile, have important person X look over my book, then a Polaroid, a handshake, and a thank-you. Some of the meetings were so short and curt—and so many gorgeous girls were in the waiting room with me—that I was sure I'd made a terrible impression and that whatever booker I happened to have met was going to call the Agency as soon as I left and say: "What were you thinking, sending this girl over here? Hideous. Really, I thought better of you. Give the beast some TrimSpa and send her back to whatever cave she came from." But at the end of the week the Agency called me and said I was going to be considered for a department store catalog shoot, which basically guaranteed that I'd be around for a while. So I'd wanted to celebrate, naturally—even though the night itself had turned into a sort of anti-celebration for both Svetlana and me. We both had gone to castings for the upcoming shows for Fashion Week and had gotten absolutely no bookings. But those problems disappear into the city night quickly with the right amount of alcohol and fun. . . .

Wearing a flirty Betsey Johnson dress borrowed from one of the girls and sporting a pair of Svetlana's Choos, I planned on making my first night at the club an unqualified success. Looking at myself in the mirror before we left, I knew that more than a few men would be turning my way.

Thursday was Marquee night for Svetlana. She had a whole schedule worked out: Monday at Butter, Tuesday at Marquee, Wednesday at Cain, Thursday back to Marquee, Friday at PM. Saturday was a wild card—try to get into Bungalow 8 or settle for somewhere in the Meatpacking District—and Sunday was, of course, the Lord's day of rest, and anyway most of the clubs had their gay nights on Sunday. Rinse and repeat.

Svetlana had trained for her party life in Moscow, where she started out as a model, brought from some depressed city near Odessa, a Russian among Ukrainians. Her father, a bureaucrat from Novograd, sent to the Ukraine by Moscow, had died of a broken heart at age forty-seven after the USSR collapsed. Her Russian mother decided to stay in the Ukraine, and they had moved into a modest flat in Odessa, where if you had a pair of binoculars, you could say it had a lovely view of the Black Sea. She made quite a splash in the Moscow modeling scene with her unnaturally svelte long limbs and unique features, and soon her Russian managers farmed her out to the Agency in New York. For a fee, of course.

In New York she'd had a bit of success—walking in the Imitation of Christ and Jeremy Scott shows during the previous Fashion Week (which made her getting passed up this season twice as galling)—but that was about it. The Agency seemed to put enough faith in her reedy body and angular face that they kept her on (and kept charging her account the thousands of dollars a month for her tiny bed in our dorm. The poor giraffe).

She seemed to be acquainted with every club promoter in the sea of "it" clubs, and never missed a chance for a free meal at a ridiculously expensive restaurant—although she usually would only politely take two bites of the sea bass and then excuse herself to the bathroom—followed by a night of complimentary drinks in the VIP room of whatever club it may be that night (refer to the calendar detailed earlier). Normally club owners actually paid promoters to get models to show up to their night. The sight of five impeccable six-foot-tall models being whisked into the club through the VIP line is enough to set the investment bankers and hedge fund assholes in line on fire—and make them dig deep into their wallets as soon as they get in, in hopes of impressing us with their Amex Black cards.

And there Svetlana and I were, speeding to Marquee, her hand creeping dangerously close to the promoter's crotch, while I pretended to innocently examine my borrowed yellow suede Louboutin flats. I was still recovering from Svetlana's little "accident" back at the restaurant. Earlier in the evening at our dorm, she'd produced from her purse an enormous bag of cocaine she'd gotten the night before from one of her rich Russian male "friends." She then commenced to inhale massive quantities of it in the bathroom, drawing out lines that seemed as thick as her wrists. All types of snorting noises were coming from behind the bathroom door. The whole while, Laura attempted to clean up the kitchen, looking stony-faced—as any good den mother would.

When we reached Japonais, she was giddy and ready for anything. Funnily enough, Svetlana's English somehow jumped to another level of speed and proficiency as soon as the happy powder entered her bloodstream.

"James, this Heather, Svetlana's friend," Svetlana had said as she introduced me to the promoter. He was in his early thirties, not necessarily attractive, but not unattractive, either. Mainly, he was short, probably only five-nine. Three stunning girls from another agency were already seated with him. Svetlana's teeth were starting to clack together already, a surefire sign that maybe she'd overdone it at the apartment with the coke.

"What are you drinking tonight, Heather?" James had asked, giving me the once-over while Svetlana tried her best to look available and not too coked-up. The restaurant itself seemed like some sort of petit-club, the fabulous and fashionable clientele craning their necks, checking the door to see who was coming in as they barely paid attention to their meals. A black male model I recognized from a Tommy Hilfiger campaign smiled at us from a table in the corner as we sat down.

We ordered the most expensive sushi on the menu and five pricey bottles of sake; James didn't bat an eyelash. I actually ate some of the sushi, while Svetlana picked away at hers with the chopsticks so it looked as if she'd been eating something, at least (a classic tactic). Throughout the meal she had been rubbing her nostrils as the numbing of the drug spread up her nasal passages.

About a half hour in, Svetlana was trying to ask James a flirty question over the din of the restaurant. I was chatting with a model from another small agency who had come up from Alabama a few months before, but noticed Svetlana attempting to make a move.

"What?" he asked, bringing his ear closer. "I can't hear you."

Svetlana leaned in to ask her question again, the promoter mere inches from her lips, and all of a sudden blood came squirting out of her nose, shooting all over the obscenely expensive toro she had barely touched. Too much coke in too little time.

"Aaaah!" Svetlana squeaked, pulling back quickly.

James, who immediately knew what had happened, practically pulled all six-feet-plus of her body out of the chair by the scruff of her neck. "For God's sakes!"

Svetlana, blood streaming out of her nose and over her hand, ran into the bathroom past a series of oblivious restaurant-goers, while James deftly covered the ruined sushi with a cloth napkin and looked a bit exasperated.

"Svetlana!" I shouted after her, when James grabbed my hand.

"Shh . . . Don't make a scene, she'll be all right in a sec."

"Everything all right, Jim?" the waiter asked, with a slight grin.

"Yeah, you know these girls, some of them haven't outgrown their allergies yet. American pollen, you know, probably not used to it."

The waiter cleared away the plate, and Svetlana emerged from the bathroom, a huge wad of toilet paper crammed under her nose, trying to look as elegant as possible under such circumstances.

She actually seemed to have regained her composure and started strutting back to our party, until she reached another table about ten feet away from us. Her left heel slipped and she practically fell head-first into a bucket of champagne a couple was sharing. She made an admirable save, though, catching herself and only shaking the table ever so slightly, spilling a few drops of bubbly in the process. The woman at the table gave her an icy glare, while her date stared slack-jawed, entranced by the creature who had nearly fallen into his lap.

I'd had to stifle a chuckle—despite the Russian girl's tall haute-couture body, she was still only a girl, like all of us, and a clumsy one at that. Although the walk down the runway had been pro-grammed into her muscles over the past couple years, in everything else she seemed just a bit off and awkward, no matter how hard she tried to be graceful around all the men. Every night there seemed to be some almost-disaster when she would nearly come lurching to the ground. And there were more than a couple nights when half a VIP room would know exactly what color thong she was wear-ing—or even better, how recently she had gotten her Brazilian wax—when, after too many glasses of bubbly, she would go clatter-ing over some couch, her skirt practically flapping up to her dainty earlobes.

Back at the table after her almost-fatal swan dive into the cham-pagne bucket, Svetlana sat down with the wad under her nose as if nothing had happened and took a swig of sake.

"Svetlana ready for Marquee."

MY HEAD SWAM as James led us all out of the town car. We waded through the masses who were trying in vain to convince the stone-faced doorman that yes, in fact, they were on the list and should be let past the velvet rope.

I'd worried for a nanosecond that we might get carded but realized that in the glitzy New York club world, being a model is ID enough, no matter how young you are.

The music inside the club was deafening, drowning out every-thing in a stream of diva house music, interspersed with the latest hip-hop anthems. Svetlana had ditched her nose-stopper as soon as we neared Marquee. She examined herself in her compact mirror to ensure no blood was crusted on her nostrils. I'd checked my hair quickly in the rearview mirror before we hopped out and assured myself I was *just* as beautiful and glamorous as any of the other girls who were going to be there.

We faced a sea of beautiful women and the men who love to spend money on them, some dancing off-rhythm to the music, some cuddling in the banquettes, and others simply watching the crowd with silly drunken grins. A group of beefy Jersey types in khakis and striped guido shirts almost visibly started salivating as we swished past toward the VIP access upstairs. James nodded to the mountain of a man guarding the velvet rope to the back room, and he held open the gate for us.

My Russian roommate turned to me with a huge smile just before we climbed the stairs. "Svetlana so excited, it look good tonight!"

Depositing us at his reserved booth, James bade us farewell—"I'll be up there in a sec, girls. Help yourself to the Belvedere on the table"—and quickly melted into the crowd. Not that we minded one bit as we giddily poured ourselves some vodka, waiting to see what, and who, we might discover.

The VIP clientele didn't strike me as so much different from the main area, except for the fact that the women were even more beautiful. People were mingling, sipping champagne or cocktails. In one corner a girl clutching her Bottega Veneta handbag was dancing barefoot on one of the small tables, while a man in a tailored suit swayed beneath her on the floor, his nose dangerously close to going straight up between her thighs. He looked like he had just won the Powerball.

A girl from a reserved table off to the side started waving in our direction, and I recognized one of our new roommates who had just arrived a few days earlier—she obviously hadn't had much trouble finding her way around the city. She was Brazilian, with a leopard-like body and incredibly thick curly black hair that always made her look like she had just stepped out of the stylist's chair. She was sitting with a couple of other girls I didn't recognize, along with a tall man dressed all in black who had his back to us. We got up from our booth, started walking over to them, and had almost gotten to the table when Svetlana performed an about-face, grabbing my shoulders. She had a panicked look in her eyes.

"What is it?" I asked, worried that maybe her nose was starting to act funky on her again.

"Heather, that Robert du Croix there!" she exclaimed breathlessly. "Is Svetlana look okay?" She turned her nose up so I could investigate.

"Row-bear du Croix?" The name didn't click for a second, since Svetlana pronounced it as you would in France, but then I realized with a thrill whom she meant. Back home, while poring over some chic lifestyle magazines, I had come across an article about him—he was the famous, fabulously wealthy owner of Shiva Bar in Paris, the hottest spot to see and be seen for the glitterati in France for the past decade (or at least so the magazine claimed). Since I'd read the article, I'd been obsessed, picturing myself in the City of Light, dancing at Shiva Bar till dawn on a Tuesday. I'd gotten all the Shiva Bar mix CDs over the past two years and had listened to them nonstop in my room, imagining what must have been happening in that club night after night, the movie stars, rock stars, and fashion designers all together in one beautiful medley. Legend had it that one early morning, after the club closed, Monsieur du Croix took Madonna and a whole crew of other people who had been partying at Shiva Bar, commandeered one of the gigantic tourist boats on the Seine, and kept the soiree going until nine A.M., when the gendarmerie had to board from rafts, taking du Croix away in handcuffs under the shadow of Notre Dame. As they put him in a paddy wagon he reportedly had shouted, *"Vive la liberté!"* before chastising the cops for scuffing his Prada loafers.

Now here he was a mere fifteen feet away from us, and Svetlana was nearly having a stroke. Once again she had me check her nostrils, and I assured her that she looked fine. But what about *me?* I took a deep breath and tried to look as nonchalant as possible as we walked to the table.

The Brazilian girl stood up. "These are my roommates, guys."

The girls, uniformly gorgeous, gave us a blasé greeting. Robert stood up and we got our first look at him. He was tall—even taller than Svetlana—and well-tanned, probably from time spent in St. Barts on his yacht over the summer. His dark hair was perfectly coiffed, swooshing back over his temples like a cresting wave, gleaming. His white teeth shone as he smiled broadly at us.

"Hello, I am Robert, a pleasure to meet you." He stepped forward as I shook his hand, and he kissed me lightly on both cheeks. Doing the same for the nervous Svetlana, he nearly smashed noses with her as she miscalculated which cheek he would be going for first. He laughed lightly, and she tried to look as unflappable as possible, even though I knew her stomach was probably doing as many backflips as mine was, if not more.

"Will you join us for some champagne?" he asked with the seasoning of a man who has indeed asked many a woman to join him for champagne.

"Yes, thank you," I said as we sat next to the other girls on the swanky couch.

Robert hailed a passing server: "Another bottle of the ninety-six. And make sure she's not too cold, no?" The cocktail waitress nodded and sped off to retrieve another bottle.

He turned to us. "Where are you girls from?"

Svetlana was stone silent.

"I just moved here from Miami—and Svetlana's from Russia."

"Miami? I have a beautiful condo on South Beach."

"Oh, me too! Well, it wasn't exactly a beautiful condo, but it was on South Beach," I managed to get out. I, of course, was overwhelmed with the impression that I must have sounded like an entire idiot, or at least that my dress must have been torn or I had a big piece of shiso leaf between my teeth from Japonais.

The champagne arrived, and Robert poured us two fresh flutes. As he filled my glass he looked directly into my eyes, and my heart performed a triple-Axel inside my chest. I nervously started playing with my necklace.

Svetlana had gathered enough courage to speak. "Svetlana from Ukraine, not Russia, but I always want to live in Paris. Paris best city in world, best nightspots!" she gushed.

"Yes, true," he said, barely paying attention to her and turning back to me. "Me, I reside in Paris half the time and spend the rest of my time here in New York, along with some weeks in London and Miami. Being too long in one place makes me, well, a bit bored."

We both nodded in agreement, although none of us really knew what it was like to be jet-setting across the Atlantic every two weeks.

He continued, looking to me, "And you are with what management?"

I told him that Svetlana, the Brazilian, and I were all with the Agency, and he nodded with a sweet smile. "Yes, they are definitely on the rise—I have spoken to my photographer friends about it. Very beautiful girls, as we can see tonight."

Svetlana, absolutely smitten, blushed brightly, and despite the corny line, my pulse began racing, too. He seemed to be the most attractive man I had ever met—charming, confident, polished, and

Jude Law beautiful. And also about twice my own age . . . but no matter.

Then he turned to a breathtaking blond next to him—whom I recognized from a Chanel campaign the year before—and began talking to her intensely, seemingly forgetting Svetlana and I. My Russian friend looked devastated. We sipped our champagne as Robert flirted with the Chanel blond. I talked to the friendly Brazilian girl while Svetlana tried in vain to catch Robert's eye from across the table. Throwing her chin back to expose her shapely throat as she sipped her champagne, flipping her hair, she looked like a lost puppy.

She became so frustrated in her attempts that she began scanning the room for new prey. Near the bar were two late-twenties lawyer types, who were suspiciously rubbing their nostrils and looking *very* excited. They caught her eye, and she smiled seductively at them. Standing up, she walked wobbily to the bar, looking over her shoulder to see if Robert noticed. He hadn't even seen she'd left. I have to say I was a bit disappointed, too—not for Svetlana, but for myself— and I eyed the blond as she laughed at one of Robert's jokes, wondering vainly whether she was prettier than me. For a moment it felt like I had been sent back to seventh grade and was having to contend with those mean girls again. Robert's companion had been in a Chanel campaign and what had I done, besides traipse around Manhattan for a week on a bunch of go-sees?

At the bar, the two lawyers were ecstatic to have Svetlana's company and summarily started ordering shots of vodka in honor of the girl's homeland. She slurped them down, constantly looking over to spy if Robert was seeing how good of a time she was having with these other men. No luck. She ran to the bathroom and came out even more jacked up, and now the entire trio was anxiously twiddling with their noses.

The Chanel girl laughed shrilly, and Robert started fingering the pendant that rested on her chest.

All of a sudden shrieking in feigned joy, Svetlana started dancing by herself with a glass of champagne in hand, and both men soon joined her, making a sandwich out of the Russian. Robert actually looked up at this point but didn't bat an eyelash before returning to his apparently riveting conversation with the Chanel ho, whom at this point I was beginning to hope would suffer some sort of cataclysmic disaster—maybe a flying champagne cork would hit her in the forehead.

Then, out of nowhere, as Svetlana returned to the bathroom for a fill-up, Robert turned away from his blonde, who was gathering her things to leave.

"Listen, I think you have much promise as a model, and I have many friends who work in the advertising and fashion world. We should talk sometime about your prospects," Robert said to me, leaning in closely—but not too close, still a gentleman.

Blood shot up my body to my face—Robert du Croix was asking for my number and wanted to help me out! I practically stuttered as I recited my cell number, which he programmed into his über-thin BlackBerry with a smile.

"Let me give you mine, in case you need anything—it is an international phone, so I can also be reached when I am in Paris or London." I eagerly punched his number into my phone, typing in his name as it sounded when he and Svetlana spoke it.

"Now, if you'll excuse me, I'm exhausted. I need to see that my friend's girlfriend here gets home safely. Say good-bye to your Russian friend for me." He took the Chanel girl's hand in his; she smiled at us all, and then he was gone.

Svetlana soon emerged from the bathroom, another few hundred dollars of cocaine evaporated. Seeing Robert was gone, she sobered up for a second and ran over to me with a crestfallen look contorting her face. "Where Robert go? With blond hooker?!"

"Don't worry, he said it was his friend's girlfriend," I said to her. "We need to go soon, anyway." Svetlana sat glumly down on the couch and looked off into the distance, her attorneys forgotten. The two men walked over to the couch with coked-out smiles on their faces.

"Hey, gorgeous, Brad here says you need another drink."

Svetlana didn't even bother looking at them. They stood awkwardly by for a second, having spent probably $100 on Svetlana and at least expecting an answer.

"Svetlana busy," she said icily.

Brad moved forward, getting visibly angry and almost saying something before his companion held him back, and they stalked off. The word "bitch" floated to us as they walked away.

TAKING A CAB WITH FARE that James had given us, we both sat in the backseat, heading toward our tattered model dorm. Svetlana, halfheartedly trying to conceal herself, spooned onto a key a large bump of the lawyers' cocaine—where she'd gotten the key I never knew, because we didn't need to have one for the apartment. It zoomed up her nose, and she smiled a bit.

"Svetlana *like* Robert—you think he like Svetlana?" she said, looking at me with an oblivious smile, trying to repair her self-esteem.

"Oh, he seemed to really like you, Svetlana, who wouldn't? He even made sure that I told you he said good-bye."

"Really?" she said. She leaned back in her seat and kicked her feet against the front seat of the taxi.

"But he is going back to Paris for a while, he mentioned. I mean, I heard him say it to someone else," I said.

The Russian looked forward with the slightest of smug grins. "Svetlana wait—she know how to get man."

My phone beeped at me—a text message. I flipped open the phone to see whom it was from. The screen displayed in bold letters: ROW-BEAR.

The message read as follows: *"Nice to meet you, Heather. Dinner when I get back from Paris late October?"*

Svetlana looked at me quizzically. "Who from?" she asked.

"Wrong number, I think," I said, flipping the phone closed. Through the window, the city lights spilled over my face as we headed home.

3

THE NEXT MORNING, after grabbing only a few hours of precious sleep, I was awake and up, trying to perform magic on my bleary face with an array of M•A•C makeup I'd picked up the week before. I knew I wasn't supposed to be going to my castings, but, well, I had a couple really good ones that day, and I didn't want to miss them. No one else seemed to miss *theirs*, anyway.

The first was for an editorial shoot for *Vogue Italia*, and I knew—and the Agency had let me know in no uncertain terms— that if I got the job I'd be on my way to making a name for myself in the industry and getting big-money gigs (along with making them a sizable commission and probably earning me enough money to move out of the dorm). So I naturally spent about three times as long as I should have deciding between every article of clothing I owned while Svetlana and Kylie snored in the beds next to me. Finally I decided on a light ruffly skirt, a top with a plunging neckline, and a pair of Svetlana's heels, and by the time I ran out the door I was running late. Within weeks—maybe even days!—I might be out and set up in my own chic apartment in the West Village somewhere.

I scaled back that vision as soon as I arrived at the casting. Occupying the same subway car I'd taken up to Chelsea were two other models, nervously holding their books. They got off at the same stop, and we marched practically single file toward the address I had been given. I kept hoping they'd veer off to some other destination, but instead, with each block, a couple *more* girls would join our line of hopefuls.

Inside the imposing building, it was chaos. Girls everywhere, primping themselves in compact mirrors, eyeing the competition. I'd sworn the Agency had told me it was not an open casting, and only girls they were interested in were being asked to come in, but it was obvious that every girl who had a booker worth his or her salt had shown up for a coveted spot. It was what they call in the industry a cattle call!

After waiting in line for a bit, I signed in on a clipboard overflowing with other names from across the world, just to get two minutes in the small casting area that was closed off by a drab door at the end of the waiting room.

So what did we do? We waited. It was like some sort of international convention, all the nationalities sticking together—the Russian-speaking girls in the center of the room, the Brazilians gossiping together by the wall, the two Scandinavian girls looking quiet and blindingly blond in the corner. The lone Asian girl looked kinda lost. I didn't recognize anyone I knew, so I kept to myself, even though I noticed a group of American girls lined up on one side of the room, their American English recognizable in the ca-cophony of international tongues. A model UN!

Throughout the room roamed the publicity people for the hot clubs, chatting up all the girls, each trying to convince them that *his* club was the best place to see and be seen, and, yes, hinting at more than a few free dinners and drinks. They looked like sharks, their capped teeth glinting through forced smiles.

The line to get in moved more slowly than a bus stuck in Mid-town rush-hour traffic, groups of girls were asked into the room and then reappeared minutes, or sometimes mere seconds later, looking variously dazed, cocky, or even scared. One girl from another top agency stumbled on her way into the casting, her gangly legs crum-pling underneath her, and when she emerged from the room, tears started welling out of her eyes. Another model from her agency con-soled her as she walked out, but no amount of hugs was going to change the fact that she knew she wasn't going to be the new *Vogue Italia* cover girl.

At last my turn came. It had been about two hours. A woman in Alain Mikli glasses, A.P.C. jeans, and a bobo deconstructed top called out my name, along with those of three other girls, and I stood up with a jerk, smoothed the ruffles in my skirt and walked into the casting room with the other models. It was time.

Two stone-faced women behind a table looked at us as we walked in. A man in a sleek suit sat next to them, absentmindedly sipping a bottle of Fiji while he typed on his BlackBerry. I handed my book to the woman who called me in.

"Hello," I said, trying to break the ice and smiling as big as I possibly could.

"Hi, ummm, Heather," one of the women said, reading my name from the comp card, which held all my stats and had a pouty pic-ture of me on it.

Mr. Sleek stopped fooling with his gadget and looked at us for the first time. He nodded to me and finally spoke. "As you probably know, this is for *Vogue Italia*. The photographer specifically requested an unknown girl, a nobody, no supermodels, which is why we have you girls here," the man said, looking at me with X-ray eyes.

"Well, I'm definitely a nobody," I tried to joke. No response. One of the women flipped through my book. The man paused before he asked his next question. The way he said it made it seem as if it were the most important question ever asked in the history of questions: "Will you all be willing to cut your hair and color it?"

Everyone nodded, although one of the Scandinavian girls looked a bit tentative. She started speaking but was cut off by a casting agent, who looked up at us from our books.

"Okay, we need Sophie here to take some Polaroids."

The jeans girl produced a camera. *Snap, snap, snap, snap.* The man displayed what seemed suspiciously like a *very* fake smile.

"Well, thank you very much for coming in. We'll be letting your agency know within a week who we'd like for callbacks. Best of luck!"

Before I knew it, we were ushered quickly out of the room, staring back at all the eager girls who were waiting to go through the same process. And that was it. Dazed, I tried to smile at the girls as I left, but I didn't feel convincing. As I left the building, my shoulders slumped a bit. The whole thing seemed to have lasted about thirty seconds, and I felt like my chances against all those other models were slim. Deep in thought, I walked back toward the east. I passed by my subway station and instead of going straight home, I ambled through Chelsea and then downtown, past the nice restaurants, the closed bars that would be humming by nighttime, my brain in a whirl—what if I never did get a big job? What if my parents were right? My time modeling in Miami had been tolerated—Mom and Dad had thought that I would have gotten it out of my system down there and come back home to finish high school. But they viewed moving to New York as a more serious step and felt that instead of running around the city getting Polaroids taken of myself, I should be in a classroom somewhere at State U., learning calculus or economics or business technology.

I found a bench outside City Hall and impulsively called my mom, just wanting to hear her voice.

"Hey, hon, I'm at work, sort of busy, had a meeting, but how's everything going?" she said. I could see her sitting at her desk, poring over her paperwork as she talked to me.

"Good. . . ." I paused. "I had a casting today."

"That's great! Do you think you'll get the job?"

"I don't know, there were a lot of girls, and . . ." My voice trailed off.

My mom knew me well enough. "Heather, is something wrong? You'd tell me, right?"

"No, nothing's wrong, Mom, of course I'd tell you. It's just a lot right now."

"Baby, you know you can always come back here if you want. We can get you in a late term at the community college. Your father and I would love to have you back."

The thought of already turning back after barely giving it a go made me feel like a coward. Hadn't I *left* all that for a reason?

"No, no, Mom, forget about it, just wanted to say hi," I said, gathering myself up off the bench.

"Are you taking care of yourself up there, Heather?"

The question was code for: Are you partying too much? My mom's vision of me getting into trouble was probably one of a stereotypical keg party from her college days, not champagne-soaked nights at exclusive clubs with my cocaine-addled man-crazy Russian roommate.

"Of course, Mom, I'm not stupid. I'm taking this seriously," I

said. For some unknown reason, I added. "I met this very interesting man last night."

"Watch out for boys, Heather. If you're going to be up there to
model, you need to focus on that. Trust me. I know how easy it is to
get sidetracked."

Boy! She probably thought I meant I had met some Joe College
just a couple years older than me . . . not a Robert du Croix. But I
didn't correct her.

"Don't worry, Mom, I'm *not* going to get sidetracked," I said.

"Okay, well, I gotta run to a meeting."

"All right, love you!" I said, putting on the most cheer I could.

"Love you, too. I'll tell your father you called. He's been wondering how you were since we haven't heard from you in a bit," she said.

"Bye."

"Good-bye, honey."

I put the phone back in my bag and walked the final leg back to
the apartment, calmed by the thought of my mom going to the local
grocery store and fixing her homemade lasagna, which I always ate
too much of. A pang hit me in the stomach. I was homesick (and
sort of hungry, to be honest). I had already staked out in Miami on
my own, but she had been down all the time to visit me. Now, a
year older, I was alone up here, going against what seemed to be an
army of equally tall sculpted girls who would also do anything to be
the next Tyra Banks or Karolina Kurkova.

Clearly it wasn't going to be as cut-and-dry as I once thought.

But little did I know as I entered the building, nodding to the
doorman, cursing the blisters I'd gotten from walking around in Svetlana's heels all day, that my problems were soon going to be nothing
compared to those of one of my roommates. Behind the scenes, the
Toilet Paper Insurrection Turned Toilet Paper Farce was starting to
come to a head. And it wasn't going to be pretty. Two-ply was at stake.

THE NEXT FEW WEEKS FOLLOWED the same formula: a daily dose of ego crushing at each casting that came to nothing. I was constantly rushed through cattle calls and was already getting used to competing with the gaggle of stunning beauties that nations would have been proud to fight over in the ancient Greek days.

As I left an open casting about a month and a half into my stay at the model dorm—it had been something for J.Crew—I even had a smirk on my face, wondering if they'd brand us with a big "J" on the way out. And what if they spooked us, the herd of panicky models trampling over a poor skinny gay intern who was just trying to get credits at the Fashion Institute of Technology? I could see the headline in the *New York Times* already: "Models Stampede—Little Billy Poked to Death by Manolos." And then in smaller type underneath: "Memorial Service for Young Designer Hopeful at Barneys this Friday. Cocktails and Great Networking Opportunities to Follow."

I could laugh about it, but it was beginning to bother me just a bit, and once again I took the long walk home, wondering when I'd finally get a job and be able to move out of the apartment. Success had seemed like it would come so easily, but now I was riddled by insecurities and doubts.

I was met with a strange sight when I opened the door: Laura was on all fours, scrubbing the carpet with a damp rag. She rubbed at a stain maniacally, cursing under her breath.

She turned and looked at me, startled when I walked in. Her eyes were red and sunken, as she'd clearly been crying all afternoon. Turning quickly away, she sprayed cleaner on the spot and scrubbed harder. Her lustrous hair was pulled back in a bandanna to keep it out of her eyes, and although a bit haggard and dressed in faded sweats, she still looked model-gorgeous.

"Hi, Heather. . . . Just . . . trying to get this spot out." She pressed all her skinny might onto the rag and offending stain.

"Laura, are you all right, have you been . . . ?" I asked.

"No, no, it's just this . . . cleaner hurts my eyes, you know. We need to make sure people wipe up stuff they spill right away, otherwise I end up doing this."

I pulled off my shoes, glanced at a blister on my foot, and walked over to where Laura crouched. She pushed her head down a bit farther as I approached. I inspected the spot she was working at but couldn't really see any stain.

"Just a bit more and it'll be perfect," she said.

A solitary tear plopped down from her face onto the rag as she said this.

"Perfect. . . ."

Another tear and another fell from her face onto the already-wet rag. Laura leaned back on her heels and looked at me, her eyes brimming.

"What's wrong?" I asked.

"The Agency—they've put me on 'final warning.' I didn't even know they *had* such a thing. Can you believe that? Rachel told me I'd been on the final warning list secretly for the past couple weeks, that they'd been keeping tabs on my 'attitude' toward modeling. She threatened to revoke my contract because I haven't been getting as many jobs as I used to, which she says is related to my 'attitude.' What *is* that? Before the last few weeks I went to every casting, ran around the city like a slave for them." (I knew she *had* in fact been going to at least a few of her castings but just nodded, keeping up appearances for the sake of the insurrection.) Laura continued, "I don't go out like all the other girls—" She looked at me, as if unsure of where I'd be heading in *my* stay there. "And I'm the only one who keeps this f-ing—excuse my French—place together. And they say I'm not doing enough."

Though she was nearing retirement age, I'd heard Laura was also one of the few girls to get any decent jobs on a steady basis, and some of the other girls at the Agency pretty much *knew* that while far from being rich, she even had made enough money to move out of this dingy apartment. But something had kept her around. Maybe the models' bizarre habits, unhealthy dieting practices, and constant crises made her feel needed, like she was the Mrs. Garrett in our *Facts of Life*.

"Final warning?" I said. "Can they even do that?"

"It's the Agency. They can do anything they want." She looked around, like somebody might be listening to us, and whispered under her breath, like maybe even though we were alone, the place *could* be bugged. "And that bitch Rachel, if you get on her bad side, she'll do *anything*. It's the toilet paper thing; I know it; somebody's telling. They know I haven't gone to my castings lately, but no one else was called in for a talk. It's suspicious. Somebody must be telling Rachel something." She looked at me again searchingly.

"Oh, no, it's not me. I'd never, I mean I just got here."

"I didn't think it was you—you seem sweet. I'm sure one of the girls outside the dorm heard about it and has been telling Rachel all these horrible stories. A mole, just like I thought."

A *mole*. And not a good one, like Cindy Crawford's.

"Why would somebody do that?"

Laura looked at me like I just fell off the proverbial turnip truck. She wiped her tears away with her sweatshirt sleeve and brightened up a bit, taking comfort in the fact that she could take up her role as den mother again.

"Sweetie, the girls at the Agency are vipers, bitchy vipers. They'll do anything to get ahead, outside of poisoning somebody's celery, and I'm not even sure some of them haven't thought about that as a last resort. Don't you see that if I'm out of the way, that's one less girl the Agency has to send on castings, one more spot to edge into?"

I nodded. The girls in high school were always backstabbing their "best" friends to get into pole position for the hottest guys, taking to keying poor Samantha Schmidt's Honda Accord and writing "SLUTTY SLUTBAG" in big red lipstick on her windshield. And it stood to reason that when massive modeling contracts, fame, fortune, and potential marriage into British royalty were involved, things could move to even more extreme measures. Maybe not murder, but character assassination . . . that seemed to come with the territory.

Laura seemed to have gotten over her bout of weakness, and she stood up, looking satisfactorily at the now-clean spot on the carpet where doubtless Kylie had dribbled Metamucil and vodka one recent night.

"Perfect," she said, turning to me. "Heather, just be careful who you talk to around here, and don't make any enemies."

She looked at me and smiled approvingly. "Well, with that face, I'm sure you're going to make *some* enemies, but try not to make it *too* many, okay?" she advised.

"Are you going to be all right with this? I mean, aren't you scared?" I asked. I was scared *for* her, but I didn't want to say.

"No, I mean, they can't bully us. If we stick together and do something, it's not like they can send us all home. Kylie and Svetlana are on my side, and you are, too, right? Rachel's just trying to whip me into submission and scare everyone else so nobody will complain about anything. But I won't back down. We're getting our T.P. whether they like it or not."

I nodded, trusting her judgment on the whole thing, feeling like she had everything under control and was protecting us from the outside forces.

"Just be careful. You can trust *us*, but you never know what kind of ambitious monster might lurk underneath those pretty faces. With Keyshia, who was in your bunk before you . . ." She paused, as if thinking of whether to tell me or not.

"Keyshia?" This didn't sound good.

Laura started a sentence, but inside my bag my phone began vibrating and ringing madly. I pulled it out quickly and glanced at the caller ID. I nearly dropped the phone. The display read "ROW-BEAR"! Robert du Croix was still supposed to be back in his native France at that very moment—why was he calling me? I glanced between the phone and Laura quickly. It rang again insistently.

"I should probably take this."

Laura sensed my excitement and patted me on the shoulder before walking to the kitchen. "Just be careful here," she said.

I nodded and ducked into the bedroom. Before opening the

phone I poked at Svetlana's bunk, making sure her willowy body wasn't hiding under the pile of blankets.

Taking a deep breath, I answered as nonchalantly as possible. *"Hello?"* It came out weird, and I was instantly convinced I sounded like I was eleven.

"Well, hello, Heather. This is Robert du Croix. We met last month at Marquee?" he said. "But I'm hoping you have not forgotten me so soon."

"Oh, *no,* I haven't forgotten." My instincts screamed at me for being so eager with him, even though I was gushing on my end. "I mean, I have a very good memory, and you're one of the first, I guess . . ." Uh-oh. No one likes a rambler, least of all Monsieur du Croix, who I'm sure was used to dealing with the most unflappable glamorous girls. And on an international scale, no less. I stuttered a bit more, then finally managed: "Aren't you still supposed to be in Paris?"

"Yes, I was to be there for three more weeks, was planning a holiday with my mother—it's her birthday next week, and I'm afraid she won't be with us for much longer. But business has brought me back for a time."

"I'm sorry to hear that." Idiot! I'm not sorry he's here. "I mean, I'm sorry to hear about your mother."

"Ah, yes, but as we all know, death is part of life—the least beautiful, but a necessary element nonetheless," he intoned, philosophizing off-the-cuff in that particularly French way that hints at the depths of their souls.

"Definitely." Double idiot! All I can come up with is "definitely"? I *definitely* sounded like I was eleven.

"I knew you'd understand such things. I could tell that about you when we met," he said. "Anyway, my dear, the reason I'm calling is that since I'm stuck here for some time, I'd love for us to meet and discuss your professional future over dinner, perhaps at Cipriani downtown?"

My answer to Robert, dear reader, shouldn't be too much of a surprise. We settled on an evening early the following week.

"I will look forward to it," Robert said before hanging up. "*À bientôt.*"

"Yes, *ciao,*" I answered, trying to sound sophisticated.

With that, the call ended. Robert du Croix was taking a personal interest in my career *and* taking me to Cipriani, one of the biggest scene restaurants in the city! I took a breath and hoisted myself up on my bunk. Lying on my back, I closed my eyes and a series of fantastic scenarios played across the inside of my eyelids. The way my leg would look for the paparazzi as Robert helped me out of a limo onto the red carpet for the grand opening of his New York club, the two of us sitting in a reserved banquette in the VIP room, bottles of champagne chilling in ice buckets as he introduced me to the hot designer du jour who had just flown in from Paris.

The grim disappointment from the casting earlier in the day, Laura's troubles, the mysterious fate of Keyshia, the fact that the shoddy bunk mattress was absolutely *killing* my back—all these were washed away as Robert's irresistibly accented voice stuck on repeat in my head. Suburbia had never seemed so far away, my certain success never so close. My Robert-tinged daydreams carried me to sleep.

A SHOUT FROM THE LIVING ROOM woke me from my nap. I looked at the red digital clock down on the floor. I'd slept for more than two hours.

Another holler filtered in through the closed doors. It was Svetlana's voice. My pulse quickened.

"What the . . . ?" I murmured, crawling down off the bed, rubbing my sleepy eyes.

Pressing my ear close against the door, I tried to hear what was happening, wondering if I had just woken up to one of those New York horror stories you see on the "hard-hitting" TV news shows, some crazed rapist having waltzed into our apartment through the unlocked door after following the trail of beautiful girls to the model dorm.

"Give it to me! Do you hear, you bloody Slav?!" I heard Kylie shout.

"*Nyet!* I know you take! You don't get back from Svetlana till you give me back!" Svetlana replied.

"You're fucking off your nut, Svet. I did no such thing!"

Satisfied that I wasn't walking into a true-life crime story, I slowly opened the door and peered outside.

Svetlana clutched a bottle of Kylie's vodka against her breast. She held a Sigerson Morrison heel in the other, raised above her head in a threatening manner, shaking it at Kylie. With one heel still on, Svetlana hobbled ridiculously as she scooted sideways to get a chair between her and her would-be attacker. My other roommate was only a few feet away, nostrils flaring while she eyed the Stoli that Svetlana held. They both looked a little tipsy, to put it mildly. Laura was nowhere to be seen.

As I opened the door, Kylie glanced at me. "Oh, hey, Heather, just in time," she said matter-of-factly before lunging at Svetlana, trying to grab the bottle from her. The Russian awkwardly swiped her heel in the air in Kylie's general direction.

"Give me it! Give it!" Kylie grabbed at the bottle before Svetlana pushed the chair against her to keep her at bay.

"Will you tell this Russian *cow* to give me back my bottle? She's lost it, Heather."

Svetlana firmly shook her head back and forth. "No! Australian *kuirva* take Svetlana stuff. *No* good. She give back or no vodka!" Svetlana hissed.

"Stuff?" I asked, innocently enough.

"She thinks I took her bloody pick-me-up, is what it is," Kylie answered. "Like I'd mess with whatever baking soda gasoline *shit* she's got. I've got enough to worry about. She probably dropped her baggy in the toilet while purging some fucking borscht."

Svetlana glared. "Look, Svetlana no have! Kylie took." She opened her Fendi clutch to show that it didn't hold her drugs, even though it was cluttered with all manner of compacts and lip gloss.

They both looked at me. I had suddenly become judge, jury, and executioner, my eyes still bleary from the nap, my mind still afire with memories of Robert's call. And then I realized . . .

"Svetlana, you no have, I mean, you didn't have that bag last night. You had the other one," I said.

Walking into the bedroom, I found the Louis Vuitton bag she'd had with us at Cain and brought it out.

Kylie rolled her eyes as Svetlana began sheepishly sifting through the bag, the Russian's fingers scouring its interior. She came out with her prize, a small plastic baggie half-filled with white powder. Svetlana held it up to the light with amazement. *"Da!"*

Kylie snatched the vodka from Svetlana as she examined her coke, but my Slavic roommate scarcely noticed. Flicking the upper end of the bag with her forefinger to get all the powder to the bottom, she began to estimate what was left.

"I told you she was losing it," Kylie said as she walked into the kitchen to prepare one of her martinis.

"You want one, Heather?" she asked over her shoulder as she pulled down the fiber to mix a cocktail.

She turned to look at me, and I shook my head no.

Svetlana disappeared into the bathroom. My head was swimming from the crisis averted, and I was finally beginning to wake up. Kylie came back in and sat in her favorite dilapidated throne, the vodka-infused queen of the model dorm.

I realized I was still wearing my now-smeared makeup from earlier in the day, still had on my now-rumpled skirt and top.

"I heard through the grapevine that somebody here was seen at the J. Crew casting?" she said, squinting her eyes at me.

I nodded slowly. "It's a huge job! Can you blame me?"

"Ha! I knew it! Don't worry, I've been going on mine, too. I'm not risking my career over some bloody toilet paper, you know?"

I felt guilty, but Kylie was right. It was just funny she was still pretending we didn't know everyone in the dorm was also going on their castings. That included Laura, although she still urged us to keep up the good fight. I skipped some of the less prestigious ones—that counts for something, right?

Snort, snort came from inside the bathroom.

"And Svetlana, too," Kylie continued. "I saw her call sheet. She's been getting sent on some coveted castings all of a sudden, like Baby Phat and Yves Saint-Laurent. Who knows how she's getting them. Anyhow, no way was she going to skip those. Rachel would send her bony ass back to the motherland.

"Have you met Rachel yet?" Kylie asked.

"No, well, at least not since I first signed with the Agency," I said.

Kylie chuckled. "Don't worry, you'll get to know her soon enough. And it'll be too soon, trust me. She'll probably tell you to lose some weight—not that she'd be wrong or anything."

I bit my tongue—it was the reality of the situation, and even if I didn't like Kylie's uncouth straightforwardness, well . . . let's just put it this way: If you're an NFL player, you have to make sure you keep beefed up, hit the weight room every day, drink those protein shakes, and are in tip-top physical condition to crush the competition. That's your *job*. Being a model's pretty much the opposite, yet at the same time very similar—a lot of people are very pretty, but when you're a model you get paid for not only being naturally beautiful but also becoming (and remaining) ridiculously skinny.

A final *snort* and then Svetlana popped out of the bathroom like a jackrabbit, bounced over to the computer, and lit up a cigarette as the machine booted up. I don't know why she even bothered hiding in the bathroom anymore. Habit, I suppose. Kylie leaned farther back and smiled to herself, turning on the TV. Apparently their near brawl two seconds ago had already passed cleanly out of their memories.

The model dorm equilibrium was back.

"Hey, Svet," Kylie casually said as she took a sip of her cocktail.

"*Da?*"

"What time you think we should get to Aer?"

"Svetlana call Tyler in few minute."

My stomach grumbled—I hadn't eaten anything all day, I realized. Popeye's fried chicken and biscuits danced across my brain for a moment, but I squashed those thoughts. Five pounds. And then just five more.

"Kylie, do you, um, think I could have one of those drinks?" I asked, pointing at the disgusting-looking cocktail.

She smiled broadly at me. I had come around.

"Well, why didn't you bloody say something before? And you're coming to Aer with us."

5

THE BEGINNING OF THE NEXT WEEK, I was back at the Agency for a check-in, which meant I'd be marched up on the scale again and roped around by serpentine measuring tapes as Luke checked my "progress." I guiltily slunk into the elevator as I realized that going to the gym the past month or so had totally slipped my mind. I'd had castings to worry about, and what I was going to wear when I went out with Robert in a day, and, well, how Laura was getting along, and just getting used to life in the city, of course, which offered so many distractions. They couldn't expect me to start a grueling exercise regimen right away. I had to become acclimated . . . right?

The elevator doors slid open. I had a view of the office through the massive glass windows. I spotted Luke far off, near the partition that walled Rachel off from the rest of the Agency's goings-on. He didn't notice I'd arrived and had on his face what could lightly be called an uncomfortable look.

Peering at the partition, as if he could see through to Rachel, Luke bit his lip and then moved his mouth, apparently answering one of his boss's questions—I couldn't hear anything, could just try to read his lips. I swear I could see a bead of sweat rise to his forehead and roll slowly down his face, but that's probably just my overactive imagination. Gone was the lithe charm, dazzling smile, and confidence I was used to seeing. He looked like a naughty schoolboy caught with his hand in a cookie jar.

His interrogation at the hands of Rachel evidently over, Luke spun on his heel to return to his desk. Head down, he smoothed his tailored blazer and sat down, still not noticing me.

I decided to give it a handful of seconds, then rang the buzzer. Luke sprang to his feet and looked immediately to be back to his old self, all smiles as he let me in. He rubbed his sweaty palms on the legs of his Tsubi jeans as he walked over.

"Hey, Heather, so good to see you!"

He kissed me on both cheeks, which I was learning was de rigueur for anyone and everyone I came in contact with.

"Hi, how are you . . . doing?" I said, careful not to let on I'd seen his interaction with Rachel.

"I'm terrific, and how are *you* doing, you're looking great! Everything all right at the apartment with the other girls? I hope they're not giving you a hard time," he said. Before I had a chance to even answer, he piped up again. "They aren't, are they? Because if anything happens, you just come straight to *us*, and we'll take care of it!"

"Okay, thanks . . ." I said.

"That's what we're here for!" he responded, flashing his $18,000 grin. "I hear you've been going to all your castings, which is just great!" Here he put on a more serious sympathetic mode. "No callbacks yet, but they're sure to come, when you're a girl as pretty as you."

He handed me another sheet with a dizzying grid of castings and go-sees, then pressed his finger down on a spot as I tried to decipher it.

"Now *this* one with the photographer Roberto di Luca is really important, so try to be on your toes, okay, sweetie?"

I nodded and gave the most convincing grin I could.

"All right—*dun, dun, dun!* Time to get measured, hon." Luke tried to play off the seriousness of my weekly face-to-face with my own potential unworthiness to be a model with this little bit, but it made me feel even worse, thinking about how many empty calories in champagne and vodka I'd slurped down since I last saw him, while not even stepping into the building's gym even for a second. I'd even walked by a Crunch gym earlier in the day and averted my eyes from the second-floor lineup of diligent people jogging on the treadmills, suddenly taking a great interest in a silly ad for Manhattan Mini-Storage that promised to help get rid of all that "summer clutter."

Brought to the scale, I stared dumbly at its blank digital display for a moment. My enemy didn't flinch.

"Okeydoke, off with the clothes!" Luke said. He may have sounded cheerful, but I felt like a guilty prisoner being prodded into a cell block, forced to strip down to my skivvies. The crime, Your Honor? EATING, OVERDRINKING, AND NOT WORKING OUT! *Bam!* Down with the gavel. My sentence: a lifetime of obscurity and cellulite. And there's certainly no La Perla on the inside, that's for sure.

I stepped onto the scale.

"Uh-oh," I let slip out, before I even thought about it.

Hmm . . . Five pounds off? I had *gained* two pounds.

Luke clicked his tongue lightly and wrote down the figure in what I now determined was his terrible, terrible little book.

Maybe it's . . . muscle? I have been walking around a lot. . . .

"Let's check on the waist," Luke said. He snared me in the measuring tape in various contortions, scratched some more figures in the book, and looked at me squarely.

"Okayyyy . . . Now, I know you've just gotten here, but we're really going to have to work on getting down to the size that's going to show exactly how beautiful you are to the world," he said. "You want that, right? We really want you to succeed. It's really your best interests we have at heart here, sweetie."

I nodded, the dutiful prisoner chained by his measuring tape.

"I mean, I've-just-been-running-around-a-lot-trying-to-get-my-bearings-and-my-mom-still-hasn't-sent-up-my-jogging-shoes-that-I-forgot-and—" I blurted out in one breath, trying to somehow compensate for my utter failure to the Agency not only to shed pounds but to not *gain* weight.

Luke cut me off and put a friendly hand on my arm. "Don't *worry,* honey; we just want you to be aware of this so it doesn't creep up on you and spiral out of control—we've seen *that* before, and it's not pretty; you don't want to look like some of the others." He paused, digging deep into his repertoire for this next one. He looked me straight in the eye with the manipulative sympathy of a parent to his child. "Let's just think how we're going to get that ten pounds off your gorgeous frame—we don't want you turning into a Miss Piggy, do we?"

The question was more or less answered by Luke's tone, but I still nodded rapidly.

"Okeydoke, that's it for this week!" With that, Luke wrapped everything up in a nice bow and started to walk me to the door. I looked furtively at the photos of the Agency's other, successful girls on the wall. *They* hadn't been putting on the pounds, that's for sure. Their perfect faces seemed to glare, and I swore a couple of the girls narrowed their eyes at me as I passed. The shot of a Mediterranean beauty who'd been particularly successful, landing a campaign for Versace last year, was the worst, and I imagined her chastising me in lilting *Italiano* as I passed, taking time from her gorgeous posing to shake her head at my clear obesity—and this when I couldn't pull a quarter-inch of skin off my ribs if I tried.

We had almost reached the exit when a voice shot out across the Agency's offices.

"Luke!" Rachel shouted. I gulped.

"Yes, Rachel?" Luke said, suddenly prey to the compulsion to wipe his hands on his jeans again.

"Is that Heather?" she asked from behind her wall.

"Yes, yes, it is," Luke said. He gave me the slightest of looks.

"Bring her over here to see me," Rachel said, as if it was a great privilege and not in fact a potentially scarring event.

"Okay!" Luke said, putting on his cheerful facade again. He gently coaxed me toward Rachel's desk. My hands started shaking a bit.

We had only met once before, and for only a brief moment. Back then, I had decided on the spot that she was the most frightening person I'd ever met. I had thought she hated me, but a call came through saying that the Agency wanted to sign me.

Rounding the thick partition, I saw Rachel for the second time in my life.

She was on the phone and held her finger up to me as she finished her conversation. I imagined maybe it was some high-powered casting agent or photographer.

"Honey, you tell your brother I'll be home early and that his room better be clean, or Mommy's going to have some words for him. Love you, too." She hung up.

She got up from her chair, poised. She stood six feet tall, with gorgeous blond hair pulled back in a ponytail. Although I knew she was nearing forty (or maybe had even passed that milestone—all the women in fashion never seemed to start gaining years on their birthdays until after thirty or so)—she was impeccable, her makeup flawless, nary a wrinkle to be seen on her smooth skin. Botox maybe? I still couldn't believe she'd had kids. The years had been kind to her, instilling a sense of wisdom into the girlish beauty that had made her such a standout model in younger years. She had an *air* about her, the kind that stops conversation midsentence when she walks in the door, an aura that emitted from her and demanded attention.

All rigid smiles, she stepped forward to shake hands, dispensing with the *kiss-kiss* I'd come to expect.

"Hiii, Heather, so nice to see you again. Welcome to the Agency," she said, shaking my hand with her delicate fingers. Her manicure was impeccable, and the rock on her left hand dazzled me in its massive beauty. She took a step back and examined me head to toe with a hawkish eye as she continued speaking. "We've got big hopes for you, and I am sure you're excited to really make your career with us."

"Oh, yes, I'm really excited. I should say, *really, really* excited to be working with you, and am, uh, just honored to be here," I said stuttering. The whole time Rachel just stared at me as I spoke, nodding slightly. Luke stood to the side, his hands held together in front of him like some solemn sentry.

"And how's everything in the apartment? Everything's *just fine,* isn't it? I know it's not the biggest space in the world, but this *is* New York, and, well, do you think I made it by worrying about silly things like closet space?" Her trademark phrase was even more brazen when coming straight from her mouth.

"No, no, of course not," I got out. Everything's *always* perfect at the dorm when talking to Rachel—even if there's a roach infestation or a broken heater or the poltergeist of an evicted model, it's still *just fine,* thank you very much!

"That's right, all I thought about was work, work, work, all the time work. I wasn't weak like some other girls—and who knows what they could *possibly* be doing now?" The way she said it was as if having any other life outside of having been a wildly successful model and now running a modeling agency in New York was a fate worse than death, on par with Chinese water torture or at least tripping at the Marc Jacobs show before all the flashing cameras at the tents.

Out of the corner of my eye, I noticed a pristine roll of toilet paper on Rachel's desk—the triple-ply, softest, cushionlike T.P. money could buy. But why did she have it right in front of her like that?

She saw me turn to it, and I quickly glanced away. I swear a slight grin flashed across her face.

"You girls should be grateful we have the apartment for you, otherwise you'd be all alone, trying to get an apartment in the Manhattan real estate market—that's no good, and let's just say it's pretty *expensive.* I'd imagine you probably wouldn't even be able to live up here to model, now would you, without us providing this perk?"

Her veiled threats shook me, and I just nodded.

"Anyway, let's get a good look at you," she said. Stepping up to me, she straightened my back so I stood perfectly straight and smoothed my shirt. She circled around me, gazing intently.

She stopped and looked me straight in the eyes. "Luke's told you to lose fifteen pounds, right?" she said.

"Well, I think he mentioned ten," I answered.

Rachel patted me on the shoulder and smiled her big terrifying smile. "Luke's such a sweetheart sometimes. Let's shoot for fifteen, dear."

Fifteen pounds? I'd fly away down Madison Avenue on a windy day if I got that thin! My heartbeat quickened, and blood flushed my face as I took it in stoically.

And that was it. She didn't say another word, just sat down at her desk and buried herself in her BlackBerry, which she had neglected for all of one and a half minutes. Luke motioned for me to follow him, and we silently left her to her own devices. When we were far enough away, Luke leaned in and whispered to me, "She's an amazing woman, isn't she?" Oh, yes, yes, I nodded, not wanting to give him the slightest hint that I could think otherwise.

"*Ciao*—and think about what Rachel said. . . ." Luke said, kissing me good-bye at the door.

As the elevator doors opened, I ran almost head-on into Laura, who was clutching her book and trying to sprint in the doors. I jumped—my nerves had been put on such an edge by this meeting.

"Oh, hey, Heather! Sorry, I was running late," she said. "Did you just have your measurements?"

"Yeah, they went really well!" I lied through my grinning teeth, Rachel's *fifteen pounds* echoing in my brain. Laura looked absolutely great, on the other hand, and I knew she never had to get measured at the Agency—she was always effortlessly thin.

"That's terrific. Listen, I gotta get up there; Luke said they had some big news they wanted to tell me in person, and I think this could be *it!* Don't tell the others, but I went to a couple—only a couple—important castings, but just because I was getting bored at home. I bet we get some toilet paper and some respect out of this. Ha!" *It* was the career-making high-profile campaign we all lusted after, the contract for something like Miu Miu that paved the future in (perfumed) gold. "Do you want to grab a tea at that new café when I'm done here?"

"Sure," I said.

"Okay, let's say in forty-five. Gotta run!"

She bounded into the elevator. The doors slid shut with a dull, tomblike *thud.*

My heart still pounded after encountering Rachel. I stopped walking to collect myself with a breath of crisp air. Standing outside the Apple store, I leaned against the brick wall, taking a moment to enjoy the beautiful New York autumn afternoon. It all felt, well, *right,* and I counted up to fifteen in my head, turning Rachel's orders into a childish numbers game as my pulse lowered a bit.

I was jolted from my daydream by a whiff of street-vendor hot dogs and a photographer who nearly knocked me over as he sprinted off the sidewalk into the middle of the street. A swarm of paparazzi materialized, seemingly emerging from manholes, hidden doorways, and unmarked cars. They all shouted, "KATE! KATE!! KATE!!!" at a woman in a black hoodie, sunglasses, skintight jeans, and knee-high boots who walked briskly down the street, trying not to pay attention to the fleet of parasitic photographers. As she steered to her destination, a friend attempted to keep the paparazzi at bay. Tourists stood, mouths agape, as the photographers shoved their way past them to this "Kate."

I stared at the woman, wondering who she was to cause such a furor. It seemed like I'd met her before somewhere. Finally, I realized it was Kate *Moss* they were stalking. The storm of photographers and shouts passed as they followed her toward West Broadway.

I decided to wander in the opposite direction, down a side street toward the Lower East Side to kill time before meeting Laura—and also get a reprieve from the hustling crowds of shoppers.

At a quiet portion of the block, sandwiched between the glossy storefronts of the luxury stores, was a humble stoop that had a sign affixed to it: GALLERY—2ND FLOOR, a vestige of old, freewheeling, art-crazy Soho. I realized I'd been so busy running around on castings and going out to clubs with Svetlana that I hadn't even *been* to an art gallery since arriving in New York—and that had been one of the reasons I'd been excited to come in the first place, the chance to see firsthand what some of the greatest artists in the world were doing in the city. I was curious to see what imaginative leaps they were putting on canvas, shaping into sculpture, cobbling together out of found objects, working long into the night in their studios, which were tucked away in buildings across the city. I decided to check out the gallery, opening the creaky door and tentatively ascending the stairs. At the entrance to the space sat a brunette girl with stylish glasses. She was poring over an issue of *Artforum* behind a small desk. It was dead quiet, and I had the irrational fear that I was inter-rupting her and that she was going to snap at me for breaking her concentration.

"Hi," she said warmly. She handed me a pamphlet on the show. "Let me know if you have any questions." She went back to the magazine. The gallery was near empty, except for one old woman dressed in vintage Chanel, wearing coke-bottle-thick glasses. She teetered from painting to painting, putting her nose to each piece to get a good look at the brushstrokes.

I walked to what looked to be the beginning of the exhibition. It was a solo show for a painter—his first, I read in the brochure. His paintings had a violent quality, the edges of the canvas ravaged by sloppy, frenetic brushstrokes. But each had a feminine figure in the center, barely recognizable, yet giving grace to the pictures. Rachel and her icy, so put-together, almost *too*-perfect presence, along with her drill sergeant weight-loss orders, melted away.

The old white-haired woman shuffled up to me and smiled. She pointed at one of the canvases. She leaned in and whispered, like it was our secret, "Beautiful, isn't it?"

"Yes, it really is," I answered, smiling back. You could tell that under the wrinkles and plastic surgery she had been a stunner once, and she still held herself together after all these years.

Leaving the gallery, I felt calm and ready to merge into the bustle on the streets again. I was going to make it, I felt—the paintings helped center me, putting everything in perspective.

The café was filled with a lazy afternoon crowd. Models from other nearby agencies dotted the room, their modeling books laid conspicuously on the café's tables so everyone could see whom they were with, the names of the agencies announced on the soft leather covers.

Laura hadn't shown up yet. I ordered a green tea from the spiky-haired Japanese man in a Loomstate T-shirt behind the counter, whose bony hips looked like they could barely hold up his faded boutique black jeans. I was pouring honey into the steaming paper cup of tea when I spotted Laura through the window. At the counter, a booker from another modeling agency was arguing with the Japanese barista: "I told you soy, and you put *whole milk* in my latte! Are you deaf or something?" she chastised him. He grimaced and took the offensive drink from her to replace it.

Laura walked up to me slowly, awkwardly. She held the roll of toilet paper I'd seen on Rachel's desk, and her eyes stared into the distance. Her face was as white as the toilet paper she held in her hand.

"Laura . . . ?" I said.

"They, they . . . dropped me from the Agency!" Laura stuttered, throwing an arm around me. The tears came. Through sobs she told me that Rachel said they'd had enough of their working relationship, that they knew she'd been skipping most of her castings and was a bad influence on the other girls. She was getting older, and the Agency wanted to concentrate on nurturing the new talent. Less troublesome talent. And just like that, they dropped her from the Agency. Which meant she was evicted from the dorm, sent home, back to Manitoba. They'd lured her in with some "big news." But instead of *it* happening, the exact opposite had. Rachel had given her the toilet paper as a cruel final parting gift to remind Laura what troublemakers met when they crossed her.

The bitchy booker from the other agency gave us a dirty look as she breezed past with her *soy* latte.

"It's going to be all right, Laura. I mean, it's not . . . not the end of the world," I told her, as convincingly as possible. She didn't believe me.

"Well, there goes my work visa," Laura sobbed.

I pulled a few sheets off the roll of toilet paper and wiped the tears from her face.

WE WANDERED FROM THE CAFÉ into the fading evening light, Laura's delicate frame nearly stumbling in her state of shock. Having no destination, we crossed Broadway, passing the Prada store and making our way through a crowd of people streaming out of the Prince Street subway stop. Laura and I kept going east into Nolita and just walked in silence. I didn't know what to tell her. The Agency had spoken.

Turning the corner, we came across a dingy-looking bar on Spring Street, some place we'd never normally go; Laura turned to me, hollow-eyed.

"I need a drink," she said. Laura, who rarely came along with us to the clubs and, if she did, kept her drinks to a maximum of two, had the urge to start throwing them back at a dive bar? Okay. . . .

We stepped into the place, which was half-filled with a motley crew of early-evening drunks, NYU kids, and a couple of off-duty fire-fighters. The bartender raised an interested eyebrow when we walked in. He probably didn't get very many models in there. He'd get over it.

"Maker's. Straight," Laura ordered definitively. She slugged it down as soon as it appeared in front of her and slammed down the glass dramatically on the bar.

A wolfish whistle came from behind us. The bartender looked the guy straight in the eye. "Shut the fuck up, Johnny."

No more whistles.

Laura ordered another Maker's, straight up.

Uh-oh. Backup may have been needed. Laura tossed the whiskey back in one giant gulp. Scratch that, it was *definitely* needed.

I stepped out for a second and made quick calls to Svetlana and Kylie.

"Laura's been evicted. Come meet us. She's already drinking like a fish. I don't know what to do! I've never seen her like this!"

When I spoke to Kylie, she complained, "Evicted?! Ah, bloody hell. . . ." A pause. "But I'm in my *sweats.*"

"C'mon, Kylie, just get over here!"

"All right, all right, be there in thirty."

Svetlana was already in SoHo, doing some shopping with one of her Russian banker "friends." She told me "Svetlana deetch" him and meet us as soon as she finished trying on a skirt at Marc Jacobs.

Back inside, Laura was chatting up the bartender, whom, I must say, looked pretty good in his faded rolled-up flannel that revealed his strong forearms. Maybe he reminded her of what she'd probably have to be going back to in rural Canada, and that slumming it in a dive like this would have to be what she got used to.

If two six-foot models showing up at the bar wasn't already spectacle enough for the regular crowd, when Svetlana and Kylie showed up, people *definitely* took notice. The men gawked. After they each initially looked around like, "You brought us *here?*" they quickly got over it and took to consoling Laura, who was already starting to get tipsy. Plenty of hugs and tears were exchanged. Svetlana carelessly tossed her Agent Provocateur shopping bag next to a bar stool. The sack was filled with kinky lingerie her Russian banker had put on his plastic just an hour or so ago.

"The Agency no fair! Svetlana *complain,"* the Russian said.

"Don't do it, Svetlana; it won't do any good. It'll just get you in trouble, like me," Laura said, having her last turn as den mother. "It's pretty obvious they can do anything they want. You saw what they did with Keyshia, and now it's happened to me."

"Who's going to clean the bathroom when you're gone, Laura?" Kylie asked. "You were so good to us. . . ." The Aussie started to get choked up a bit.

My ears had perked up at the mention of this mysterious Keyshia, whose bed I was now filling.

"Keyshia . . . ?" I asked the veteran model dorm trio. They all looked at one another. Laura decided to explain.

"Keyshia was this beautiful, absolutely stunning black girl from New Orleans. She was getting jobs, was really gonna make it, we all thought."

Kylie nodded. "Definitely." I sensed maybe it wasn't such a bad thing for them she wasn't around anymore.

"Keyshia so nice. Also, very good dancer," Svetlana said.

"Okay, and . . . ?" I asked.

"And . . . well, Keyshia went and got herself pregnant, by a club promoter in Meatpacking," Laura revealed, coming a bit closer. I could smell the bourbon on her breath. "It turns out the father was one of the bookers at our Agency. I didn't even know any of them were straight. She knew she was going to keep it—she'd already had one abortion that sent her into this deep depression. Anyway, before she was even starting to show her pregnancy *at all*, Rachel caught wind of what was going on—and evicted her right on the spot. Like I said, there's a mole out to get us girls in the dorm. I bet the bitch is threatened by us. So just watch it."

Kylie, Svetlana, and I sat silently at the bar for a moment, thinking about the treachery that could destroy our potential careers in a second. Dreams? *Gone.* Just like that. Laura took another sip of her whiskey, and the tears started coming to her eyes as she once again realized what she was losing. The model dorm was her home, and the girls there pretty much all the family she had.

Kylie broke the silence. "I'm surprised the Agency didn't let her keep the baby—they could have charged her double for having it in the dorm." She took a more serious tone. "I bet if they hadn't sent her home, just let her have some time off, she would have done all right after having the kid. She was gaining momentum and getting lots of attention." Kylie complained, "But the bloody Agency doesn't want it to be known at all that its girls are getting knocked up by its own sleazy bookers. Bad for business."

We all kept drinking as night descended. Laura flirted with the bartender some more, and he started giving us free drink after free drink. Some older banker types, who had ducked in for a drink after their twelve-hour day, started hitting on Svetlana—even here she managed to attract them, like moths to a flame. But Svetlana wasn't interested tonight. She brushed them off and instead had her eye on a tall skater-hipster who was sitting in the corner, whom she wouldn't normally run into at one of the big clubs. His perfectly mussed brown hair fell barely over his blue eyes, and he had a strong sexy jawline, even looked like he might be a male model himself. You could see he had a lean, strong body underneath his ragged jeans and T-shirt that read THE CLASH in bold letters. After

Svetlana gave him more than a few flirtatious looks, he came over to her and started talking.

I settled for chatting with Kylie, who seemed a little out of place when finally dragged outside of her natural habitat, the living room. The time blurred together as we all got good and drunk, trying to forget for a bit what had happened to Laura.

Svetlana and the skater hottie snuck off to a booth in the corner and were starting to make out a bit, her hand moving closer to his crotch. She whispered something in his ear, then sprang up and disappeared into a bathroom. Skater guy looked around, gave it thirty seconds, then followed her into the bathroom. Ten minutes later Svetlana emerged, smiling from ear to ear, her face flushed. She walked over to us to get another drink. The skater guy she'd just had unfettered raunchy bathroom sex with came out a minute later. He couldn't stop smiling and goofily waved to us when he sat down at the table.

"Svetlana *like*," she said deliciously, motioning to the guy. "He swimmer, very big, you know." She motioned downstairs—apparently skater/swimmer boy was carrying quite a package. Kylie yawned and rolled her eyes.

Then, as if she hadn't just been bent over the sink by this guy two seconds earlier, Svetlana leaned toward me and whispered excitedly, "Oh, Svetlana forget! Robert du Croix, he still in town. I saw earlier shopping. I wave, but he must have no seen Svetlana!" She became really excited and nearly started giggling. "Svetlana *must* see Robert. He so sexy, so cool. Did *Heather* hear he still in New York?" Her competitiveness did not go unnoticed.

"Umm, *no*. . . ." I think I did a pretty good job lying. I'd hoped Svetlana's infatuation with Robert was just a passing thing, induced by the alcohol and coke. Apparently not.

"Heather go out with Svetlana this week to see Robert, yes? You think he like?" she asked about herself.

"Oh, yeah, I bet he'll love you once he gets to know you!" I forced out. Faked cheerfulness, always fun. Not that I hadn't already smelled this, but I began to suspect Svetlana was maybe, *maybe* just a little crazy. What would she do if she found out I was going out with Robert? I mean, it was technically just to talk about my career, of course, but . . .

I tried to push the whole thing from my mind by ordering another gin and tonic. My Russian roommate switched gears back to the matter at hand—the guy whose penis had been *in* her hand just minutes before.

"He want to go back to his dorm—he on NYU swim team and live with them." She smiled salaciously. "You come with Svetlana? Hot guys—we have fun!"

I figured I already had enough on my plate, given that I was supposed to go out with her huge French crush the next night. Plus dealing with *one* dorm, was more than enough, so I shook my head. Kylie shrugged.

"Why the hell not, I'm already out of my bloody sweats, may as well make the best of it," she said. "Just make sure they've got some vodka, and I'll be happy. I think our work here is done."

"Svetlana tell." She walked as gracefully as she could over to the skater guy in the booth, who was about to become the most famous boy in whatever NYU dorm he lived in. A scrap of toilet paper stuck to Svetlana's shoe, a reminder of her flagrant bathroom tryst.

I took a sip of my fifth or so gin and tonic and pulled my phone from my bag to check for messages. The phone beeped—two new voice messages. I quickly stepped out on the street to check the messages.

"You have TWO new voice messages. First voice message," the computer voice told me.

The first message began. It was Robert! With his fetching French accent, Robert sounded honestly sorry, and charming as ever as he told me he had to break our date: "Hi, Heather, this is Robert. Listen, I'm terribly sorry, but something's come up. This just came out of the blue, as one says, and I'm afraid I'm going to have to cancel our plans for tomorrow night—" The message clicked off. My heart sank, and the moment froze as a trillion thoughts and emotions tore violently through my head, at once.

"End of first message. To save this message . . ." I was in a daze and didn't even press the button to save it. A group of guys in baseball caps and polo shirts walked by and whistled at me. I scowled. I was sort of stunned. I mean, it wasn't *that* big of a deal; he was not supposed to be around, anyway . . . but I was really disappointed. I had been looking forward to this ever since he'd called me that night. All that seemed like girlish fantasy, but still, after the rejection and frustration from the open casting calls, after Rachel essentially called me a porker, after Laura, whom I'd come to think of as my friend, had been brutally evicted . . . an evening with Robert had seemed like a step in the right direction. Careerwise, of course. What "came out of the blue"? Did he have to go to Paris suddenly, or did he just not want to see me and was trying to be nice about it? But what could I have done to scare him away—I hadn't even *talked* to him!

"Second voice message." The nice computer had decided to stop waiting for me to decide whether or not to save the first and just get along with the second. Probably from my mom or dad or someone. But, with a jolt, I realized it was Robert's voice again!

"Hi, Heather, it's Robert—my battery died while I was leaving the last message. As I mentioned, I'm sorry I have to cancel but was wondering, rather *hoping* you'd be free on Thursday instead. I truly hope I haven't inconvenienced you at all. I'm sure, like me, you have a very busy schedule. Please do let me know if this works for you. *Bisous.*"

He wasn't canceling, only postponing! I looked back at the onslaught of pessimistic thoughts that had come upon me from the first message and thought how quick I had been to assume the worst. And it wasn't bad at all, just a little postponement, as he said. Nothing to worry about.

"End of new messages. To save this message . . ." I pressed to store the message so I could listen to it again later and slowly put my phone away into my bag.

I still was a bit frazzled by how suddenly I'd reacted to the (false) news that Robert was going to be ditching me. I stood on the sidewalk for a little longer, my face looking strangely blank. Svetlana stumbled outside with a cigarette in her mouth.

"They no let Svetlana smoke inside!" she said incredulously. I must have still had a puzzled expression on my face, because she took one look at me and thought I was upset about Laura leaving. And I let her think just that.

"Don't be too sad; Svetlana still be here!" The Russian hugged me, and I wondered if she would have been leaping for joy if she knew what'd just happened.

Inside, Laura, three sheets to the wind, laughed with her new bartender friend. Svetlana's hot swim-team-slacker guy impressed Kylie with stories of whom she was going to meet in just a few minutes.

I was the only one who went home alone that night.

6

THURSDAY. It couldn't come quickly enough, keeping me going as I skipped through my castings. Would this label request me? Nope. What about the lovely people doing this campaign? Nope. The rejections didn't weigh much on me, though, as I spun daydreams about going out with Robert. For a couple of days I was living under a spell. Even though she had been going through the solemn ceremony of getting a plane ticket back to Canada and packing up her meager belongings that had fit in the tiny apartment, Laura's eviction and imminent departure didn't even seem to strike me as a possibility for *me*. The terrible round of measurements and blatant criticism from Rachel were shut away, locked up in the dusty cellar at the back of my head, where I wouldn't have to think about them. Of course *I'd* be safe.

Thursday afternoon, Svetlana had been practically tugging at my sleeves, whining, trying to get me to go out to the clubs on a Robert du Croix scavenger hunt.

"DJ Misto is in town for spinning. I think Robert big Misto fan. We go to this?"

I declined, making up a BS excuse about having to go out to dinner with a great-uncle who was in town. She seemed *very* intent on finding him that night, but it wasn't until later that I'd discover that her "crush" on Robert was more than just a passing fantasy. So I didn't pay her much mind and slipped out of the dorm, scot-free, while she powdered her nose in the bathroom. The Frenchman was waiting.

In the cab on the way to Soho, I tried to clear my mind of Svetlana and prepare to meet Robert. The taxi pulled to the curb in front of Cipriani. I paid the fare and got out. Despite the cool autumn evening, West Broadway still bustled. I checked the time on my phone—I was just a couple minutes late—took a deep breath, and went inside.

Cipriani buzzed with multilingual conversation. Its decor, high ceilings and walls covered in oversize artworks, gave it a cosmopolitan non-American feel. Well-dressed waiters whisked by with plates of delicate food for the diners. Robert had said he would meet me at the bar, but I didn't see him anywhere. I walked to the back to see if he had already taken a table. A waiter tried to get by me with handfuls of empty plates, and I moved to let him pass, slightly bumping a table behind me.

"Sorry," I said, turning to the couple I'd disturbed. The girl threw me a bitchy glare, and with a jolt I realized I'd interrupted a date of a certain high-profile Oscar-winning actress whose marital problems had been blasted all over the gossip pages for the past week. She was *definitely* not with her husband. I wondered if Page Six was going to pick up on this tomorrow.

"Um, yeah, sorry," I spit out, beating a retreat back to the bar. But where was Robert?

I decided to just wait, taking a stool at the bar, sitting next to an older guy in a tweed jacket who was looking over the latest issue of *The New Yorker* through thick round glasses.

"Yes, may I help you?" the bartender asked in accented English.

"A Bellini, please," I said as confidently as possible. Even though I'd been to a couple upscale dinners, I still felt a bit out of place here, my nerves already on edge waiting for Robert. The bartender mixed the champagne-and-peach-juice cocktail and placed it in front of me with a flourish.

I took a sip, throwing back my head slightly, waiting for the Frenchman to arrive. I seemed to vaguely recognize everyone in the restaurant, the well-heeled architects behind the city's glitz and glamour.

The door swung open, and there was Robert! He shook hands with the host, who immediately had one of the staff take his coat to be hung up. Robert spotted me at the bar and smiled broadly. A group of people near the entrance started whispering to one another when they saw Monsieur du Croix enter, then looked at *me* with great interest as he walked over to the bar, his tall frame and movie-star looks commanding the attention of the entire restaurant. I felt a thrill of delight, like I was onstage, wondering if they'd be trying all night to figure out who I was.

"Heather, a pleasure," Robert said simply as he kissed me on both cheeks. If it's possible, he seemed even *more* handsome than when I had met him at Marquee. Butterflies twittered in my stomach. "I'm so sorry I was late, the taxi driver got in—what do you call it?—a fender bender on Houston, and I had to dash the rest of the way here on foot. I hope you are not angry?"

"No, no, that's all right, Robert; I just got here a minute ago," I said. At that moment, I felt that even if he had been two hours late, rather than fifteen minutes, it would have all been worth it.

"Good—I would hate to sully your delicate face with frowns." He took my hand and pointed to a table the host had waiting for us. "Shall we?"

"Sure," I said, taking my half-drunk Bellini from the bar.

"Michel, just add that to the dinner bill," Robert said to the bartender, pointing to my cocktail.

"Oh, no, for a young lady with you, it is on the house," he said, smiling at me.

"Well, thank you," I said, smiling to myself.

We took our seat at the table, and without even ordering, a waiter brought a bottle of champagne to the table in an ice bucket.

Sitting there, across from Robert, surrounded by the highly refined crowd of the restaurant, I felt nervous and nearly tongue-tied. While this was the world that Robert lived in, I felt like a mere trespasser—enjoying the good life before the stretch limo turned back into a giant pumpkin.

I finished my Bellini, trying to look as seductive as possible (and maybe not fully succeeding, since I choked a bit on the last sip). Robert could sense my nervousness, though, and tried to warm me up.

"Well, I'm glad we have made time to see each other," he said, pouring me a glass of champagne. "And how have you been keeping yourself?"

"I've been good, thank you," I said. "How were things back in Paris?"

"Work is work, you know. People think I have the most glamorous life in the world. What they don't realize is how much it takes to keep things running smoothly," he said. "Just like those who think being a model is the easiest thing in the world, when I know you women must work *very* hard to be beautiful."

I nodded, thinking about the measurements at the Agency.

"How has your work been going? Has your agency been treating you well?" he asked.

"Yes, it's great. I mean, not *too* great, but I've been going to a lot of castings. . . ." *Everybody goes to castings,* I thought. So I continued. "And I think I may be getting a hold put on me for a shoot for Paul Smith later this month," I lied. A "hold" is when a model is an option for the shoot, which is still up in the air—the Agency won't book you for anything else that day, in the event they want to use you.

"Very good. I do not know how much it is worth, but if you have any questions or need advice about the fashion industry, please ask. I know a lot of photographers here and in Paris," he said, smiling at me and sipping his champagne. I thought that if someone had a way to bottle just a fraction of Robert's charm and sell it to other men, they'd become a billionaire overnight.

"And how is that girl—you live together, no? The Russian one, what's her name . . . Olga?" Robert asked.

"Olga? Oh, Svetlana, yes, she's just doing terrific," I said, notably avoiding the fact that she was getting ready to hunt Robert down that night. "Yes, we still live together in the, uh, *loft.*" I wondered if Robert realized by "loft" I meant "cramped model dorm."

"Svetlana, now I remember," Robert said reflectively. "She struck me as a bit . . . psychotic. I'm sure she's a lovely girl, though."

All this talk of Svetlana got me paranoid for a moment. I wondered if she'd be passing by on the street and, thunderstruck, see Robert and me seated together. I checked over my shoulder and determined with relief that she wouldn't be able to see in through the fogged windows.

"Is everything okay?" Robert asked, an eyebrow raised. "Are you waiting for another man?" he joked.

"Yes, wait, no, I mean, everything is okay. I was just looking for the waiter to get more water," I said, covering.

We ordered dinner and passed the time with great conversation, Robert asking me about my family, how they were treating me at the Agency, what I had dreamed of as a little girl. . . . My nervousness had totally washed away by the time the steaming mussels arrived. I barely stopped to eat, just talking as Robert listened, his handsome face always showing interest. After a while I realized I had pretty much been dominating the conversation. Not having really gone on any dates since I got to New York, just spending evening after evening with other models and club promoters, trying to shout over the club music, I was now bubbling in Robert's gracious company.

"Sorry I'm going on like this. You must be bored," I said to Robert.

"Bored? Not at all. I doubt anything you could say would bore me," he answered, lightly touching my hand for a moment.

I blushed. My heart did pirouettes inside my chest. I felt like I had wandered into someone else's life, midscene, and that this whole thing wasn't happening, that it was like a movie that would end, lights coming on, and I'd realize it was all make-believe.

Did he really like me? Or was this just how he treated everyone, his smooth demeanor and charm impossible to turn off? I tried to stop second-guessing everything and just enjoy the moment.

Robert moved the conversation to what I should be doing if I really wanted to model. He talked about the contacts he had at magazines, the photographers in Paris who were his childhood friends, the designers who would absolutely fall for me if they had a chance to meet me. . . . I felt lost in the world of names and personalities he was introducing me to, but I smiled and told him how grateful I'd be for any help he could give me, how unbelievably nice it was of him to offer.

At least four times during our dinner, Robert's friend, the maître d', came to ensure that everything was perfect for us.

"This is Heather, a model," Robert introduced me. "Keep an eye on her—you can see from her beauty that she's going to be incredibly successful."

"A great pleasure to meet you, Heather," the host said. "Enjoy your meal."

When we finished dinner, the waiter brought a dessert menu, but I abstained, not wanting to look like a pig, even though I'd eaten only a couple mussels and had barely touched the seared tuna. I was getting trained well.

Robert, thankfully, didn't insist on my eating dessert—although he did order two espressos to settle our stomachs after the meal. He sipped his coffee and looked at me with his devestatingly blue eyes that any girl would give her left foot to wake up to in bed every morning.

"I am so glad we were finally able to catch up. I have thought of you often, wondering how things were," he said. "I've been working so hard that the chance to just spend a dinner with a beautiful smart girl like you is very welcome. And now that the plans for Shiva Bar here in the city are seeming to roll, as one says, we will perhaps get to see each other more often."

"I'd like that," I said softly, smiling.

"Would you like to go out now, or are you too tired?" he asked. "A friend of mine from Paris is spinning at Bungalow tonight, and I'd love to say hello. I haven't seen her since her last set at Shiva Bar, which seems like ages ago."

Bungalow 8 was one of the most exclusive clubs in the city, nearly impossible to get into—Svetlana and I had actually only succeeded twice in getting past the doormen, and those were on slow nights. Too many times had we been drinking at Cain, Prepost, or

Bed and then decided to try to get into Bungalow, only to be humil-
iated at the velvet rope by the unsmiling bouncers who guarded the
gates to exclusivity. Unless you were somebody, or were the close
friend of somebody, chances are you'd be left out in the cold. And
now to go with Robert! But I paused before eagerly agreeing, remembering that back at the dorm, Svetlana had said she was going
to try to track down Robert wherever—what was the name?—DJ
Misto was at.

"Is your friend DJ Misto?" I asked, trying to sound as innocent as
possible.

"Oh, no!" he said. Then, lowering his voice: "Just between you
and me, I can't stand all that trance music shit."

I nodded in total agreement, even though I didn't really know
anything about it. Svetlana was off Robert's scent. For tonight, at
least.

"Let's go, then!" I said.

Robert settled the tab, and he escorted me by the arm, like a
gentleman. Along the way I felt like the eyes of all the women in the
restaurant were on me—I was convinced I was with the most handsome man in the place.

A refreshing breeze wafted down the street, a few golden leaves
falling gently to the ground. Even in the heart of the city, the scent of
autumn hung in the air. Everything seemed so perfect, the elegant
dinner, the conversation, and now him standing there in the fall night,
holding my arm, waiting for the town car the host had called for us.

If there was ever a more perfect time to kiss a girl in the history
of kissing girls, this was it, and I coyly looked to Robert, my eyes
fluttering. Was it going to happen? He was occupied with looking
down the street for the car. *Look here!* my eyes said.

The car wheeled around the corner on Broome Street and
stopped in front of us. Damn!

He opened the door to the car for me, and we both got in.

"Twenty-seventh between Ninth and Tenth, please," he said to the driver, who nodded silently and sped us uptown to West Chelsea and the glitzy Bungalow 8. He turned to me. "I hope you'll have fun tonight. Just let me know if you get bored, and we can go."

I didn't say it out loud, but I was pretty sure I wouldn't get bored, given Bungalow's reputation.

We pulled up in front of the club, which sits on a strip of clubs on Twenty-seventh—but it's the haughty beauty queen of the block. Outside was a mass of wannabes trying to get inside, whining, cajoling, even threatening the grim-looking doormen. Groups of four or five girls, all beautiful and dressed to the nines, were turned away at the velvet rope, where pretty much anywhere else in the world they would've been welcomed with VIP treatment. It seemed to be an especially busy night.

A man in a suit yelled into his cell phone, pacing back and forth. "Goddamn it, Susie, come out to get me. They're not letting me in! What? What? Speak up. What do you mean they're not letting anyone get people from outside? Don't they know who I *am?*"

Robert coolly led me to the edge of the jostling crowd, and I wondered for a second if even *we* wouldn't be able to get in.

The doorman known as "Disco" spotted Robert. "Move! Move! Let them through!" he barked at the crowd, pointing to Robert and me. The sea of commoners parted, and Robert led me to the entrance.

"Robert, my man, what's going on?" Disco said, opening the rope to let us in. "Amy's inside, say hello."

I heard the man in the suit yelling as the door closed behind us: "Hey! Why do *they* get to go in?! I thought you were full! I'm partner at Southall, Cleary, and Williams!"

I smiled.

Inside, I saw why they were being such bastards at the door. It was as if every young A-list starlet and socialite had converged on this one spot for the night. As we walked past the couches on the side, down the narrow walkway in the middle, I recognized a famous face at practically every table. The two times Svetlana and I had been here before, I'd seen a couple people I recognized, but nothing like this—that's probably why they had let us in, figuring that if there weren't celebrities at the ready, a couple of models wouldn't hurt.

The club was full, but not so crowded that you were constantly jostling into people. (The moneyed celebrity classes like to have their space.) As we walked toward the rear, I still looked fearfully behind the potted palm trees, like Svetlana might jump out, wielding a stiletto heel, even though I knew there was probably no way she would have gotten in.

Robert led us to the last booth before the bar. "Excuse me just one moment," he said. "I must say hello to Amy." "Amy" was Amy Sacco, the mastermind behind the club Lot 61 in the nineties and now Bungalow 8. She was holding court in *the* prime booth, surrounded by a cast of dazzling friends. On her left sat a certain famous blond twenty-year-old actress who was a born-and-bred New Yorker—she was getting tons of buzz for a movie she had just starred in, playing an American trying to find her way through British high society. She was dressed down in jeans and a tight-fitting T-shirt and, to my shock, had a bullring dangling from the front of her nose—some girls wore a stud on the side of their nose, but not something like *that*. On Amy's right was another young actress, who, if she hadn't been getting the *critical* acclaim of Amy's other friend, had been getting a lot more attention than her competitor—a highly publicized eating disorder and alleged drug problem had been tracked by the press as closely as a presidential election. From the empty glasses in front of her, it looked like she was slugging down a few too many cocktails for her current rail-thin weight.

Amy's face lit up when she saw Robert, and she stood up to kiss him on both cheeks. Robert was wise enough to just give his brief hellos to her friends and then let them all be again.

"Is that . . . ?" I asked Robert when he turned back to me, discreetly nodding to the booth.

"Yes," he said, smiling. "I'll introduce you to them later. They both love Shiva Bar when they come to Paris. Let's get some drinks."

He went to the bar and shook hands with the bartender, who took his order before everyone else's—Robert seemed to know *everyone*. My date introduced me to Mikael, a colleague of his from Shiva Bar. We didn't bother him too long, though. Mikael was busy: The handsome comanager was with *two* Estonian models that night.

We walked back to the booths, and I sipped my mojito, trying not to stare too much at the club patrons. All of a sudden there was a bit of rumbling in the crowd, as the impeccably groomed heiress to the Donovan family resort fortune entered. She was the queen of the gossip rags, on Page Six almost daily for every little thing she did. Trailing a few steps behind her was a gigantic bodyguard, who held her tiny dog in front of him on a satin pillow. I even recognized the dog from the gossip pages. I think its name was Heinrich von Doesenflieger VIII. Or maybe VII. I can't remember. The girl's Venezuelan oil heir boyfriend was nowhere to be seen—the Internet had been buzzing with speculation that they were on the outs. After saying hi to Amy, she sat down in a booth where some friends of hers were waiting. She reached nonchalantly out to the bodyguard without even looking at him, and he handed her the dog, which she gave a few gentle strokes to, before handing it back to the bodyguard/dog holder. He put the spoiled pooch back on the pillow he held in his hands before him and looked suspiciously at the crowd.

"Robert!" an über-tall, blond girl called to my date in a crisp British accent as she spotted him while dancing. She had been swaying on the dance floor, her cascading hair flipping back and forth in between sips from her champagne flute. She looked like she was a model herself; though in her mid-twenties, she would have been reaching retirement age for most. Jealousy lurched up in my chest.

Laughing, all smiles, she came over to us, a towering man following behind her.

"Trina, darling, how long has it been?" Robert said joyfully, greeting her with a *kiss-kiss* on the cheek.

The broad-shouldered man with her stepped forward and shook hands with Robert. His hair matched Robert's in intense stylishness, dark in its luster as it swooped back. He looked to be twenty-five at most. And *hot.*

"And Mark, how have you been keeping yourself?" Robert asked.

"Well, you know . . ." the man answered, winking at Robert as he took a swig of a drink that looked like straight vodka on the rocks.

It seemed like an eternity, but he finally turned to introduce me.

"Heather, this is Trina Raniski, talent manager and producer extraordinaire, and Mark Powers, of the very 'it' firm, Mark Powers PR."

Powers looked at me. "*Spicy,*" he said. But in a playful way.

"These are very old, dear friends of mine. We summered in the Hamptons briefly this year," he said.

Powers chuckled at this. "Yes, we did. You know, I'm surprised Charles never mentioned anything about how we left the guesthouse after that last party," he said. "But he was so drunk he probably thought *he* did that to the carpet."

They all laughed, and I felt, well, just a *bit* left out, having, of course, no clue who Charles was or possibly being able to imagine what happened to his carpet, nor even if it was shag or short or . . . you get the idea.

"And what do *you* do, Heather?" Trina asked archly.

"You know, I work in . . . fashion," I said, suddenly feeling a bit less accomplished than Robert's two young friends, who already seemed to have the world in their hands. Besides, being *just* a model, with so many other girls running around like cloned giraffes, seemed a bit—I don't know how else to put it—*just* being a model. I didn't want the conversation to grind down because I was trying to get paid to put on clothes. I could imagine them treating me like a two-year-old if I started talking about anything besides stylists and dieting habits.

"Don't be so modest!" Robert cut in. "Heather's going to be the next top model; she's with a very good boutique agency." Robert seemed very eager to let it be known that I was a model. I tried to ignore that and focus on how glad he was to introduce me.

"Oh, that's great," Trina said while sending off an e-mail on her BlackBerry.

"Robert, you and the models," Mark said, giving him a bit of a nudge in the ribs. What was *that* supposed to mean? Powers then turned and looked me up and down. "What'd you do last?"

I started to blush, knowing full well I didn't have *anything* in the bag in New York. Before I could start stammering, Robert jumped in to save the day. "She's on hold for a shoot for Paul Smith, and I'm sure she'll get it—she's just gotten here, already doing great. Big things in the future for her," Robert said. I liked that he was sure enough of me as a model to tout me to his friends. But I also didn't want to go deeper in my white lie about Paul Smith. I tried to shrink a bit beside him, hoping that the conversation wouldn't go further, that they'd go back to reminiscing about the Hamptons.

"Oh, I love their winter line. Have you seen it, Robert? You'd look great in the striped cashmere sweater they're pushing," Powers said. Then, without missing a beat, to me: "Do you live around here?"

Oh, shit. I imagined Bungalow's chic interior morphing into the threadbare stinky living room that was the model dorm and what he would think. At least we'd gotten away from the designer I'd fibbed about.

"Yeah, I . . ." I paused. "Live downtown, I mean pretty far downtown."

"Oh, like the Financial District?" Powers asked. "I love it down there. There are some amazing lofts," he said, obviously assuming I lived in one of the sprawling apartments and *not sharing bunk beds* in a shoe box with a cantankerous alcoholic Aussie, a promiscuous Russian, and a slowly rotating cast of strangers. I didn't correct him.

Robert looked to the DJ booth and saw his friend. He turned to Trina and Powers. "Can you keep Heather entertained for a few minutes while I say hello to my friend upstairs?" he asked. "Well, don't entertain her too much, just keep her away from the Donovan girl— don't want her going down *that* path."

Trina looked over at the girl with the dog and rolled her eyes. "I know what you mean," she said.

Robert leaned in and whispered in my ear, "You look lovely. I'll be back in a minute. If you need another drink, just tell the bartender to put it on my tab."

"Okay, no problem. Your friends are nice," I said.

Robert made his way through a trio of drunken dancing socialites as he aimed toward the DJ.

"Have you known Robert long?" Trina asked me, stuffing her

BlackBerry away in her gold water snake Louis Vuitton bag—this season's must have—which must have cost as much as three months' rent at the model dorm.

"Not too long, I guess. This is our first . . ." I almost said "date," but didn't want Trina to report back to Robert. "Our first time hanging out since I met him. I mean, he's been in Paris for a bit."

"Well, good luck," Trina said rather mysteriously, I thought.

Powers whispered something in her ear, and she snapped around to look at the super-skinny actress, who had gotten up from the booth. She teetered and swayed as she pushed her way through the line to the bathroom, obviously pulling VIP peeing status.

I looked around again and saw a woman sitting on one of the couches by herself, obviously out of her mind on some combo of alcohol and drugs, playing air guitar to the remix of an eighties tune that pounded from the speaker. Then, with a shock, I saw what looked like the child actress from the classic TV show *Big Home* putting back a shot of liquor with the comedian who had played her *dad* on the show! In her teens she had built a multimillion-dollar empire branding herself and was now a freshman at NYU, although I had read that she had maybe lost her class schedule and thought lectures were held at the clubs every night. Her TV dad puffed on a cigar and ashed it in his empty shot glass, chatting intensely with the girl.

"Hey, that's . . ." I said to Trina, tipping my head toward the actress.

"Yeah, one of my old boss's clients when I was an agent trainee," Trina said. "Can't stand her . . . but don't tell *her* that! She's here practically every night."

Turning away from that spectacle, I saw a man in an impeccable black suit with a skinny black tie weaving his way down the "runway" in the club between the palm trees. He looked vaguely uncomfortable, like he wasn't used to this sort of hoopla. He came to a halt upon seeing Trina.

"Trina, how are you?" he said, greeting her with a broad warm smile, in strangely accented English that sounded like a mix of French and German.

"Willem!" Trina said. "I've been meaning to stop by the new gallery, but I've been trapped out in B.H. trying to get this feature off the ground for the past couple months. How have you been?"

"Ah, no problem. The gallery, with any luck and a bit of hard work, will be there for decades," the man answered. Although he looked to be in his mid-forties, he carried a sense of boyishness about him, like life still held a lot of wonder for him.

"Oh, I'm sorry, Willem, this is Heather," Trina said, remembering she was supposed to keep an eye on me. "Heather, Willem."

"Nice to meet you, Willem," I said, shaking his hand.

"And you, Heather," he answered. "What is it you do to keep yourself busy in the city?"

"I, um, model a bit," I answered, hoping that I wasn't going to get the third degree about what jobs I had done, in which I would be forced to pull out my resume of all the jobs I *hadn't* gotten, the ones I'd *almost* been chosen for. . . . But Willem spared me.

"Lovely, lovely, a fine way to spend a bit of time as a young woman," he said. The whole time he looked me in the eyes and didn't do an up-and-down glance of me. His eyes were warm and genuine, and I could tell immediately he wasn't interested in trying to pick me up.

"And I take it you run a gallery of some sort?" I asked, a bit shy about broaching art-related things, assuming people would immediately think: *What would she know about that? She's just a model.* After Svetlana mistook "MoMA" for "Moomba," I'd been carrying around my interest in art like a burglar who stashes his loot in a hidden barn, far away from the public eye.

"Not just *any* gallery, Heather," Trina said before Willem could answer. "*The* gallery of the moment right now, just moved to a bigger space in Chelsea. They show *everyone,* from Damien Hirst to Basquiat to Serra."

"You have Jean-Michael Basquiat?" I asked breathlessly. He was one of my favorite artists, a fearless painter from the early eighties in New York.

"We show our fair share of his work, had a large show last year at the old space," he said. "What do you think of him?"

"I *love* his stuff. I mean, I've been meaning to buy a book on him and . . ." I realized I was on the verge of babbling, I was so excited to meet someone who, instead of shutting me down as a nitwit model who had no right discussing anything besides fashion, was actually encouraging me. "I guess I really, really like him, yeah." I said, a little giddy.

"Ah, you'd have really, really liked the Palladium, then, if you had been born in time to enjoy it," teased Willem playfully.

"The Palladium?"

"It was, perhaps, the Studio 54 of the eighties. Basquiat had a mural there. A pity that the club is now history. You could pay homage, but the building was demolished to make way for an NYU dorm. Anyhow, we have some Basquiats in the back that haven't been shown for years that I might even let you see."

He handed me a thick two-tone business card. It read:

WILLEM CLIJSTERS
CLIJSTERS GALLERY

The address, in Chelsea, was engraved on the back.

"I'd love that," I said, thinking how amazing it was that I'd been wanting to see some galleries, and here I'd just met someone who had his *own* space, and pretty big, if I was to believe Trina. I put the card carefully in my bag, where I wouldn't lose it.

A funny thought crossed my mind: I'd never met a Belgian before, or at least not that I knew of, although I'd eaten a couple Belgian waffles back in the day. This seemed like it'd be a pretty funny thing to say to Willem, but I realized that all the booze was probably catching up to me, and I wisely kept my mouth shut.

Out of the corner of my eye I saw Robert leaving the DJ booth to come back to us. I waved. Willem had begun talking to Trina about something or other, and when he saw me wave, he looked over toward Robert. A bit of color drained from his face.

He snapped out of his conversation, strangely nervous. "If you'll excuse me, ladies, I need to find my colleagues, but it's been a pleasure talking to both of you, and a great pleasure meeting you, Heather," he said. He hurried away toward the bar. I thought it was weird that he would just bolt like that, but Trina didn't seem to notice anything strange, or at least didn't show it.

Robert finally made it through the dancing socialites again and was back at my side. He was all charm still, and I thought he looked even hotter than earlier in the night—but that was probably due to the mojito more than anything else. He put his arm around me, and I felt a jolt, as if he had just blasted pure electricity into me.

He looked off to where Willem had disappeared.

"How's everything, Heather? Trina hasn't been boring you with stories about Hollywood, I hope," he said, touching my arm lightly.

"Oh, Robert, *stop,* just because you always wanted to be a big movie star doesn't mean that you need to trash the industry. Anyhow, love, where would you be without stories of those trashy starlets dancing on the tables at your Shiva Bar?" she joked.

He had a strange forced smile and moved close to me.

"Who was that man you were talking to earlier—was that Willem Clijsters?"

"Yes, why? Do you know him?" I said.

"Yes, only in passing, I suppose," he answered. He looked around the club for a bit, his arm still holding me against his side. "I've heard some things about him and know that perhaps it isn't in the best interests of a girl like you to be around him."

"Oh" is all I said, confused, and not daring question Robert further.

His body felt tense, but it didn't last long, as he turned to look down at me, smooth Robert once again.

"Listen, Heather, I hope this won't disappoint you, but I've been working all day, and I'm starting to feel a bit tired—would you be disappointed if we left now? I'm sure you have things to do in the morning. I wouldn't want your bookers getting me on the phone and screaming about how I keep their models out all hours of the night!"

"Sure," I answered, still wanting to stay a bit longer, but knowing that one more mojito would probably send me off into drunkyland, and I'd be dancing on the tables soon enough if I stuck around, embarrassing my date.

We said our good-byes to Trina and Powers, who were busy dissecting a washed-up teen star's embarrassingly revealing outfit.

"I think I see nipple . . . again," Mark said, shaking his head.

As we left, the actors and actresses, heiresses of the world, producers, Belgian art dealers, PR people—they all faded into a dull roar and continued to party as the door shut behind us and we stepped onto the street. The block was fairly deserted, even though a group of diehards still stood outside the velvet rope, shivering, maybe figuring that if they hung around long enough, the bouncers of Bungalow would feel sorry for them and let them in. They never do.

Robert and I stepped off to the side. We faced each other, close, his eyes looking into mine. Even though I'm tall, he still stood above me, which is always catnip for us model girls who tower over even the normally tall men of the world.

"Thanks so much, Robert. This was a really great tonight, the dinner was amazing, and I really enjoyed meeting your friends," I said.

"No, thank *you*, Heather. It's spending time with a girl like you that reminds me it won't be that terrible at all to leave Paris and move here," he said. "I'm meant to return to Paris later this week, but should be back in a month again. I hope we can meet then."

He leaned down, his lips coming close. . . . . I closed my eyes. . . . He kissed my forehead and pulled me in close. *Forehead?* I thought for a second. That passed and I just let go, warmth flooding my body. I put my arms around him and held him tight.

At last he pulled delicately back and gave me a million-Euro grin.

"Let's find you a cab—what would your mother think, staying out all night with a French stranger?"

I laughed and held onto his arm as he waved down one of the waiting taxis. He handed the driver some money as I got in the cab.

"Don't worry, the fare's taken care of. Good night!" He pecked me on the cheek before closing the cab door. It lurched forward and sped off, back downtown.

Returning to the model dorm, I found the living room eerily quiet. Kylie had already gone to bed, as did Laura, who was counting her days until her flight. Svetlana probably wasn't back yet. I didn't go directly to sleep but instead threw my bag down on the floor and fell into the lumpy couch, staring at the ceiling, my mind replaying everything that had happened.

I could still taste the crisp fresh mojito, could feel Robert's presence, how he'd been the perfect date. And Bungalow's unabashed glitz and glamour, the playground of the rich and famous, allowing themselves to be unashamedly, well, rich and famous. The worn-down surroundings of the apartment only reminded me how far I was from leading that life full-time, not just as a tourist. Why *couldn't* I, though? I just had to stick it out here, make sure I go to all the castings, really work on getting those pounds off. . . . I'd make Rachel proud!

I brushed my teeth, exfoliated, drank a liter of water so I wouldn't have a hangover, and then slipped into my comfy pajamas, ready to sleep. But, lying in my bed, I turned over in my mind one odd thing about the evening: What was it that had caused Willem, who had otherwise seemed so easygoing, to leave the conversation suddenly, and why had Robert been asking about him in such a strange way? I pondered this mystery as I rocked gently to sleep.

A few hours later, just after four A.M., I was woken by Svetlana, who stumbled in after a night out. She came to the side of the bunk and poked me in the ribs with a slender finger, obviously drunk (and probably a bit more).

"Heather, *Heather!*" she said, whispering in that loud shouting voice that only drunk people seem to know how to pull off.

"What is it, Svetlana?" I asked groggily.

"Svetlana no find Robert." She seemed on the verge of tears.

JEANETTE. EVEN NOW, writing the name sets my teeth on edge just a little. She was our newest roomie, but not for long.

After Laura was sent packing back to Manitoba a week after Rachel dropped her from the Agency, we were down to just three, the smallest group of girls I'd see at the dorm. Kylie, Svetlana, and me. We settled into domestic routines together, and everything seemed to fall into what I guess could be called normalcy.

Without Laura around, the dorm had gotten a bit shabbier and a lot dirtier, as if she had been the slender piece of twine that barely held the place together. Dishes (mostly cocktail glasses) cluttered the sink, and Svetlana's mug of cigarette butts started to overflow. A suspicious odor started to cling in the living room, but we never bothered to investigate it. We had more important things to do, like deciding what club Svetlana and I were going to go to, and Kylie watching marathons of *Project Runway* on TV while getting blind drunk.

Robert du Croix was never far from my mind. It seemed that with each day that passed, the memory of his smile, his ease of manner, his depth of charm grew in my mind, so that he took up all the space that other men I was meeting could have had—his current distance only made my idealization of him stronger. Out with Svetlana on the usual model party circuit, I still talked politely to the cute boys we inevitably attracted, but never had any interest, despite the amount of champagne that'd been bought for us at the VIP tables. (The men were never without enough attention, however, with Svetlana and the other girls around!)

Maybe a week after Bungalow, I came across the card Willem had given me for the Clijsters Gallery. I'd wanted to start going to galleries, expand my interest in things outside of clubs and fashion, cultivate my knowledge of art. Willem would be a perfect guide into that world. But Robert's cryptic comments about him kept me away. His disapproval of Willem mattered to me, when I normally wouldn't have cared at all. I wondered what Robert would think if I went to the gallery—I knew when I cared that much what somebody thought about me, I was starting to tread in serious crush territory! Potential jealousy came, too.

I thought about the blond I'd seen Robert with at Marquee the first time I met him, and I began imagining what he'd be doing in Paris, how he spent his nights, if he was seeing women over there, if he had a mistress he kept who whispered sweet French nothings in his ear at night in his floor-through apartment in the Marais. On a whim, I bought a French phrase book, which I peeked at when the other girls weren't around and stuffed in my luggage to hide when they were.

I managed to stamp down my idle thoughts of Robert and his

imagined French wench by trying to focus on how I was going to get my modeling career off the ground and get out of the model dorm. Besides, that's what had initially drawn me to Robert, right? The fact that he would have sound advice and good connections, that he wanted to help out a girl like me. I mean, could he really be interested in a no-name model, when it came to romance? I'm sure he was just a nice guy and that I was blowing things out of proportion, that he genuinely just liked to help people out, as undoubtedly so many had done for him when he first began his career as a club impresario. That's what I told myself. And I started thinking about Rachel's "suggestion" about my weight the day they evicted Laura— but just for my career, of course.

I poked my head into the gym in the building—but I didn't actually *work out*. It's important to survey a gym before you actually use it, I told myself. Besides, my mom still hadn't sent up my gym sneakers, and who had the money to buy new ones in the most expensive city in the country? There are priorities for a girl, and investing in pumps at a Barney's warehouse sale is more important than some Adidas sneakers (Or at least I assured myself at the time . . .).

Even though I wasn't exactly hitting the gym hard, I'd managed to whittle down my meals to one and a half a day or so, which was some real progress. Plus I was walking around to my castings, which I convinced myself was just as good as going to the gym. When I went back for my next measurements, I'd dropped the two pounds I'd mysteriously gained, and although I was still just back where I started, Luke had acted like I'd just won the New York City marathon when the scale showed the tiniest of dips. I also got a callback for a small catalog shoot and had a good feeling I was going to get the job. Though the pay would cover maybe one-twentieth of a Marc Jacobs dress, it was a step in the right direction. *If* I got it. But it seemed the Agency still had faith in me, which was important.

And Rachel hadn't called me in yet for any "pep talks," so I'd dodged that bullet so far.

Then Jeanette arrived.

It was early one evening. Svetlana was blasting some horrible Russian techno in the living room, half-naked in her pink bathrobe. She'd been sashaying around entirely nude after her shower, and I'd convinced her to at least put on the robe, which she did, grudgingly, of course.

All of a sudden, there was a small knock at the door. *Rap-rap.*

"Uh, come in?" I said. Nobody had told us about a visitor. Typical Agency behavior.

The door swung open to reveal a beautiful dirty blond saddled with suitcases. She had freckles on her angelic face, and you could tell that underneath her oversize sweatshirt and out-of-date acid-washed jeans was a perfectly shaped body. She just stood at the threshold and smiled at us, oblivious, as the door slammed behind her.

"Hi, I'm Jeanette," she said innocently. She looked gorgeous and picturesque standing there, so sweet. "I'm from Utah."

I think I may have heard Svetlana hiss, and even Kylie called from the bedroom, where she lay in a bunk, nursing a hangover. This new girl carried a certain presence noticeable at first glance, and maybe Kylie's radar went off. "Who's that?!" she shouted before groaning and going back to sleep, not bothering to wait for an answer.

The doorman stood behind Jeanette, grinning foolishly. I had never seen him leave his post, but apparently this beauty was enough to rouse him from his laziness and help bring up a bag or two.

"Come in, Jeanette, the Agency must have sent you," I said as Svetlana narrowed her eyes and turned back to her computer chat with whatever hairy Russian horn dog was on at that moment. I helped her with her bags. "I'm Heather, and this is Svetlana." I motioned to the Russian.

Svetlana barely moved to look at our new arrival. "Svetlana busy," she said, taking a studied drag off her cigarette.

"Great to meet you!" Jeanette exclaimed.

"Svetlana feel same," she barely acknowledged, clicking to another message.

I took one of Jeanette's bags from her.

"Thanks, Heather," Jeanette said to me, all smiles. "Wow, this place is *great!*" she exclaimed, looking around at our dingy unclean surroundings.

"Yeah, it's really *something*," I said, wondering what planet this girl could be from. Unless my sense of smell was totally off, there was still an unbelievably funky odor invading the living room, but this girl didn't seem to either care or notice. There was something charming in her obliviousness. She was going to have a hard time in this cutthroat world, I thought.

As Jeanette set her bags down and took in the place, I couldn't help but feel the slightest twinge of jealousy already. She was picture-perfect beautiful, very slim, but still with an hourglass figure, unlike a lot of the twiggy, almost androgynous models out there. Even though she didn't look a day over eighteen, she still looked like she was already in control of her body as a *woman*, unlike Svetlana. My Russian roommate, like I mentioned earlier, stood tall and model thin, but often struggled with her gawky limbs. In contrast to Svetlana's more abstract beauty, Jeanette seemed down-to-earth in her gorgeousness, like a woman a man would want to take to bed and maybe, just maybe, have children with, not an expressionist Russian art exhibit to display for an evening or two, to deck out in beautiful clothes but ultimately feel cold toward.

"Are you guys hungry? I could go for some dinner. I had a tiny breakfast, and I had lunch really, really early," Jeanette said.

Three meals in a day? This could be interesting. . . .

.   .   .

JEANETTE HAILED FROM A SMALL TOWN in the mountains outside Salt Lake City. Quite early on, it was obvious something was special about her, and now, after graduating high school, her parents had gone against the wishes of the elders in the Mormon church and let her go to the teeming pit of vice, iniquity, and sin generally known as New York City to become a model. But we weren't her first agency, and you'll forgive me if I digress to tell the story of how she ended up standing in the doorway of apartment 1480, looking pretty as a peach and immediately making an enemy of poor Svetlana and pretty much every other girl in the Agency.

It was a gift from God. That's what the church said of her beauty. She must take a husband, they said, and begin having children to spread her gift to new generations. Her parents were of a more, shall we say, liberal type in the community and knew she had some potential. They sent her to one of those silly model searches often used to raise capital for unscrupulous owners and give a chance for bookers at agencies to be showered with free trips and dinners. Jeanette turned out to be one of the very few success stories from the model searches, as a junior booker at a rival agency signed her on the spot. She was that good.

Jeanette had arrived in New York, never having set foot anywhere east of the Mississippi, except for a school trip to D.C. during her freshman year of high school. But her good cheer and utter inexperience kept her afloat, people were willing to go to great lengths to help this mountain flower. That was just two weeks before she showed up at our place.

She had signed with a boutique agency that did decent business and had a small but select roster of girls to send out to castings. It was owned by a forty-five-year-old ex-banker who definitely, had an eye (among other things), for true talent.

They put her up in another model dorm, similar to ours—except there was one gigantic sleazy middle-aged catch. The owner of the agency lived in the apartment too, in a massive adjoining suite to the bedroom in which all the girls were crammed. It apparently was an amazing spot in Tribeca, huge and outfitted with all the latest technological marvels. All the girls just happened to share the space with the owner, who was decidedly not following the trend of most males in the fashion industry—i.e., he liked girls. As in liked having sex with them. A lot. He even refused to hire any males on his staff. A favorite saying of his: "I want to be the only cock in the henhouse."

So basically he had his little model harem set up, and things were running smoothly. Until the naive young Jeanette from Utah showed up.

Jeanette had been in equally good spirits about her spot in her first model dorm. She tucked herself in early every night and said her silent prayers, content after another day's castings.

The agency owner gave it a little over a week before he approached Jeanette. During that week, Jeanette said, every other night he would come into the girls' bedroom. Raising a bushy, slightly graying eyebrow, he would look around the room, find the model he sought for that evening, and tell her he had something "important" to discuss with her. The selected girl would dutifully shuffle off with him to his master suite, not to be seen again for another hour or so; and then she would dutifully shuffle back to her bunk to go to sleep (or, more likely, sneak out to one of the clubs). The others didn't seem to mind the arrangement—just another thing to put up with on the road to fame.

As you can imagine, things didn't go as smoothly with Jeanette. Her night came, the agency owner entering the bedroom. He asked if he could have a word with her, and she said okay, even though she knew what was up. (She was naive, but no girl's *that* naive.) Jeanette told me this story, but she refused to go into details about what happened in the master suite, only that it was "absolutely disgusting!" I can only imagine what he had waiting for her to "discuss," something that probably involved unbuckling his slacks and exposing his unit to her. Needless to say, Jeanette, spotless as a lamb, wasn't about to drop down and start sinfully servicing Mr. Middle-aged just because she was in that agency's stable. After saying something about how she had to excuse herself, she sprinted out of the master suite, back into the bedroom, and mouthed her silent prayers to save the soul of that wicked man next door. The other girls were amazed—apparently no one had thought it worth her trouble to deny the owner his sleazy treat.

Everything seemed normal until the next night, when the owner once again requested Jeanette's presence, obviously thinking that with a bit of persistence he'd be able to crack her.

"I'd prefer not to," Jeanette said. Even though she was young, coming from Mormon stock, she knew a thing or two about how males try to throw around their power; and leaving that culture, she had no intention of succumbing to it in her new home of New York City.

"*Prefer* . . . not to?" the owner asked, incredulous.

She nodded.

"Prefer?! Who do you think you *are?!* I run things around here—if you're not in my room in fifteen minutes, well, maybe you can *prefer* to find other management to book you!" the owner shouted before storming off into his suite. Fifteen minutes passed, and Jeanette did not go to the owner's room. Instead, she began packing a few of her belongings.

About an hour later, the guy came out and asked Jeanette's Brazilian roommate if he could see her for a moment. She smiled wickedly at Jeanette and skipped into the bedroom—she enjoyed the visits. (Apparently the Italian girl did, too, and they were even known to go in together for a "group" discussion . . .)

Jeanette finished packing, and the next morning, with the help of a girl she'd met at the other dorm, went looking for another booker. Two days later she was standing in our doorway, as you met her. And even if I didn't hiss like Svetlana, I have to admit that a pang of envy hit me—though I tried to choke it down with smiles and "how are yous," it didn't totally work. Without any jobs booked yet, I saw Jeanette, with her amazing features and to-die-for body, as definite competition. We'll see how she handled the model dorm.

THE NEXT MORNING I WAS JOLTED AWAKE at 6:30 A.M. by the creak of a bunk. Was somebody just getting back from a night out?

"Sorry, Heather," Jeanette whispered as she quietly climbed out of bed. "Going to the gym."

The *gym?* At this hour? She quietly pulled her workout gear from an open suitcase. Svetlana snored, and Kylie was still as a log, a half-drunk martini that she'd brought in for a nightcap sitting next to her bed. Svet and I had been out until three A.M. starting the night with some Tommy Hilfiger male models at PM, before following some Dior Homme boys to a *Vice* magazine party. My woozy head pounded in pain, and I unsteadily climbed down and went to the bathroom to fish out some Advil. I looked at my bleary face in the mirror and decided that wasn't such a good idea. My eyes were bloodshot, and lines creased down my face. Ugh. I soaked a washcloth in cold water to use as a compress, hoping maybe I could get back to sleep if I pressed it on my head, which felt like it was likely to explode at any moment.

On the way back to the bedroom, I ran into Jeanette, who was dressed in her workout clothes.

"Gee, I hope I didn't wake you up, Heather. Just thought I'd get a jump on the day!" Jeanette said.

I murmured something to the effect that it didn't bother me and tried not to look at her fresh-as-a-daisy face, comparing it mentally to my own puffy one.

"Maybe I'll see you for breakfast?" she said. "I'll be done in a couple hours."

Deciding it was way too much physical effort to make it back to the bedroom, I threw myself down on our couch, lying on my back, the washcloth covering my eyes and forehead. I groaned and slipped back to sleep.

When I woke up for good, afternoon sun streamed in through the dirty windows of the model dorm. The Advil had done the trick; my head cleared. I pulled the now-dry washcloth off my face and groggily sat up.

Jeanette poked her head out of the kitchen. She was wearing superslim jeans and a tight V-neck top that showed off her cleavage to full advantage.

"Oh, hey, Heather, you want some lunch?" she said. "I'm cooking some chicken breasts. I had the best casting earlier today! I really hope I get a callback!"

Not only had Jeanette gotten up at the crack of dawn to work out, she had also come back, showered, put on a cute little outfit, gone to a casting, and bought groceries to cook herself lunch. Up to that point, I hadn't even been sure we'd had pots and pans.

Kylie came out of the bedroom, yawning, in some silk pajamas. Her eyes were red-brimmed slits.

"Is someone . . . *cooking?*" She said it as if cooking were about the strangest thing anyone could ever possibly think of doing, besides using gin in a martini, that is.

"Oh, hey, Kylie, right?" Jeanette said. "You want some chicken? I've got plenty!"

The idea of food sliding into Kylie's hungover stomach sent her bolting to the bathroom. I heard some barfing.

"Oh, okay, guess not!" Jeanette chirped.

Later that afternoon, Svetlana returned home from a day of castings. I had been sleeping my hangover off on the couch a *long* time, it seemed.

"Hi, Svetlan—" Jeanette started, but the Russian moved quickly to the bedroom, not even looking at our new roommate, her face screwed into an icy Slavic mask. Jeanette shrugged and smiled sweetly, "I think she was at the casting earlier today, but there were some other girls, and I don't think she saw me. Plus I was talking to the woman in charge of the campaign for *such* a long time. She was sooo nice."

Hmmm . . . maybe things hadn't gone as well for the Russian at the casting.

Jeanette went back to obliviously cooking her chicken, humming what I could only imagine was some sort of church tune. She moved a bottle of Kylie's Stoli out of the way as she cooked, then did a double take on how empty it was. The Aussie had, of course, been in rare form the night before in honor of our new roomie's arrival, tossing them back like nobody's business, yelling at the "fucking morons" on the week's new episode of *Survivor.* Jeanette hadn't said anything, but I imagine that back in Woodshack, Utah, she hadn't exactly run into a lot of conspicuous vodka consumption. Jeanette looked around her as if she had just discovered the worst secret in the world. She spoke in a hushed tone.

"Holy moly, did Kylie drink *all* of that last night? No way! Does she have a . . . problem?" Jeanette looked at me with the biggest eyes, like Kylie's mortal soul was in danger because she liked her vodka a bit too much.

"Umm . . ." I didn't know how to answer. "I don't think she has a problem, no. Last night was just an exception," I lied.

"But why does she drink so much—is she sad?"

"No, Kylie's perfectly happy," I said.

But then I thought about it for a second—every night with the Metamucil martinis, night after night, afloat in her bottle of vodka. If she'd made it and didn't have to live in the dorm, would she be doing the same thing? She'd been here the longest, even longer than Svetlana. And I'd heard that after a while in the dorm, the Agency began to examine what you did more closely, how you were handling yourself. Maybe Kylie was even on some sort of secret final warning, just a mistake away from eviction, like Laura or my predecessor, Keyshia. If she knew she was on thin ice and hadn't told us, maybe her nightly sousing kept those fears at bay, allowed her to sleep on the damn uncomfortable beds. . . . She'd been optioned a few times for big deals, but she was always beaten out by just one other model each time. Striking distance, but never managed to grab the grand prize, the big shoot that would've sprung her from captivity. Maybe that's why she drank so much. Maybe Jeanette was onto something. Maybe she wasn't so—

My reflections were interrupted.

"*Pssst!*" The sound came from the bedroom, and even though it wasn't really a word, I could still hear the thick Russian accent in it. I looked over. Svetlana was poking her head out at me. She motioned for me to come into the room, making sure Jeanette didn't see her. Kylie came out of the bathroom, still looking green, and we all convened near the bunks, the door closed. The room was dark, the curtains still drawn, and our meeting had a conspirational air, like we were plotting a coup.

Svetlana kicked off the proceedings, looking us both earnestly in the eyes before beginning.

"Svetlana smell something wrong. Jeanette—no good." She arched her eyebrows at us, which had the effect of making her look more silly than menacing. "Svetlana, Kylie, Heather find what go on with *beetch*. She make look bad, go gym."

"I don't know, she seems all right. . . ." I said, not entirely convinced that Jeanette was putting on some act for us all. I couldn't argue with her making us look bad, though.

"Svetlana's onto something. I knew when I first saw her that she was going to be trouble. We better get to the bottom of this mess before she screws us all."

The aroma of grilled chicken wafted into the bedroom under the door, as Jeanette's humming segued into full song, something about Jesus. Svetlana glanced at the door and gritted her teeth. Kylie looked like she might puke again—I couldn't tell whether it was from the scent of food or the religious ditty.

"Maybe it's all part of some evil plot to brainwash us with that Church of Former Day Saints or whatnot. They have some evil plan to get us all onboard, know what I mean?" Kylie asked. "They need more women over there, with all those multiple wives and bollocks like that."

"*Latter* Day Saints," I corrected gently.

"Whatever. All we're saying is that this has to do with *you*, too, Heather," she said.

I felt a bit of guilt simmer in my stomach as I silently took part in this cabal formed against Jeanette, who seemed so harmless. But if she was taking away jobs from Svetlana, which it seems she may have done at the casting today, what about when I was up against her in the future? It dawned on me that I had yet to get *any* job, but I pounded that thought down quickly.

Svetlana looked at her appointed drawer in the shabby IKEA dresser, which spilled over with all the ill-gotten booty she'd received from rich men by putting out with her own, well, *booty*. A floor-length Proenza Schouler gown dangled near to the ground. She proudly admired the stacks of fantastic shoes she'd piled in the corner, a frenzied mass of designer footwear most any woman would have killed to have.

The Russian gave her judgment on the situation, coming up with the most dire punishment she could think of at the time for Jeanette: "She no borrow *any* clothes from Svetlana."

This pattern with Jeanette was to continue: the Utah girl playing it straight and narrow, getting up every morning to hit the gym, going to castings that always "went great"—in comparison with mine, which always seemed to go terribly—and cooking full-on meals. Svetlana and Kylie could barely contain themselves. They knew something was up, they just needed to find out what. They sniffed around Jeanette like hungry panthers, trying to find something, *anything* they could use against her. Her beautiful unstudied presence in the dorm was a threat not only to their own potential livelihoods as models, but also to their chosen dissolute lifestyles, Kylie with her homebody alcoholism and Svetlana with her girl-about-town party-girl promiscuity. Jeanette never even so much as *mentioned* going out with us, despite Svet's best efforts to get her drunk.

"Maybe she get pregnant, then sent home!" she conspired.

Even though Svet and I tended to hit up parties every night, I tried to stay away from the horny men, whereas the Russian would indulge them, embracing her sex appeal as she flung her arms around them. This made me feel like I was still on the side of a nice girl like Jeanette, although I must admit I had the occasional fantasy of her stumbling on the treadmill as she so cheerfully jogged along, while I snoozed with my roommates into the late morning.

SOME DAYS LATER, I FINALLY GOT THE CALL. It came in the morning, Luke's always-polite voice waking me.

"Hey, Heather?" said Luke.

"Yes?" My breath caught, wondering what was up.

"I've got some good news."

It took me a second to process what he was saying. I had gotten my first modeling job in New York!

As clichéd as it may seem, I involuntarily pumped my fists and literally jumped for joy in the living room. Collecting myself, I looked around, checking that nobody had caught me, even though Kylie had left early for a casting, Svetlana was sleeping, and Jeanette was probably lightly toning her triceps in the gym.

It wasn't a big booking, but it was at least *something*—a shoot for the look book of Vena Cava's upcoming line. A look book is a catalog of shots that usually just goes out to press and fashion buyers. I'd had a go-see for it earlier in the week and had come away feeling pretty good about things, as if the Polaroids and small talk went better than normal. I'd walked out of the casting, past the other anonymous beauties, with my chin up a little higher than normal. Turned out my instinct had been right.

The pay for the job was going to be peanuts, not enough to really even put a dent in the running tab the Agency was keeping for housing me in the dorm, my small weekly stipend, printing costs for my comp cards, all the little things they charged us for, but I felt like maybe I was on my way at last to earning my keep and having something to show for the time I'd already spent here. I was really doing it!

I went to the mirror in the bathroom and looked at myself, grinning. It was one of those rare days when, away from the judging eyes of casting directors and disdainful looks from rival girls, I was happy with what I saw. I slipped off my pajama bottoms and T-shirt I had been sleeping in and checked myself out in the full-length mirror on the back of the bathroom door. I felt like I had never looked better, sexier, more appealing. I pinched the skin above my hips to assure myself there wasn't any. Nope. Well, maybe just a *little*. I was so caught up in the moment that I pranced out of the bathroom without a stitch of clothing on, feeling light as a feather. Kylie was just walking in, looking quite chic when not in her cocktail-slurping uniform and actually going out on go-sees and castings.

The Australian looked at me with one eyebrow raised and smiled, peering around to see if some boy was lurking behind the couch, caught in the act.

"Well, hello, sunshine!" she said, giggling, as I blushed, realizing I was totally naked.

"Yipes!" I ducked into the bathroom and came out quickly, dressed again in my PJs. "I got booked for a job!" I burst out to her. "A small one, but still!"

She squealed and we hugged each other, the competitiveness of the dorm melting away as we both acted our age for once, letting our better natures take over in the moment, replacing the supermodels we played in the clubs every night. I was washed back to that beach where I had initially been discovered, before the half-square-foot bedroom at the model dorm, and before the depressing open castings I was running back and forth to. Maybe, just maybe, I was going to make it.

I HAD FOUR DAYS UNTIL THE SHOOT, and I was going to make the most of them. Cutting back on my food intake, I decided I was perfectly satisfied with dinner consisting of a clump of rice smaller than Svetlana's tiny fist, covered with select steamed vegetables. Despite Svetlana's complaints, I even stopped going out with her to the clubs every night, even though she always promised the "hot-teest guy" was going to be waiting for me there. I didn't want to be all bloated and distended from alcohol when the shoot came, some Stay Puft Marshmallow Woman for our age, perfectly cast in *Ghostbusters III* if they ever decided to make it.

Speaking of guys, Svetlana was beginning to worry about me, since I didn't show much interest in the wide variety of male specimens we had as our de facto servants every night—from twenty-year-old singers in up-and-coming bands to the middle-aged private equity managers who could buy the entire club we were sitting in and still have enough cash to last through retirement. The previous week, during a drunken night at the Pink Elephant, when a crew of us girls had helped a flashy guido guy finish his three bottles of Grey Goose vodka, she turned to me very intensely.

"You no like man?" she said, with a bit of mischief in her eyes, as if maybe she was hoping a little bit that was the case. "Svetlana know love for you." She motioned to an amazing-looking girl, probably not yet eighteen, who was from Spain; Svetlana knew her from the club circuit. The Spanish girl eyed me intently—Svet had obviously planned this. The end of the Spaniard's tongue flicked out of her mouth to keep some wayward vodka from running down her chin and onto her breasts.

"No—no—no—no, you've got it all wrong, Svetlana," I said to her quickly, a bit panicked by the young Spanish girl's heat-seeking eyes, which alternated between my face and breasts in a seductive manner. I took a napkin and wiped Svetlana's nose before anybody noticed the powder boulder ready to drop with a thunder to the floor from her nostril. "It's not *that,* I just, you know, need to think about my, um, career," I said, and even sort of believed myself.

"Some else already?" she asked.

"What?" Even though I normally could decipher her spotty English, I didn't have my codebook of broken Russian-English on me to make sense of that. A terrible remix of an R. Kelly song pounded in the background.

"Some *else* already?!" she repeated. I realized she meant, was there *someone else already?*

"No . . . let's just drop it," I said, taking a quick swig of my vodka cranberry, thinking that maybe she was right about that. In my thoughts, I had carefully avoided my growing crush on the absent Robert.

The Russian became giddy, convinced she'd just revealed some huge secret. Little did she know. . . .

"Svetlana *know!* Heather have some else! What wrong? He old?"

She laughed like she had just told the funniest joke in the world and grabbed me tight, nestling her delicate face against my collarbone and wiggling in drunken coked-up joy.

The Spaniard looked at us jealously.

On the couch, a successful South American model from another agency was lying in the fetal position, covering her face, drunkenly sobbing after having one too many cocktails. She rocked back and forth.

"I want to go *home, home,*" she moaned. I couldn't tell if home was her apartment here in the city or whatever Brazilian favela she had been plucked from by her top-flight agency. "I have a casting, I have to—" She didn't get the chance to finish, as she suddenly lay flat on the black leather couch and puked over the end of it. After evacuating a night's worth of champagne and vodka, she sat up straight, wiping the spittle from her plump lips with the back of her hand. Her face was ashen, and I highly doubted she'd be able to pull it together in six hours to make the casting looking anything like what her comp cards advertised her as.

"Water," she croaked.

Svetlana fixed up an extra-strong vodka soda and handed it to her.

"Thanks," the girl said, dim-lidded. She gulped it voraciously, apparently never noticing the difference.

The Russian winked at me.

"Svetlana have same casting tomorrow!" She laughed shrilly and started dancing to the music, forgetting about her supposed discovery of my "some else already."

The night before my shoot, however, brought everything out in sharp relief, the proof tacked on the wall before my very eyes.

During the day I'd taken a long walk around downtown, bundled up in an H&M winter coat—though I'd been telling people it was Marc by Marc Jacobs. If you squinted and didn't touch it, I guess it was believable. Late fall was drifting into winter, and earlier in the morning a couple snowflakes had even whisked by the window, like they were sent ahead from the Arctic by the months of winter to come, just to make sure everything was still okey doke down here in New York. My stomach grumbled at me as I walked through Washington Square Park, past the clusters of students sprinting to classes and a couple of masochistic wannabe hippies playing Hacky Sack shirtless in the freezing cold. I popped a piece of sugar-free gum in my mouth and began chomping on it to cut my hunger—the shoot was less than eighteen hours away.

A couple of guy students stared at me, mouths wide open, as I walked past—I was at least three inches taller than both of them. Living in the model dorm and hanging out with other models all the time sometimes made me forget how I stood out in a crowd. I put an extra sass in my walk as I passed them, maybe to give them something to talk about in the dining hall with their friends, I thought. I cut across to Broadway and walked north, up to the Strand bookstore, just enjoying the chance to stretch my legs and get out of the stale claustrophobic dorm for a while during the day. I'd seen the Strand while zooming by on my way to dinner at a restaurant on Park Avenue with Svetlana the week before and had wanted to check it out. Inside the jam-packed store, I went to the art history section and looked through the books on display. I decided on a big coffee-table book on Jean-Michel Basquiat, who had become famous twenty years earlier on the same downtown streets I had been wandering today. The book was expensive, but I had a little bit left from my weekly stipend from the Agency, and besides, it was on sale—half off. I thought back to Willem at the Clijsters Gallery. Maybe I should make a visit; after all, it couldn't hurt—plus

he probably wouldn't even be there. Robert had said it would be better for a girl like me to stay away from Willem. And if the Belgian *was*
there, maybe I could find out why Robert had acted so strangely when
he knew I was talking to him. I just wouldn't go to the back room.

The cashier at the Strand, a bearded guy wearing glasses and a
knit cap, raised an eyebrow when I handed him the Basquiat book,
like a small-town gas station owner who thinks he's selling *Penthouse*
to a minor.

"Basquiat, huh?" he said, ringing it up, but not before giving me
the once-over.

I just smiled at him a bit icily, as if to say, *Yes, I do have a brain.*

The temperature was dropping outside, the cold starting to settle in my bones (my diet ensured I didn't keep too much insulation),
and I took the train back home downtown, chewing two more
pieces of gum in a vain attempt to quell my protesting stomach.

In the lobby, a stocky Russian-looking guy sat in one of the
chairs, antsy. He was in his early thirties, wore a leather jacket, and
had slicked-back hair. Russian mafia, or at least wannabe. When he
saw me enter, he gave a start, as if he recognized me, but soon realized he was mistaken and sat back down. The doorman kept a hawk
eye on him. The guy pulled out a cell phone and started jabbering
in Russian. I would've bet a thousand rubles he was waiting for
Svetlana, but I said nothing.

Outside the dorm, I was met with the unmistakable scent of
french fries wafting from under the door, and inside I saw why: In
one of their ploys to derail Jeanette, Kylie and Svetlana had gone out
and bought cheeseburgers and fries for the girl to "enjoy" with
them. They sat around our unsteady table, Jeanette chomping happily on the burger, piling the fries down her throat, and—horror of
horrors!—even drinking a chocolate milk shake. Svetlana and Kylie
had barely touched their food, and a couple crumpled-up napkins

led me to believe that they may even have resorted to the childish trick of chewing up food and then hiding it in a napkin when Mom's not looking.

"Have some of my fries," Kylie said, pushing her carton slowly toward Jeanette with two hands.

"Oh, thanks, Kylie, and thanks for getting this for us!" Jeanette said, dumping some of the Aussie's fries onto her plate.

"Anytime," Kylie said icily.

Jeanette kept eating like a horse, oblivious to the fact that her pals were literally trying to fatten her up for a slaughter at Rachel's hands. Apparently they didn't take into account that Jeanette's metabolism, ramped up from hours of cardio every day, would have her body greedily consume the food, leaving her just as thin as before.

I shook my head and went to the bedroom. I pulled out the glossy Basquiat book, then started flipping through *Paper* lazily. I sat on the top bunk, my legs dangling over the edge like I was ten and at summer camp again.

I skimmed a few articles, yawning a bit—it had been a long day of walking around the city, and my feet ached pleasantly. I planned on going to bed nice and early, so I'd be chipper and rested for tomorrow's shoot, making a good impression on the photographer and stylist.

I turned a page, and my breath caught: There, staring out at me from the magazine, was a full-page black-and-white photo of Robert du Croix, wearing a tailored YSL suit and crisp white shirt with the top few buttons undone, his smoldering eyes ready to burn a hole through the paper. The city lights of Paris blurred behind him, but he was the brightest light in that picture. He looked cool, suave, and sexy. The magazine was running an article on Robert entitled: "Believing in du Croix: A French Superstar Brings Parisian Nightlife to

NYC." The story was about the scheme of the Shiva Bar's owners to open the glittering star-packed New York version, with Robert leading the charge, bringing a taste of Paris sophistication and cool to downtown Manhattan.

Flipping to the next page, I was met with another black-and-white picture of Robert, but this time he was standing in front of the Shiva Bar's entrance, wearing Dior sunglasses at night. Flanking him on both sides were two magnificent models, decked from head to toe in couture. They also wore sunglasses. Their pouty lips perfectly showcased their nonchalance to the glamour of the shoot. Even though they were surely just models, paid to show up and then leave, irrational jealousy shot through me, seemingly out of nowhere—*I* should be the one next to Robert there, my delicate limbs covered by the best fashion the euro could buy, *not* sitting on the top of a creaky bunk in an apartment that had started to take on the odor of a heap of garbage.

Dammit.

The whole thing was depressing. Why should I have to do this small shoot for this baby designer when I should be in the pages of magazines, my face emblazoned on giant billboards and on the sides of buses?! This was the first time I actually thought about it: What if I *never* got out of the model dorm? At first the whole thing had seemed funny, maybe even a little cute—it was like a dingy waystation everyone has to stop in at on the way to the big time, to the paparazzi flashes and lofts and vacations to the Côte d'Azur. Instead, being a model was becoming all about waking up way too early, hungover, to make it to castings, dealing with stupid issues like toilet paper, and having to sleep in bunks, like inmates in a prison. And the whole time we lived under the ax of Rachel, who could drop us at any point if we displeased her.

I looked at the two girls on each side of Robert and became even more pissed off. Not that I hadn't been counting or anything, but I once again realized I hadn't heard anything from Robert since he left, after our first date—was he back in New York and just not calling me, had he found some other girl who didn't live in a dilapidated shoe box who actually had work? It'd only been a little over a month since I last saw him, but I felt he was in danger of just disappearing.

I knew this wasn't like me at all, but I rode the tidal wave of jealousy and paranoia, pulling out my cell phone with the intention of texting Robert, "innocently," to congratulate him on getting in the magazine—but more to check up on him and see what he wrote back.

An internal debate started . . . and a sickening possibility struck me in the gut: But what if he doesn't even respond? Isn't it worse to expose yourself as overeager—it may scare him off. . . . But what if getting the text reminds him of me? But, again, what if he ignores it? Well, he *is* international, it *could* get messed up over the Atlantic. You never know if you don't hear back from him, whether he ignored it or not. . . . I knew my friend Linda had tried texting me from Germany this summer and I didn't get any of them. But I thought I remembered something about Robert saying his number definitely worked overseas. . . . Arrggh!

To hell with it!

I typed out the message quickly—and then changed it about twenty times to make it sound as casual as possible before I sent it.

It read: *hey, robert! saw u in paper, u looked great. very cool. what r u up to?*

I pressed the SEND button with finality and took a deep breath. No taking that back now. Nothing to do but wait and see. Wait. And. See.

I immediately regretted sending it—did I mention my imagination is not always the most optimistic? I suddenly had a vision of Robert at Shiva Bar getting the text while dancing with the two girls from the picture, pulling the phone out of his pocket with a "What the hell?" look on his face, then showing the text to the girls, who would be in disbelief that a *nobody* like me would even think of texting *the* du Croix. "American cow!" one of the girls would shout. They would all then laugh hysterically, he would hit DELETE, he'd put the phone in his pocket, then they'd continue dancing, except Robert would move closer to one of the girls, his hand resting on her hip while he brought a champagne glass to her lips and she sipped seductively. WHY HAD I SENT THAT STUPID TEXT?!?!?!

The phone beeped at me, and I nearly fell off the bunk: one message received! At that exact moment, Svetlana burst in, scaring the hell out of me and almost making me fall off the bed again. (Side note: Even though Svetlana seemed indifferent all the time, she was actually obsessed with what everyone was up to in the dorm, and probably couldn't stand the fact that I'd spent five minutes in the bedroom alone, doing god knows what.)

"Svetlana *hungry*," she complained to no one in particular, even though she'd had more than enough chances to eat at least some of her burger.

I wanted nothing more than for her to turn around and leave. My heart pounded—was the text from Robert? I was dying to know but didn't want to check it in front of the nosy Russian.

BEEP! The phone once again let me know that I had something waiting for me, but I had no clue what it was—it could be from Robert, or it could just be something from my mom, reminding me we needed to think about plans for Christmas. I don't know if I was just imagining things, but Svetlana seemed to sense that I was acting a bit weird.

"Heather have message," Svetlana said, edging closer, hungry for some gossip. I gripped the phone tightly.

But then all of a sudden Svetlana shrieked, like one of those girls you see in the old footage of Beatles concerts.

"ROBERT!"

The blood drained from my face—how'd she know?!

I had totally forgotten that the magazine with the article on Robert lay open on my lap. Svetlana had spied the full-page shot of Monsieur du Croix in front of Shiva Bar with my two mortal enemies and was now basically having a seizure of delight.

"Give Svetlana!" she said, grabbing the magazine from me and greedily flipping through the pages. "Robert *sooo* hot!" She pointed at the sexy picture of him solo. I nodded mutely, having avoided a potential disaster. Svetlana grabbed her English-Russian dictionary off the floor. She pointed to the magazine. "I bring back Heather?" she asked, or demanded, really, before running out to the living room to try and struggle through the article with her dictionary.

I counted silently to three and then jumped down to close the door. I flipped open the phone and hit the button to check my message. The phone stalled for a second as it moved to the message screen. . . . The message was from him! ROW-BEAR plainly appeared on the screen.

God-I-had-been-stupid-thinking-he'd-be-with-those-dumb-hos-he's-a-nice-guy-it-was-just-a-photo-shoot-I-mean-would-he-really-not-have-answered-of-course-he'd-answer-he-likes-me-he's-just-been-busy-I'm-such-a-moro—

I forced myself to cut the crap and just check the message.

It read: *"So good to hear from you, was thinking of you today! Thank you for your compliment, though I am a bit embarrassed by the press. I return in two weeks and will see you then."*

My self-pity from just a minute before was scrubbed away by

each word I read in his text. He'll be here in two weeks! Everything else that had seemed so life-threatening just moments before now transformed into great opportunities in my mind. Of *course* I'm going to have to start small with working, that's just how the nonfat cookie crumbles in the modeling business—the shoot was going to be great exposure. And I'd get a free dress too! With that under my belt, and with Robert to help . . .

Svetlana burst in again. "Robert no have girlfriend!" Svetlana said to me in delight, apparently uncovering this vital bit from the article. Well, *that* was good to know. I flipped the phone shut quickly.

"Oh, ha, uh, that's great!" I said to Svetlana, remembering what happened when she thought Kylie had stolen her meager bag of coke. What would she do if she found out I was "stealing" her huge crush?

I didn't have time to ponder this too long, as Svetlana bolted out again and started rummaging in the kitchen drawers for something. Her phone rang and she answered in a stream of Russian, ending in an emphatic English "SVETLANA BUSY!" It must have been the shady guy waiting downstairs.

I felt totally disoriented by everything that had just happened, feeling the immediate need to get out of the dorm, away from my friend who was in love with the guy I had just secretly texted, away from the magazine and its seductive photos, away from Kylie's grilling of clueless Jeanette, away from that funky smell. I bundled up and took a long walk, telling myself I needed to focus on the shoot tomorrow, not all this brewing model dorm drama. I *tried* to focus, at least. I walked and walked until I had tired myself out, until there was no way I wouldn't just fall asleep as soon as my head hit the pillow.

I got back a little after eleven. Kylie and Svetlana were both out.

(If I remember right, it was a Tuesday, so they must have been at Marquee.) Jeanette was already asleep; she had probably hit the hay at 9:30 like a good girl.

I washed my face, made sure to moisturize, and drank several glasses of water.

When I got to my bunk, yawning, I realized what Svetlana had been searching for in the drawers earlier: scissors.

Taped on the wall next to her lower bunk were the two photos of Robert from the magazine. Except the one in front of Shiva Bar had been modified by the handy Russian—the two models were no longer. Svetlana had cut their figures out of the picture so that only Robert peered out from behind his sunglasses at her, to watch over her as she dreamed, a thin cutout silhouette on each side of him.

I gulped. How do you say "creepy" in Russian?

Well, at least she hadn't taped a picture of herself in there, right? *Right?*

THE NEXT DAY I ARRIVED at the shoot half an hour early, fully rested despite the slightly psycho tendencies Svetlana was starting to display—my long walks had worked.

The shoot for Vena Cava's spring/summer line was in a gorgeous loft in West Chelsea. When I showed up, a whole crew of people was already there, getting everything set up. The photographer's assistant scurried around, setting up lights, adjusting the umbrellas used to cast soft light. The hairstylist, makeup woman, and clothes stylist were all there, ready and waiting for me. Seated in front of a mirror, I was transformed by their expert hands, the hairstylist taking my hair and turning it into a lustrous flirty mane that screamed high-fashion seductiveness, the makeup woman expertly covering my face so that I looked flawless. To die for. I practically squirmed in my seat, I was so excited.

The stylist then had me try on different outfits to see which fit me best, and as I looked at myself in the mirror, I almost giggled at how *different* I looked. Pulled out of the dingy climes of the model dorm, made up by professional hands, I looked like, well, a real model!

The photographer arrived and immediately started yelling at his assistant to change how the lights were set up.

I towered over him, a short man who was wearing a thinly striped black-and-white shirt and blazer, like he had just walked out of a sixties French movie or something. He was manic, and I vaguely suspected that he was partaking of Svetlana's favorite "pick-me-up." He flitted from light to light, adjusting them, cursed at his assistant, and then cursed at no one in particular.

Then we were ready! I slipped into the first outfit the stylist had decided on and was posed against an iron spiraling staircase that went to a raised second-floor portion of the loft. The lights were adjusted just so, and the shooting began, the photographer yelling out instructions as I posed. Everything went well, and we took a lunch break, which was catered. I only had a half of a half of a sandwich, my stomach churning with nervousness as we went through my first shoot in New York.

We shot the second outfit in the "living room" section of the expansive loft. It had an Eames couch, glass-and-metal coffee table, and Le Corbusier armchair. They were going for a modernist vibe, which jibed nicely with the line, or at least that's what the stylist told me.

The assistant placed me where I was to be photographed in the first shot after lunch and started waving a light meter around me, shouting out numbers to the photographer, who was installed feverishly behind his camera, consumed by a world of F-stops, focus rings, and framing.

All of a sudden I noticed that on the coffee table was the same exact book on Basquiat I had bought the day before! I resisted the urge to pick it up while the assistant finished with the light meter and posed me.

"Okay, chin down, chin down, no that's too far down, all right, hold that—OPEN YOUR EYES wider, let's see those beautiful eyes!" The photographer instructed as the camera went *snap, snap, snap* and flashes blinded me. "All right, that's it for that position. George?" His assistant sprang to his side like a faithful cocker spaniel. "Adjust the 550 and then let's get her ready for the seated shot."

George went and fiddled with one of the lights, and I assumed I had at least thirty seconds off.

I leaned down to pick up the book on Basquiat. "Whose is this? The person who lives here? Or did you guys bring it especially for the shoot?" I said, flipping through a few pages, taking in the painter's frenetic energy. "Isn't he amazing?"

The photographer looked at me like I was absolutely, utterly, completely insane.

"What is she doing?" he asked his assistant, like I wasn't even there. "What is she *doing?*"

"Umm, looking at a book . . ." the ever-helpful George offered. The photographer gave him a dirty look.

The blood rose to my face. I hadn't expected quite that kind of response from him. "Sorry, I just bought this same book the other day, and I was thinking that—"

The photographer cut me off. "What are we playing, fucking art-world Trivial Pursuit?" he chided me. He snatched the book from my hand condescendingly, like a father taking a dangerous knife away from his young child. He looked at me squarely. "You're a model. Don't think, honey—it'll give you wrinkles. We just need you to look beautiful, got it?"

I nodded, lips tight.

He walked back to his station behind the camera. "Okay, George, now get her . . ." His words trailed away as the blood pounded in my ears with a mixture of anger and embarrassment—I mean, I wanted to do a good job on this shoot, but I couldn't even say something about a fucking book on a table? I remembered the look the cashier at the Strand had given me and wanted to prove to the photographer how wrong he was, how I could have a conversation with him about Basquiat if I wanted to. . . . All those things I wanted to say, I, of course, didn't. I let George manipulate me into the correct pose after he once again read off light readings. My face was still flush after the incident.

"Christ, she's all fucking red," the photographer shouted. "Makeup!"

The rest of the session went more smoothly, as I veered away from any art-related conversation. The photographer thought I was doing a great job, as long as I kept quiet. *Seen and not heard.* As the shoot finished and I changed back into my street clothes, I realized the shoot had been a success—mostly because I kept my mouth shut, pouted at the camera, and was moved where they wanted me. I was an object of beauty, just like the Eames sofa and Le Corbusier chair I had shared the frame with. George had an easier time repositioning me than the sofa; I guess that was one difference. . . .

On the way out of the studio, the photographer came up to me, all smiles. "Absolutely *terrific* job, you looked gorgeous," he said, kissing me good-bye on each cheek. I wondered if he even remembered my name.

Back at the dorm, Kylie and Svetlana had a Metamucil martini waiting for me in celebration of my first job. The Australian would use any excuse for celebration, so she didn't have to drink alone at home, I suspect. I guess I was happy. But the photographer's treatment of me kicked around the back of my mind, making my smiles plastic around the edges as I received Kylie's sloppy congratulations.

She had been drinking since at least four P.M.—I found out, during a drunken confessional, that a hot, late-twenties married guy she'd been having some fun with on the side, unknown to any of us, had given her her walking papers earlier in the day. His wife, an interior designer, had begun to suspect something and had somehow dug up Kylie's number. The wife had launched into calling her all sorts of names, screaming at her, then dissolving into sobs. The guy had called an hour or so later and told Kylie never to call him again. "He couldn't go very long, anyway," Kylie consoled herself. "His wife's a disgusting bitch, too."

"You *knew* her?" I asked.

"Yeah, I met them at the same time. *She* said she wanted a threesome to begin with, not him. I can't be blamed if he liked me more than her and just wanted to see me!"

I decided not to ask any more questions.

My mom called halfway through my second drink, knowing I had my first shoot today.

"It was so great, Mom, the apartment was beautiful, the clothes were just really amazing, and I met some great people," I said, my enthusiasm feeling a bit fake, just like my smiles to my roommates when I'd first gotten back. I could still hear the order from the photographer—"DON'T THINK"—and knew my mom would be disappointed in me for putting up with that, since she herself was a woman making her way in a man's business world and had to fight tooth and nail for everything she got.

"That's terrific, honey. Can you scan and e-mail us the photos when you get them?" she said.

"Sure, sure. I mean, it may take a while, but when I get them, you and Dad will be the first to see them," I said.

"How's everything else going?"

"Good, I mean, great!" I panicked. She could always smell my half-truths. Digging in my purse to get some lip balm, I inadvertently found the card for the Clijsters Gallery. I looked at it like it was some strange omen, then quickly stuffed it back in my purse.

"Are you all right, baby?" my mom asked. Her voice still touched me across those miles on my cell phone.

I wanted to tell her everything, about how I had met this guy who owned a gallery, how I was going to go on another date with a Frenchman my semi-crazy roommate was infatuated with, how Jeanette's goody-girl act was getting on my nerves, how I'd like to try to talk to Kylie about maybe getting out of the dorm a bit more, how the promoters bought us dinner and we drank Dom Perignon free all night, how terrified I was of the weekly measurements and of Rachel, how shitty and un-high-fashion-like our dorm was, how the girls just embraced the crazy fun of being a model and threw sexual boundaries to the wind, how a part of me maybe wished I could do that myself. But I didn't tell her any of that.

"Yeah, Mom, everything's great, just feeling a little emotional. Can you send me those running shoes I left in the closet?"

I would have continued talking to my mother, just to hear her comforting voice. But I had to get off the phone. Svetlana was ready to go out. A car was waiting for us downstairs.

9

CLIJSTERS GALLERY

THE NAME, ENGRAVED ON THE HUGE GLASS DOOR, seemed to hang in midair, frozen. I stood on a Chelsea street outside the gallery a few days after my first shoot, thinking about Robert and Willem's interaction, wondering what I'd be getting myself into. *Whatever. Sometimes I think too much.* I pulled on the handle, and the door swooshed open, leading me into a foyer before the main space.

I'd been a mess of emotions after the shoot (and the partying the waiting car had brought Svetlana and I to that night). Luke had called to say how much great feedback they'd gotten on me from everyone, which was gratifying and exciting. My job had been to model, and I'd done it well, and it was probably going to lead to more jobs, which filled me with the same girlish excitement I'd felt when I first got to New York. But I also was stung by the photographer's brusque words, treating me like an infant who had no right to do anything except stand there, certainly not to start a conversation about anything besides mascara.

Lying on the couch in my pajamas—no castings a couple days after my shoot, thankfully—I flipped through my Basquiat book, getting more and more indignant at how I'd been treated, even though I'd been as meek as a lamb when shot down by the photographer.

Things like Basquiat actually interested me; I didn't fake liking them just to be "cool." I looked at all the reproductions of the paintings, and even read the essays in the back, learning more about the artist's style and influences.

Just because I was a model, that meant I couldn't have anything else to say? *Hmph.* Having gotten myself fairly well riled up at this point, I decided I was going to go gallery-hopping, do something that *didn't* involve thinking about fashion photographers, castings, my weight, which promoter's throwing what event where. . . .

Kylie was padding around the apartment, vaguely watching some TV and helplessly trying to sort her laundry, since it was getting too expensive for her just to pay to have it done.

"Hey, Kylie," I said. "Do you want to go to Chelsea?"

She was in the midst of determining whether or not to put her pink thong in the wash with her black one.

"Chelsea? Like right now? It's only four in the afternoon," she answered.

"No, not to go out—I want to check out some galleries," I said. "You should come."

"Galleries, like art galleries? I'm pretty busy," she answered.

"Never mind, then," I said, a bit defeated. I'd hoped that at least

Kylie might have had some interest in going with me—I guess I should have lured her with the possibility of free wine. Jeanette probably would have trailed along, clueless, but I'd remembered that she said she'd had a casting. Or had she been called back? I couldn't remember—she was always so bubbly about them all.

I put on some clothes and took the subway by myself up to West Chelsea, the epicenter of art in New York. I'd poked my head into a couple galleries, both of which were fairly disappointing—the first had a show of lame landscape paintings, and the second was full of what looked like comic book art, but not even executed that well, or with the playful sense somebody like Roy Lichtenstein had. Nothing too exciting.

After a few hours, I started to make my way over to the Clijsters Gallery. It had a modern concrete exterior with thin slivers of windows and big heavy glass doors. I looked at the card again, like the address could have been mistaken, but the graven letters let me know I was in the right spot.

To tell you the truth, the reason I hesitated outside wasn't just that Robert had given me a cryptic warning about Willem, who had seemed so nice, at least on the surface. The larger reason was that I was wondering if maybe Willem had been drinking a bit that night and wouldn't remember me. Or even worse, he *hadn't* been drinking at all and *still* wouldn't remember me. Or, even more worse, he'd remember me and regret that he'd ever tried to start a conversation about art with some *model*. Maybe he was just like the photographer, maybe he just assumed that I was dumb, and he would totally nod and grin but not really listen. Like I said, sometimes I think too much.

I consoled myself with the fact that he probably wasn't even around, perhaps off buying some oversize painting in a castle in Germany.

Whatever. As I said, I plunged in.

The first thing I noticed in the gallery—besides the dazzling array of oversize artworks hanging on the walls—was that I'd definitely been wrong about the whole Belgian-off-on-business-at-a-castle-in-Germany thing. The only person there was Willem, wearing a sharp pressed suit and crisp tie. Despite his clothes, he looked decidedly frazzled, like he was going forty-three ways at once.

He smiled when he saw me, though. He had a zany charm that warmed you to him.

"Heather, I was wondering if you'd come say hello to us," he said, coming up to shake my hand. "Quite wonderful to see you."

He *did* remember me, even my name. I gently shook his hand.

"I am sorry, you have caught us at a crazy time. As the fates would have it, one of my assistants has come down with a nasty bug, the others are all off running errands, and, worst of all, my receptionist scheduled for today did not appear," Willem said. "I had a long and distinctly rambling message from her this morning—apparently she decided it was in her best interest to escape to Thailand with her sculptor boyfriend. Today. Young love, may it last. I believe they're being married in the jungle somewhere."

"I can come back if you're busy. . . ."

"No, no, oh, no, don't think anything of it!" he said.

The phone rang, and he sprang over to the desk where the absent girl should have been sitting. His compact frame was bounding with energy. He loved every minute of it.

"Clijsters Gallery," he said into the phone. "Oh, hello, Mr. Wasserstein . . . Yes, yes, Virginia is not here today. . . ."

The whole time he was talking on the phone, Willem craned his head nervously, looking out onto the street, as if he were waiting for someone. Two figures appeared outside the glass door.

"Excuse me a moment," Willem said to the person on the phone before covering the earpiece. "Daniel! Daniel!" he shouted into the back. He turned to me and quietly mouthed: "My colleague." Then shouted again, *"Daniel!* Mr. Smith is here!"

The door swung open as the two people entered, and Willem was stumped for a second, having a client on the phone while this mysterious Mr. Smith arrived.

"Hello, Mr. Wasserstein?" he said into the phone after a second of thought. "I am going to have to hand you off to Heather for a moment, and I will be back."

WHAT?! To *me?*

Before I even had a chance to process this, Willem thrust the phone into my hands. He whispered to me, "He hates being put on hold, he'd just hang up. Ask him about all the empty wall space in his new chateau."

And with that he walked briskly to the well-heeled couple who had just entered, greeting them as old friends.

I held the phone in my hand like it was a poisonous snake. *What the hell . . . nothing to lose.*

"Hello?" I said.

"Hello, is that Heather?" a man with a gravelly voice and German accent asked me.

"Yes, I'm Heather." What did Willem expect me to do?

"Oh, hello, Heather, how are you? Willem's stepped away?"

"I'm fine, thanks. Yes, he'll be back in just a second," I said, although it didn't look like it. He was escorting Mr. and Mrs. Smith to a towering Richard Serra sculpture in the corner. What was I going to say?

Château.

"Willem mentioned you have a new chateau? That's . . . great." I was shooting from the hip here, all right?

"Yes, and the *verdammte* thing's filled to the brim with all sorts of terrible Victorian claptrap," he said. "That's why I had to get in touch with Willem. I heard he has access to the family in the Poconos who found the stash of uncatalogued early Lichtensteins. Have you seen them?"

"Oh, me, no, no, I mean I've *heard* they're great, though. Quality," I said, having no idea what Lichtensteins he was talking about.

A tall lanky man with glasses came trotting in from the back office—this must be Daniel. Willem passed the couple to his colleague and came back to me at the phone. Mr. Wasserstein was rhapsodizing about the virtues of Warhol's early career by this point.

"Mr. Wasserstein, I hate to interrupt, but Willem's back. Nice talking to you," I said, handing the phone to the Belgian, who gave me a look of gratitude. Willem finished the conversation.

"Uh-huh, yes, Wednesday at three P.M. is perfect. We can take tea and then I'll show you the pieces. Mmm-hmm. Yes, Heather *is* a delightful girl . . . I'll tell her. . . . Till then, Mr. Wasserstein . . . *Ciao.*" He hung up the receiver and wiped his brow, sneaking a peek to make sure Daniel was doing all right with Mr. and Mrs. Smith.

"Mr. Wasserstein gives you his regards," Willem said, smiling. "I'm quite sorry about throwing that at you, but he is a very important client for us, and I don't want him to think I am not catering enough to him."

"That's no problem. I was glad to help." What had I just been thrown into?

"Let's go to the back where we can talk without disturbing Daniel and the clients," he said. I followed, forgetting entirely about Robert's hints that Willem was less than an up-and-up character. When we were out of earshot, Willem turned to me and nodded toward the main gallery. " 'Mr. Smith' is what we call Isaac de Bourgh—all of the sales are done in the name of Smith so would-be thieves won't know the millions he has in art stored at his residences. One must be very discreet in this business sometimes." He winked.

In the sleek office, we just talked. Willem made me a cup of tea, and we chatted about Basquiat. My head was full of everything I'd read earlier in the day, and I rattled off interesting things about the artist. Willem was delighted that I took such an interest. I felt relaxed, at peace, not constantly under the gun. My brain was dizzy by the end—it was getting tired after having been put on hiatus for so long.

We walked into a back storage area. Most of the pieces were still crated. Daniel poked his head in. "Looks like Mr. Smith may take the Serra. I'm giving him a moment to talk it over with his wife," he said.

"Great, make sure she doesn't change his mind. That's a top-notch piece he *needs* to have for his sculpture wing," Willem said. He turned to me and pointed at a huge Warhol silkscreen—it was the standard picture of Chairman Mao, done in wild colors. Classic Warhol.

"What do you think about this?"

"It's great!" I said.

"My colleague doesn't agree," Willem said. "Daniel! Daniel!" The tall man poked his head in again. "Heather thinks the Warhol is terrific, just like I told you it was. Let's get it up and shown by tomorrow."

Just because I had said something? This was a far cry from being told to pipe down for even mentioning an artist during the shoot.

Willem escorted me back to the main part of the gallery, making me promise I'd visit again. "I cannot thank you enough for talking to Mr. Wasserstein. It was 'clutch,' as they say," he told me, delighting in his use of the American word. We had walked to the door, but his eyes wandered back to the unoccupied desk where his receptionist would have been sitting. The proverbial lightbulb flicked on above his head. "Listen, I know you're probably quite busy with your work, but would you be interested in working here, just a few days a week? It's not as glamorous as modeling, but I would let you take off any time you had a casting that came up. You did a good job with Mr. Wasserstein."

I didn't know what to say . . . a *job*? Did models get those? Willem noted my hesitation.

"It would pay thirty dollars an hour," he said.

Thirty an hour?! A bit of shock came across my face due to the high figure. I started to speak, but he cut me off.

"Okay, I know that's low. You drive a hard bargain. Let's say forty dollars an hour," he said. "You would be great for Clijsters Gallery; you have a good energy, plus you liked the Warhol, which fuddy-duddy Daniel was all against. I *knew* it was good."

"Um, I don't know, I'm just . . ." What about Robert, his beef with Willem—was there still something I couldn't sense about the Belgian? But he had made me tea, I hadn't gotten that "modelizer" vibe from him at all, he seemed like a nice—once again, thinking too much. *Forty an hour to answer phones and hang out at the gallery.* When my bank account looked like a pauper's. "Okay, I'll do it," I said.

"Great!" We shook on it. "Come by next Monday, say, and I will show you how we operate here." He had an ear-to-ear grin. "Daniel! *Daniel!* We have a new employee!"

It'd taken me almost two months to get my first job as a model in New York. Job at an art gallery? Forty-five minutes.

10

"SO JEANETTE'S LEAVING," KYLIE SAID to me gravely when I got back from the gallery that night, newly employed. The Aussie spoke under her breath in the kitchen.

"What happened? Did you finally chase her away, or reveal some terrible secret from the mountains to Rachel? Did the cheeseburgers add too many millimeters onto her waist?"

"Noooo—" Kylie said. She was cut off by Jeanette's chirpy voice.

"Heather!" she bubbled, coming out of the bedroom. She was folding a pair of jeans to pack in her suitcase. "Did you hear the great news?"

Svetlana, who was sitting at the computer in her bathrobe, listening to some Russian techno, turned the music up and lit a cigarette, taking a violent drag, even though she already had one lit. It burned in the makeshift ashtray of a coffee mug, neglected.

"No, I didn't hear."

"I've been requested for a campaign—for Ralph Lauren! And it's going to be an exclusive!" she gushed. "Isn't it just unbelievable? I mean, just a small-town girl from Utah, and now *this!* An exclusive for Ralph Lauren!"

A sea of envy washed over me in a cascading splash. She'd only been here a hot minute, and she got a *campaign* like that?! And getting an exclusive meant even though she couldn't appear in another campaign that season, she'd be making more money. A *lot* more money. I *had* been planning to tell my roommates about getting the job at the gallery, but now I realized that working as a receptionist was a bit smaller potatoes than being emblazoned in magazines for a national campaign.

"Wow, that's, really, um, *great,* Jeanette. I mean it's fantastic, congratulations," I said.

Kylie, fuming with jealousy, unscrewed the bottle of Stoli and took a swig of straight stuff, not bothering with the Metamucil and a glass. She held it in front of me.

"You should have a nip—makes it all go down a bit easier," she said, burping a little. I shook my head.

The Utah girl continued, totally clueless that with every word about her great success she was sending us all a step further into good old-fashioned, unadulterated jealousy. "And like I was telling Kylie and Svetlana, I couldn't have done it without you guys, bless your hearts!"

Jeanette, always beautiful and one breath away from being basically perfect, glowed with all this news. It made her look even more gorgeous, damn her. I tried to be as happy as I could for her, but this was the big time. She'd snaked us all for the big job. My shoot from earlier in the week suddenly felt small and inconsequential.

Yet I couldn't help wanting to chuckle to myself about how Kylie and Svetlana had schemed to get her out of the dorm—but not *this* way! Their cheeseburgers and extra fries and clumsy interrogating sessions had slid off the irrepressible Jeanette's back like water off a duck's, and cheerfully she'd kept on, going to the gym, making great impressions at her go-sees and castings. And now she had it. That envy wave crashed down around my ears even harder. I wondered how much money Ralph Lauren was tossing at her to become its new face (and body, of course).

"So, where are you going, I mean with all your stuff?" I asked.

"Well, first things first. My mom's flying out here from Utah, and the Agency's arranged a hotel suite for us until I find my own place," she said.

I remembered what it was like to have a place called home, not sharing bunk beds with a clutch of other girls, not having to deal every minute of the day with mysterious odors and squabbles over bathroom time.

"Gee, that's. Just. Great," I said. I was the runner-up at one of those beauty contests, who has to screw on the fake smile and then pile on the phony congratulations and hugs and tears to the girl who's beaten her, just not to look like a sore loser.

"You guys will have to come visit when I have my own apartment. It's going to be really neat."

Kylie coughed loudly at this last straw, the use of *neat*. Svetlana kicked the computer and let out a stream of Russian in frustration.

"Do you think the West Village is a cool place to live?" Jeanette asked, genuinely not knowing that the West Village was *the* best place for a fashionable girl to live, rubbing elbows with celebrities on hiatus from Hollywood. About a hundred times better than the Financial District the model dorm was in, which turned into a ghost town past six P.M. "Rachel was saying she could maybe get me in a nice one-bedroom there, right around the corner from the Magnolia Bakery." I hoped she ate too many of those tasty Magnolia cupcakes and got fat. "I'll definitely be able to afford the apartment with this campaign!" she said.

Too much, too much . . .

"Just a minute," I said, holding up my finger. I stepped into the kitchen, grabbed the bottle of Stoli from Kylie and poured myself a quick shot. *Slurp.* It burned, but in a good way.

I stepped back out, where Jeanette still had that smile plastered on her beautiful face. "Did I ever tell you how neat you are, Jeanette?"

JEANETTE'S DEPARTURE TO BIGGER and better things, along with my job at the Clijsters Gallery, marked the beginning of a new stage in the model dorm for me. Outside, on the streets of the city, winter began its assault on New Yorkers, forcing everyone to scurry faster than ever, bundled up in scarves, hats, and full-length jackets, millions of different destinations for millions of different people. Inside the apartment, Kylie, Svetlana, and I were starting to realize that far from being short-timers, we were becoming the de facto model dorm veterans, a dubious honor, at best. The stuffy apartment, which seemed a million miles from the glitz and glamour of what we should have been doing as models, came to be our fate in life for the time. And every month on our accounts the Agency would mark up another $2,000, along with all the other charges we mysteriously managed to incur, which I began to think were total bullshit—I mean $400 for Internet booking charges? For what? But I didn't dare question anyone at the Agency, remembering Rachel's wrath. Laura was probably back home, waiting tables, having to avoid the wandering hands of the beefy lumberjacks of her hometown in remote Canada as she sashayed between the tables with plates full of flapjacks and sausage patties.

The job at the gallery was a welcome break from the model dorm. Instead of wasting away my free time suffering in the apartment, I earned a decent wage greeting gallery visitors, answering phones, and accompanying Willem to the occasional art opening. Always a gentleman, he never forgot to tell me how much he appreciated my being there. Sometimes we'd talk about different artists, and I began to learn a lot about contemporary art. I liked being at the space—it relaxed me. I'd told Kylie and Svetlana about my job, and how excited I was to be mixing it up in the art world, but they'd reacted as if I'd told them something as banal as: "The sun is shining somewhat today," or "I just saved ten cents by buying a pack of gum from the other deli across the street." They couldn't have cared less about anything outside of the fashion world and its siren call.

The only problem with my job at Willem's was that I still felt some of the others in that circle didn't respect me. If there was an event, or I went out for drinks with Willem and Daniel and some of their friends, and someone asked what I did, besides being a receptionist, they'd sort of nod, like "Oh, I have you figured out. You're just a *model*." But Willem's talks with me let me know he considered me more than eye candy—plus he never hit on me. I treated him like a quirky older brother who just happened to dress in tailored French suits and who wheeled and dealed in million-dollar pieces of art. And even though I didn't want to answer phones and greet people for the rest of my life, the job *was* helping me survive as I waited for the big modeling job to come in that would set me up.

But I knew there were no guarantees. My parents, concerned that I had dropped out of high school to model, had of course wanted me to think about my "future" and had suggested I take the GED to earn a high-school equivalency. The fact that I was "just" a receptionist at this gallery only made them more insistent. I mentioned taking the GED to Willem, and he thought it was a fine idea, that I would certainly pass. He helped me set up a time to test in January and even brought me a study booklet. This was just insurance, though, I told myself. I had to be patient, and the big modeling job would come.

My shoot for Vena Cava's look book certainly hadn't put me on easy street: It barely put a dent in my account with the Agency—I think they paid me something like $500 and, unlike commercial print work, it's not as if I'd be seeing money over the coming year every time they used it. I never saw a cent of that money; it went directly to the Agency. I did get a free dress, though, which I only wore on special nights out, it was so delicately chic. Jeanette, on the other hand, now that Ralph Lauren was going to be using her for their catalog and campaign, would be seeing big fat checks coming through each and every time they used her image in an ad, whether on a billboard, magazine, or side of a bus. I wonder how much she gave to the church, which had been so against her coming to New York in the first place.

Every so often we'd get a new model who would only be there for a few days, sent from her mother agency to work in New York on a special job. Each girl would show up, crinkle her nose at the pathetic state of our living quarters, stay a few nights in the bunks, and then disappear, checks in their designer bags and relief in their heart, glad they didn't have to put up with the dorm much longer.

I realized with a bit of a shock why Svetlana and I had been going out pretty much every night: to get out of the confines of the model dorm, pretend we were really making it, while most of the girls who were doing well, booking shoots, making money, were home in bed in their nice apartments—they had to wake up for actual jobs, looking beautiful and sexy, where we just had to stumble to a couple cattle calls and go-sees we probably wouldn't get callbacks for, anyway.

But I knew it wasn't because we just weren't cut out for modeling. Svetlana had had some editorial jobs in the past, been on the runway, opening some of the best shows in Moscow. And the fact that I had just gone on a shoot and the Agency seemed comfortable with having me around said that we had what it took. There were just so many other beautiful girls running around in this city, with the other agencies, that it was a lot of luck—you just needed that one break, the one casting person for a campaign to suddenly feel that *you* were the one— in order to make it. And all those other girls were in the same boat as us, all the models you see on the street and think, *What glamorous things are they up to tonight?* Well, odds are they may be stuck in some miserable apartment, pining for home and cooking up half meals of vegetables and rice, dreaming of the big time while arguing about who took down the full-length mirror and used it to cut lines of coke on the night before. The coke wasn't the issue—the fact that the culprit hadn't cleaned it off and hung up the mirror again was.

A WHILE AFTER JEANETTE MOVED ON, I had one of those crazy nights you never forget. Svetlana was, of course, the ringleader of this particular circus. I had become a bit quieter around the dorm. Maybe it was the weather that had turned cold and gray, maybe it was that the Utah girl had upstaged us all, or maybe I just got tired of getting blank stares whenever I mentioned anything about Willem's gallery. At any rate, Svetlana sensed something was a bit off with me, and she had a brilliant idea to get me out of my slump: She was going to take me to "real Russian club—very fancy, very fun!"

I was a bit tentative. I mean, I had seen her chats on the Russian "dating" sites and could only imagine what would be awaiting me if we went out on a good old-fashioned Russian extravaganza, but she insisted, getting more and more excited. She normally kept her relationships with the Russian mafia-type guys to herself, and I could tell this was a step further in our friendship, like she was trusting me a bit more—enough to show me this side of her. (Not that her shadowy Russian "friends" ever stopped her from nattering on and on about Robert, nor did she take down her mini-shrine to the Frenchman she'd hung next to her bed. I still hadn't thought about how to deal with what was going to happen when he got back, but, like anybody who's great at denial, I would just happily forget about it.)

"Just like Moscow! Many rich guys for Heather," Svetlana had promised, not that I was particularly looking to date a Russian ATM machine that walked around on two legs and wore shiny Moschino shirts. "Heather only non-Russian, very exclusive."

The night came, and Svetlana teased her hair and put on a gaudy Moschino dress—she was going to go all out in Russian fashion tonight. The slit on the side showed off about eight miles of flesh. She covered her face with even more makeup than usual. I put on a simple black dress and wondered what I was getting myself into.

A black town car arrived for us downstairs, and we slid into the plush backseat. We didn't have to tell the driver where to go; he'd already been instructed. The driver and my roommate exchanged some words in Russian, and he smiled wolfishly at us through the rearview mirror as he kicked the car into drive. Svetlana hadn't told me where we were actually going, and I panicked as we passed City Hall and then got on the Brooklyn Bridge, leaving Manhattan.

"Um, Svet, where's this club?"

"Oh, Svetlana forget—Brighton Beach, by Coney Island. Very fun," she said, then went back to looking at herself in her compact mirror.

Brighton Beach? I thought I had heard of it; I guessed it was in Brooklyn somewhere. Brooklyn seemed like a whole other country across the East River, which I had no clue about, since I hadn't laid eyes on it since the car had brought me from the airport. I remember once when a bunch of us girls had been out at Cain, a club next to Bed on Twenty-seventh Street, and had been talking to a tall dark artist type who had been making eyes at Yelena, the successful Ukrainian girl at the Agency. But when everyone found out he lived somewhere in Brooklyn—and not Williamsburg, maybe it was Park Slope—everyone disappeared, as if he'd just confessed to being a leper, leaving him clutching a half-drank Red Stripe, stunned by the mass departure of beautiful models he'd been surrounded by only moments before. I hadn't quite understood what was so terrible about Brooklyn, only that it wasn't Manhattan.

Well, if I hadn't seen Brooklyn before, Svetlana was about to introduce me to a *very* peculiar part of it. The town car with the grinning Russian at the wheel sped expertly down the expressway, past what looked like downtown Brooklyn, a mini-version of Manhattan with smaller skyscrapers that still would put most cities' downtowns to shame. Anonymous neighborhoods streamed past, going from nice areas to dilapidated spots that looked like war zones. Brighton Beach seemed pretty far away, as Manhattan disappeared into the night smog behind us. At last we peeled off the freeway and onto surface streets. It felt like I was in a totally different country, all the storefronts written in Cyrillic, every single person walking down the street sharing the features that distinguished Svetlana so much from everyone else when we strolled together in Manhattan. In an indescribable way, I could feel Svetlana's awkwardness, her tentativeness, start to fall away from her—it was like she was home.

The car came to a screeching halt in front of a club with a bright neon blue sign announcing its name: KLUB ILIRJANA. A whole crew of Slavic bruisers in black suits stood at the entrance, guarding its exclusivity.

One of the men came and opened the door for us, speaking to me in Russian as I stepped out.

"Hi . . . Uh, party?" I said, confused, looking to Svetlana for help.

She said something to him in Russian, and he helped me out.

"Vell-come to Klub Ilirjana," he said in an accent even thicker than Svetlana's, if that's possible.

"Thank you," I answered, worrying what the hell I had gotten myself into, or, rather what *Svetlana* had gotten me into. She stopped and exchanged small talk with the bouncers before they opened the thick chrome doors for us—it seemed like they knew her already. Inside the door stood another tall doorman, who manned a small podium with a clipboard. Apparently he'd been expecting us, as he held open a royal blue velvet curtain to let us in the main room without even looking at the list.

We entered into a huge glittery area lined on the edges with booths and filled in the center with round tables. The place was jammed with patrons, the men in shiny suits, even a couple in tuxedos, the women in various little black dresses. Candles, on each of the tables, flickered, giving the room an ethereal glow. At the back was a raised stage, which was curtained off by the same royal blue velvet as the entrance. The room was filled with Russian chatter, competing with the Russian pop playing over the club's speakers.

Svetlana, clutching my arm in excitement, craned her head to find the guy we were supposed to meet. The stocky man who had been waiting for her in the lobby at the dorm earlier in the week caught her glance and waved her over, bellowing, "SVETLANA!" She took my arm and we walked to the banquette.

Ivan—I learned that was his name—was sitting at a table with two other men and a coltish young woman who gave us a freezing stare as we came to the booth. Used to being the center of attention, it was obvious she wasn't too excited about having two models from

Manhattan share the spotlight with her. Svetlana stared her down as we seated ourselves. It seemed the two Russian girls maybe knew each other.

"Heather—Ivan, Alexander, Piotr, and . . ." Svetlana searched for the girl's name, as if she hadn't been important enough to remember.

"Alina," the Russian said, icicles in her voice.

"Hello, Heather, nice to make acquaintance," Ivan said, taking my hand and kissing it, like a gentleman. I could tell these guys weren't gentlemen, though, despite the luxurious surroundings. There was the scent of dirty money clinging to the whole place. Svetlana told me later that Ivan's nickname was *Ivan Grozny,* "Ivan the Terrible," in honor of the old Russian leader. The bizarre thing was that Svetlana thought it was funny. As for Ivan's associates, Piotr was wearing Gucci sunglasses and his mole-pocked face was swollen red with the vodka he had already been drinking. A drop of sweat rolled down his hairy chest, which was partly exposed, since he had unbuttoned his tacky Eurotrash shirt two buttons down. Alexander kept leering at Alina, and she would swat away his un- wanted hands from her exposed thighs in mock outrage. I could definitely imagine Alexander's hands opening those thighs later that night and Alina not being too upset about it. None of the men were particularly attractive, all a bit overweight and older.

"Please, enjoy," Ivan said, pouring us tall flutes of champagne. That was some of the last English I'd hear that night, as everyone, instead of struggling to speak English, decided it'd be easier to just stick with Russian. Every once in a while the group would burst into laughter—everyone except me, of course—and then Svetlana would lean over and try to explain what the joke was, to disastrous results, of course. I didn't mind being left out, though, since it left me time to take in the bizarre otherworld I had just been dropped into. Svet- lana, for her part, was perfectly comfortable there; there was a certain glow around her, like she was finally famous, a *somebody*, not just some girl trying to make it as a model and living in a shitbox in the Financial District. Men would come by and pay their respects to her politely, as if we were back in the Old World.

On nearly every table stood a bottle of chilled vodka. The men poured it into water glasses and drank it straight. The women sipped it as well, or threw back champagne, careful not to overdo it while the males got more and more drunk. The girls were the darlings of Russian-American society, beautiful and scary in that blond Eastern European way.

Ivan ordered food, and ridiculous amounts of beluga caviar arrived, along with fresh bottles of champagne and vodka. We snacked on the delicate sturgeon eggs. Svetlana made eyes at me, as if to say, "See, Svetlana told you! Very fancy!"

I hadn't quite acquired the taste for caviar—this was the first time I'd actually ever tried it—but I didn't want to seem like a serf, so I carried on, one briny bite after the next.

Without warning, the blue velvet curtains on the stage opened up, and the crowd erupted into enthusiastic applause. Assembled onstage was a small band. From behind a curtain in the backstage emerged a woman in her late twenties who had on a formfitting glittery gown, her breasts practically bursting out into the crowd. The vodka-soaked men hollered loudly as she appeared, the applause increasing twofold.

As if we had just transported ourselves eighty years into the past, the singer began a series of sultry Russian torch songs, backed by her enthusiastic band. The audience was held rapt by her presence, her red lips never far from the microphone, singing about god only knows what. As she finished her first set, the audience rose to its feet, thunderously applauding her performance. Alina yawned. Svetlana had been too busy talking to Ivan to notice much.

He pulled out a small jewelry box and handed it to my roommate. She opened it and revealed a pair of small diamond earrings. Giggling, she threw her arms around Ivan—but not before making a quick assessment of the diamond's color and clarity.

Ivan looked at me apologetically.

"Ivan sorry, next time I have gift for you?" he said.

"Oh, that's all right, I don't need . . ." I tried to answer, wondering if this was common Russian mafia courtesy extended to everyone.

The show over, the club started playing Russian pop again, and a man dressed in a black suit appeared onstage, shouting in enthusiastic Russian—apparently he was asking the ladies to come up, because some of the younger women started making their way to the stage. They lined up on each side of the MC, rhythmically swaying to the music, throwing back their heads and laughing, the men in the audience whistling. They gathered their dresses up to show their legs off to the best advantage.

Maybe it was the caviar or all the champagne, or the disorientation from feeling like I'd parachuted into St. Petersburg, but my stomach started feeling a little queasy.

At Ivan's urgings, Svetlana stood up to go onstage. She grabbed my hand, trying to get me to go up with her. The earrings shone from her ears, and she had a big smile.

"Heather come Svetlana, dance?" she asked.

"No, Heather doesn't feel good, Svetlana, you go ahead," I said.

She made her way to the stage and took some side stairs to ascend. Ivan whispered something to one of the suit-clad employees of the establishment, who then in turn went up to the stage and whispered something in the ear of the MC.

He shouted something in Russian into the mic that ended with a protracted "SVVEEEEETLANNAAA!" and then a spotlight fell directly on my roommate, who couldn't have been more delighted.

Everyone clapped, and Svetlana had her time to shine. When she danced, she was perpetually a bit behind the beat, and her stilted steps made her look like a stiff mannequin, but nobody seemed to mind. The audience loved her. Here, miles away from the harsh world of the Agency and the castings, Svetlana was getting her due. The Odessa Swan was finally in front of her adoring public.

Ivan, Svetlana, and I all took a car back to Manhattan—although a lot of Ivan's "business" was conducted out in Brighton Beach, he lived in the city and was going to drop us off. It had been quite a night, but Svetlana wasn't finished.

The three of us sat in the backseat, me on the outside, with Svetlana in the middle. She was cozying up to Ivan, cooing in Russian. I pretended not to notice as she got closer and closer to him. He grunted a bit, and out of the corner of my eye I saw her clutching his crotch through his pants. She giggled, and then I heard a distinctive *zzzzzzip* as she undid his fly. I didn't flinch, just tried to look out the window at all that suddenly *very* interesting scenery as we went back to the city.

I figured Svetlana would be content just to feel around inside Ivan's boxers for a bit but, no, she really didn't want to let things stand at that. Unbuckled came Ivan's pants. I stole a glance, seeing as she sprang his erect piece out. Not bad, Ivan.

Svetlana leaned down and started sucking him off, right then and there, as if I wasn't inches away, nor the driver, who kept his eyes fixed on the road ahead. I moved farther against the door, not believing my ears as I heard the *slurps* paired to the moans of the Russian man as Svetlana did her damnedest to give him a blowjob he wouldn't forget.

Now Svetlana started speeding up and moaning herself, even placing Ivan's hand on the back of her head to control how fast she went, and the whole backseat became a symphony of Russian sounds of pleasure. I tried to make myself one with the passenger door, pressing myself up as close as I could and hoping Ivan wasn't a thirty-minute man.

Ivan's breathing sped up, and he started involuntarily kicking a bit with his leg, like a dog whose belly is rubbed in just the right place. Svetlana attacked with even more force, moaning louder and louder as she brought him to pleasure. I could tell the big moment was coming as Ivan burst out with a stream of what I could imagine meant "OH GOD!" in Russian, followed by "THICK LIKE KIEL-BASA!"—which was shouted in English, I think just for my benefit. I instinctively shielded my face as he groaned in ecstasy.

But, as it turned out, I didn't have to worry about it. I'm sure, dear reader, you've been wondering since you met Svetlana what her preference was when performing oral sex on Russian men in the backseat of cabs after a night of caviar, champagne, and dancing on-stage. I'm here to tell you that, when it comes to spitting or swallow-ing, well, Svetlana definitely wasn't about to make a sticky mess on her dress, Ivan's pants, or the town car's backseat.

Wiping her lips and zipping Ivan up, Svetlana sat up and acted like nothing had happened, although she did give me a little mis-chievous wink while fingering her new earrings. Blowjobs are for minutes, but diamonds are forever.

11

A BLANKET OF SNOW FELL ON THE CITY over the next few days, the first real accumulation of the winter, just in time for another date with Robert. It seemed to have taken an eternity but was finally going to happen.

After the backseat blowjob incident, Svetlana asked me in hushed tones back at the dorm not to mention anything to Kylie or the other girls at the Agency. I could tell she didn't care if I revealed that she sucked off a guy in the backseat of a cab with me sitting right next to her. Rather, she didn't want me to blab that the guy she'd been servicing was an unattractive, overweight, middle-aged sugar daddy. If it'd been a young male model stud, I'm sure she would've asked me to tell everyone!

Unfortunately these escapades hadn't taken Svetlana's focus

away from Robert at all, since she had started bringing him up *constantly* since hearing rumors he had returned to New York. Which, of course, I knew already, since we had been texting back and forth and had talked on the phone a couple days before to set a time for us to meet at a spot downtown, as promised. I'd tried not to think about Robert too much, but Svetlana's chatter had the unintended effect of getting my mind worked up about the Frenchman again.

The day of my date with Robert, I had to go into the Agency for my measurements. They'd finally gotten the prints from the shoot, and Rachel was ecstatic. I looked gorgeous! The people had loved me! I had also dropped another two pounds since the last measurements, due more to cutting back my caloric intake than any exercise regimen I'd put myself on—even though I'd received the shoes from my mom, I hadn't really had time to make sure they still fit and go down to the gym. Rachel seemed to be really happy with my progress and even called me "honey." As if I'd suddenly become her best friend, she sat me down and asked how everything was going back at the dorm. I could tell her *anything,* of course.

"I just want to make sure all the girls are doing well, that nobody's having any problems or losing focus. We don't want anyone getting off track, because god forbid they ruin their career by maybe partying too much or something silly like that. Do you think I made it by going out every night?"

Oh, no, of course not, Rachel, and I never go out, either, no, ma'am, my vigorous nodding conveyed. In bed by ten every night, lights out!

"So . . . nobody's overdoing it, partying a little too hard, things like that, I trust?" She smiled to bring me into her confidence, but I could tell a viper lurked underneath. She was trying to turn me into an *informer!*

"No, we're all very serious about our careers, Rachel, very, very serious, practically all we talk about," I lied.

"Good. That's what I wanted to hear. Everyone is carefully chosen here, and each has the opportunity to be a top model, and we give her all the opportunities to do so," she said imperiously. "If that doesn't happen, well, I don't see the blame falling at *our* feet," she finished, essentially dismissing me with this.

If things had started out chummy, they definitely had finished with a bit more, shall we say, normal Rachel flavor. Not only had she tried to get me to inform on the other models but she also had basically told me that it was entirely *my* fault if I didn't end up on the cover of *Vogue*—not that of genes, taste, or just plain luck.

Rachel definitely didn't need to know about my job at the gallery—I was sure she'd tell me to quit wasting my time being a *receptionist,* that instead of answering phones I should be working out in the gym four hours a day, focusing on the business of modeling. I could see her saying, "Do you think I made it by wasting time with piddly-ass jobs that took time away from my career?" I couldn't dare mention that I was starting to survive on the money I got from working at Willem's—she'd surely say that if I was spending more time trying to make it as a model, the *real* money would be coming in soon enough. Rachel, of course, didn't take into account the possibility that maybe that career-making job wasn't necessarily just around the corner and that you need money to survive on. She'd probably think it was a *good* thing we didn't have money to buy food!

So I began treating my time at the gallery as a double life, where I left the dorm and put on a new disguise as an artsy girl. At a drugstore one day, I'd considered getting glasses to complete the disguise but thought that'd be a bit over the top. I'd stopped talking about the gallery with my roomates, worried that if they told some other girl at the Agency, then it'd get back to Rachel and who knows what would happen. But, knowing Rachel, it would probably involve yelling in some form.

As if all of this weren't enough to set me on edge as I got ready for my date with Robert, when I got home, Svetlana was having a near-fit. Yelena had seen Robert out the night before during dinner, confirming the rumors, and had told my roommate he was back in town. Svetlana was beside herself, plotting where he could possibly be going that night. Little did she know I was going to be seeing him in less than two hours. I bit my tongue.

"Heather go with Svetlana to PM—Robert maybe be there. He go to that party a lot," she said to me with eager eyes.

I should have just told her right then and there, instead of hiding this silly secret, just laid everything out on the table, told her how I was going to see Robert, how he probably wasn't going to be interested in her, how he was interested in me. I didn't, of course.

"No, Svetlana, Heather's busy tonight," I said.

"*Busy?*" Svetlana asked. She, of course, was incredibly interested in what I could possibly be doing more important than going out with her to try to hunt down *the* Robert du Croix.

"Yes, um, I have to go to, a, uh, thing," I spit out before fleeing into the bathroom and closing the door behind me quickly.

I decided to start doing my makeup to get ready for the date—at least Svetlana couldn't get to me in the bathroom.

Our blond Icelandic roommate, who was only there for a few days, knocked on the door meekly, seeing how long I would be.

"Hello, please?" she asked, a six-foot blond version of Björk.

"Just a second!" I answered. Shit! I could almost smell Svetlana waiting for me to come out. What was I going to say?

The Icelandic girl knocked again insistently.

"Yes, pee?" she said.

"Okay, okay, I'm coming out," I said, my makeup nearly finished.

The Icelandic girl, whose name I've forgotten, darted into the bathroom when I opened the door to do her "Yes, pee." Svetlana was installed at the computer, laughing at something written to her in the chat rooms. I bolted to the bedroom to get dressed.

Shimmying into my skintight Diesel jeans, I couldn't help but look at Svetlana's shrine to Robert that she'd made from the cutout magazine photos. I was going to be filling in the empty spot by Robert's side in just a little bit! The thought thrilled me but also made me wonder—would Svetlana have cut *me* out?

I checked myself in a small hand mirror we had in the bedroom. I looked great, my hair teased out just enough, and I had to say those jeans looked damn good on me, despite the wriggling it took to get into them. Now just to get out of the apartment without getting the third degree from Svetlana . . .

I opened the door slowly, quietly, could smell wisps of cigarette smoke from the Russian's puffing. She was still there, that was for sure. Open the door a little more, say good-bye, walk out, that was it, right?

I went out into the living room, and Svetlana immediately spun around.

"Heather go out?" she said, wondering why I'd be leaving her behind, of course.

"Um, yeah, I have a dinner, with, a, uh, family friend, Svet," I mumbled, trying to escape.

"Friend? You dress sexy for friend," she said, raising an eyebrow. "Who friend?"

"No, no, I'm not sexy, not at all, just a friend. Gotta go!"

"Svetlana go out later," she said. "If 'friend' not work out, Heather call, *da?*"

"No problem. Look at the time!" I said, dashing out of the apartment with a sigh of relief.

I'd only gone out with Robert once, and things were already headache-inducing complicated! I'd definitely have to tell her after this date. She was my roommate and partner-in-crime going out every night, and maybe even my friend. I had to let her know, just to save her feelings. Well, depending on how things went, of course. No use hurting her feelings if things didn't work out, right?

Outside on the street, fat snowflakes fell lazily from the sky, adding to the layer of white stuff already on the sidewalks. While I tried to hail a cab, I had the opportunity to witness two guys in their mid-twenties, businessmen dressed in suits and overcoats, scooping up clumps of snow and having a good old-fashioned snowball fight. They saw me watching them and stopped pelting each other for a second. They waved at me, and I smiled and waved back. Then they went directly back to assaulting each other with snowy missiles.

That night out at Nobu, Robert was as suave and charming and seemed as well connected as ever, the waiters paying special attention to our table, as usual. But there was a strange subdued air to him, as if he were distracted. I should have been bubbling with excitement about the potential post-dinner activities—I was getting a little tired of Svetlana having all the fun, so to speak, and my hormones had been telling me that it was maybe time to get off the celibate wagon. I'd even had a nice painful visit to a waxer the Russian had recommended.

Conversation lagged in between the appetizer and main course. On a whim, I decided to bring up Willem Clijsters, curious why Robert had reacted the way he did at Bungalow—the other potential question on my mind was exactly what he had been doing in Paris for such a long time, but I didn't want to know if there were some other women he had lined up. So I asked about Willem. In e-mail or on the phone, I hadn't said anything to Robert about my working for Willem, and I also hadn't mentioned to Willem that I was going out with Robert tonight. I'd asked the Belgian once about his connection to du Croix, and he had said to me seriously, looking me in the eye: "You've gone out with him, right?" I nodded. "I'd prefer if we didn't bring him up," Willem said, only furthering the mystery. What *was* it between these two men?

"Robert, remember when we were at Bungalow?" I asked.

"Just one second," Robert said, pulling his BlackBerry out. "I have to take this really quickly." He began speaking on the phone, something about square foot this or square foot that. He tried to end the call quickly. "Listen, we'll have to talk about this later; you're interrupting my meal with a beautiful young lady," he said to the caller, smiling at me. "Now what were you saying, Heather?"

"I was just saying, remember when we went to Bungalow in October?"

"Certainly."

"Well, I was thinking about that man I met, the friend of Trina—Willem Clijsters," I said, trying to be as casual as possible. "You know him, right?"

A grave look flashed on Robert's face, and he deliberately looked down at his plate, poking at the remnants of his miso black cod.

"Yes, I do have the . . . unfortunate pleasure of knowing Mr. Clijsters," Robert said solemnly. This was a new side to Robert, who always was so effortless and cheerful in his talk and banter.

"Unfortunate?" I asked quietly, wondering what the gallery owner, whose outward appearance came across as so innocuous, and who seemed like an utter gentleman and stand-up guy, could have done. "What happened? I mean, I don't want to pry, but . . ."

"Let's just say I would not trust him as far as I could pitch him," he said, slightly mangling the English expression. "Especially with you—he is a noted womanizer."

"Really? I didn't, I mean, I didn't talk to him for so long," I said, trying to make it seem like I hadn't been talking to him a couple times a week at the gallery. *Willem?* A womanizer? Was he hiding something from me—was it all part of some act?

"*Trust* me, Heather, he's a snake." The way Robert said it made it seem better to keep quiet. I didn't want to upset him. But it already seemed too late for that—the rest of the dinner Robert seemed quietly agitated, finishing his meal with machinelike determination.

At one point I decided it'd be best to apologize for bringing the thing up at all.

"Listen, Robert, I'm sorry for bringing up that man; I didn't know it was such a . . . sore subject," I said, trying to patch things up.

"Do not be sorry; it's quite fine; there is no way you could have known," he said, sincerely at that. "It is just some time since I have had to think of that man and his . . . deeds." Deeds? Willem *was* pretty sharp when doing business deals—was I just another potential victory for him, but instead of business, something *else?* It seemed unlikely, but Robert was so earnest that a seed of doubt was planted in my mind.

Now I was burning with curiosity about what had transpired between Willem and Robert, but his uncharacteristic seriousness kept my mouth shut.

We finished our meal, and the waiter came with the digestifs and dessert menu.

"Perhaps it's best if we skip dessert. I'm quite tired. I've been working too much lately—the American way has been getting to me," he said. I nodded obediently.

Stupid, so stupid! Why had I even brought up Willem when I could already sense it was something that had bothered Robert? I felt terrible. Who knows what bad memory I'd dredged up for Robert, ruining a perfectly good meal?

Outside, I still had some vain hope that I'd be ending my streak as a nun, and Robert would invite me back to his place. But that was foolish thinking.

"You can take the car; I'll just hail a cab," he said. He turned to me as the black sedan pulled to the curb. The sky had cleared, and it had turned colder, bitterly so. My cheeks were reddened by the frosty breeze. The icy snow crunched under our feet.

"Heather, I'm sorry, I don't want you to get the wrong idea," Robert said to me gravely.

My heart sank, my stomach turning sour. *Wrong idea? Uh-oh . . .*

"The wrong idea about tonight. I had a lovely time, and I don't want you to think I was not happy to spend time with you."

Okay. . . .

"But when we brought up Monsieur Clijsters, it just sent me back to a bad time," he said. "And I couldn't shake the dark cloud that came with that name."

"I'm sorry, Robert, I didn't mean to . . ."

"Shh, shhh," he told me gently. "Not your fault at all. You see, there was a woman. . . ."

He didn't have to say anything more. I understood.

"I'm sorry," I said, imagining what Willem had done to wrong Robert, who, even though he bristled with confidence, was showing me a vulnerable side.

"You should be getting home. As always, you were lovely tonight," he said. He kissed me lightly on the cheek. I guess that's better than the forehead, but not by much.

He helped me into the cab and closed the door. As soon as I was alone, my mind was like a jack-in-the-box just sprung open into chaos—whom could I trust? Robert's pain had made an impression on me. And he had actually talked about the situation. Willem hadn't, had just wanted to drop the subject entirely. I vowed to keep a closer eye on the Belgian art dealer, just to make sure I wasn't being duped somehow—but as long as his checks kept clearing, I couldn't afford not to work there, especially just because he may have some bad habits with women.

I thought of all this as the cab sped away, leaving the tall Frenchman to fade into the distance, a shrinking dark silhouette against the beam of a solitary flickering streetlight.

THE NEXT DAY BROUGHT two unexpected deliveries: one in the form of an enormous bouquet of flowers and the other in the form of a new roommate—while she wasn't technically a "delivery," the poor girl was left as crudely at the curb as a stack of newspapers heaved from a *NY Post* truck.

The snow kicked in again in the morning, and with no castings that day I didn't really have anything to do except hunker down inside the dorm and weather the storm. Luckily I also had the day off from the gallery, giving me time to digest the information Robert had passed along about Willem, which had truly unsettled me. Was he really the charlatan Robert claimed him to be? I wanted to ponder these things alone, but unfortunately Svetlana didn't have any castings that day either (or just decided to skip them on account of a particularly nasty hangover). I was sure she'd start asking me a trillion questions about the previous night. Whom had I seen? Where had I gone? Was it fun? And then she'd complain about not having found Robert and start mewling like a forlorn kitten, while the whole time *I'd* been with him.

So I spent most of the day trying to avoid her, which isn't exactly the easiest thing in the world when the two of you are sharing a broom closet of a bedroom. I even took the extreme measure of going down to the gym to avoid having to deal with her. But after only a little while of running on the treadmill, I was winded and bored, and slunk back to the apartment, where Svetlana lingered, never changing out of her pink bathrobe, just padding around, smoking cigarettes out the cracked window and clacking away on the computer.

What was I going to tell her about Robert? What *could* I tell her if I didn't even know if we'd be seeing each other again? With how things had ended the night before, with him subdued to begin with, and then downright solemn after I brought up Willem, were things a no-go with the Frenchman? Had I missed my opportunity? But it was only *one* night—maybe he'd just had a bad day.

I kept my mouth shut and just let Svet complain about how she couldn't find Robert *anywhere* the night before, how she'd gone to Marquee, the Pink Elephant, and even made it all the way down to the Soho Grand, hoping she'd run into him. And the whole time I'd been with her prey, talking, eating at Nobu. I felt sorry for her but, in all honesty, I didn't feel *too* sorry. I mean, she didn't even know Robert, right? How could she know she had this amazing connection with the man if she hadn't even spent some time with him? But deep in my heart, I knew I was already trying to justify my deceit, secretly hoping that I was the one who had the connection with him—even though we hadn't even kissed at the end of either date, which troubled me to no end. Was it even really a date, then, with no kissing? Maybe it was better to worry about Svetlana rather than that little hiccup in the night, when everything was just right, just perfect, and he was supposed to lean down and gently pull my face toward his and . . .

I mulled this over as I tried to relax and watch TV, wishing the day would end or Svetlana would leave, when there was a thundering knock on the door.

"What the . . . ?" I looked to Svetlana to see if she was expecting anyone, but she barely acknowledged the knock at all.

The rapping began again, and I jumped out of my seat. The Russian didn't even look my way, she was so engrossed in whatever flirtatious messages from the Igors of the world were flashing across her computer screen.

"I guess I'll get it," I said, hopping up.

That turned out to be one of the best decisions I'd made in a long time.

I opened the door, and a deliveryman stood, holding a huge bouquet of flowers. He was shivering, a layer of snow covering his shoulders.

"Delivery, Heather Johnston," the man said in language thickly accented from his native Mexico.

At this, Svetlana, the nosiest of the nosies, spun around to get a look. Damn! She saw what they were, and also that I was going to be the recipient.

Immediately I *knew* the flowers must be from Robert—sixth sense—so I tried to push the deliveryman out the door. I succeeded (barely), and straddling the threshold, out of Svetlana's line of sight, snatched the small card from the flowers and stuck it down my bra. The deliveryman raised an eyebrow.

"Ah, you sign?" he asked, a little freaked out by my eyes, which were a bit wild, I imagine.

"Oh, yeah, yeah," I said, quickly scribbling a line on his clipboard before slamming the door shut.

I turned around, holding the fragrant bouquet, and was face-to-face with Svetlana.

"Who from?" Svetlana asked, poking her little Russian nose around to find the card.

"Umm, just my, uh, mom and dad, it's um, their anniversary," I made up on the spot, seconds later realizing how stupid you would have to be to believe that parents would send their kids flowers on their own anniversary. "I mean, *my* anniversary . . . um, the anniversary of my conception!" If that wasn't as stupid, it was twenty times more disgusting to think that my parents would send flowers in commemoration of the day they *did it.*

"Heather anniversary?" Svetlana asked, the weak fabrication not even fooling her. "You *hiding* something!" She paced around me like a detective, sniffing at the flowers. "Svetlana find out who secret man is!"

"No, no, no secret man, why would you *ever* think that? Just some friendly flowers, ha!" I said. "Let's get these in some water!" I was freaking out and needed to get away from the Russian's glare. I put the flowers on the kitchen counter and then slipped past Svetlana into the bathroom. I shut the door and locked it, drawing the card out from my bra. I opened the small envelope.

The message was simple and succinct: *Lovely seeing you last night, Heather. I'm sorry my thoughts were elsewhere. You were the bright point of the day.*

Instantly the night's memories washed over me in abstract warmth, Robert's jaw, the way he took my arm, his confident voice. I snapped out of it soon, though, thinking about Svetlana and her crazy ways, separated from me by only the cheap door.

I thought about eating the message, just to make sure Svetlana wouldn't find it, but that seemed silly. I slipped it back into my bra and reflected for a moment. How did Robert find my address? He must have called the Agency. But then he knew . . . knew I lived in a model apartment??? My face blushed—I hadn't lied to him, but I also hadn't volunteered that I lived like a guest in a roach motel. But if he knew I was at the dorm and still wanted to send flowers, maybe it wasn't such a big deal after all? I didn't know what to think anymore and just wanted to teleport myself out of the dorm so I didn't have to deal with Svetlana, so I could work through everything on my own, think about everything that happened the night before, what the flowers meant. Instead I reluctantly went back to the living room—I couldn't stay in the bathroom all day.

She wasn't at the computer anymore, instead was sitting on the couch, waiting. She was in a fit to find out whom the flowers were from.

"Svetlana want know where expensive flower from! Tell me, tell me, tell me, tell me!" she said, going into a girlish rage and actually using "me" for once, instead of "Svetlana"—could she actually speak better English than she let on?

"Svet, there's nothing to tell. I mean, I told you already—there *is* something to tell—but it's really boring, just from my mom and dad, you know."

"Svetlana *no* believe!" She went to the kitchen and started foraging through the bouquet, looking for the card. "Svetlana want to *know*," she at last said, putting her final ace on the table, her whiny tear-trembling voice that seemed to work on all the men. I wouldn't back down, though. I realized that despite all the dinners and clubs and castings and everything, deep down Svetlana was just *bored* of everything and would cling onto anything that could give her any excitement whatsoever.

"Where card if from parent?" she asked. She had me there.

"Listen, Svet, they called ahead of time, I, um, mean e-mailed me the message, so there was no need for a card," I said. My lies were starting to get more and more convoluted, and I became afraid of getting snared in them. *This isn't like me,* I thought. *My parents raised a nice honest girl.* Just a few months in the model dorm had started to erode my sense of right and wrong before my very eyes. And I was getting tired of Svetlana's little turn as Sherlock Holmes.

Should I just tell her?

I thought about Svetlana, Svetlana the girl, not the would-be model who loved to put on airs about how glamorous she was, desperate for men's attention. Not that I thought she was getting exploited—she seemed to enjoy the sex just as much as the men, if not more. But this Robert thing, what *was* it? Did he represent something to her, something that became missing when her father lost his battle with the bottle, his liver corroded, leaving just her and her mother to fend for themselves, stuck in some cold-war apartment in the post-Soviet world? Robert was older, this was true. Maybe he seemed like the daddy she never had, the exact opposite of hers: Instead of drinking rotgut liquor, Robert sipped fine Bordeaux; instead of working in a greasy factory, Robert ran the swankiest club in the City of Lights. Instead of leaving her and her mother near-penniless, Robert had a bank account bursting with euros that could take care of her.

I actually felt bad for her. Sort of. Mostly I was just tired of the stress—it was time to just get it over with, you know, better to pull the Band-Aid off in one quick *rip* rather than prolong the pain.

"Hey, Svetlana," I said, gathering my courage, driving from my mind the image of the cutout girls from the magazine. *She's going to take this just fine.*

"*Da?*" she asked, still dissatisfied with my earlier explanations but certainly not expecting the bombshell I was going to drop on her.

"There's something Heather has to tell you," I said, adopting her way of talking for a second. I chose my words carefully and took a deep breath. "I have to tell you, actually *need* to tell you that—"

I was interrupted by the hollow dinging of our front doorbell.

My confession stayed sealed, the *ding* stopping me cold.

Someone else was here. I bounded to the door, just in case some other damaging evidence was arriving, like a man about to perform a singing telegram detailing every minute of last night's events, before I had a chance to tell Svetlana myself. I hastily peeked through the eyehole and realized I had nothing to worry about: A brunette girl stood outside, surrounded by a cluster of bags. She was alone.

I opened the door.

I was met with a tall Slavic girl, whose shoulders slumped a bit. Definitely a runway and editorial model. She looked defeated and hollow-eyed. Her upper lip quivered like a kid who was trying to prove she was tough after skinning a knee.

"Hi . . . I'm Heather," I said, trying to introduce myself. She didn't reciprocate, only started to whimper a bit, then burst into full tears.

"Waaaaaaaaaaaaaaaaahhhhhhhhhhhh!"

And this was before she had even seen the size of the bedroom.

THE GIRL CRIED. AND CRIED. It turned out this poor stranger had been saving up those tears for some time. She had remained stoic while she packed up her things in the posh apartment she had been staying in with her now ex-boyfriend. She hadn't even whimpered a bit all along the drive to the model dorm in his luxury SUV, where he just dropped her off at the curb outside the building with her luggage.

"I'll call you," he'd said as he sped away, merging into the uptown traffic. She'd even managed to hold the tears in through the agonizing elevator ride she shared with a yuppie type who lived some floors above us. As soon as I opened the door and introduced myself, she decided it was time and opened up the dam, showering her face with big fat tears. She shook and shook and shook. I led her to the couch, and she kept it up for a good fifteen minutes. I tried to calm her down, stroking her hair, handing her Kleenex.

My talk with Svetlana would have to wait. (I will admit, I was sort of glad. And this strange arrival shifted Svetlana's attention away from Robert's flowers.)

Svetlana dipped into Kylie's Stoli and poured a small glass, hoping to calm her down. At last the mystery girl emerged from her fit and, slightly sitting up, took a sip.

"Th-th-thank you," she said, the first understandable words that had left her mouth since she got here. Her accent was Slavic but different from Svetlana's. She wiped her tear-wetted hair away from her face, took another sip of the vodka, and then downed the whole glass. "I—I—I'm sorry, I don't know what came over me, I just—*waaaaaah-hhhhh!!!!!*" She lay back down again and had another good cry.

Svetlana rolled her eyes and moved away, having done her duty as a Good Samaritan for the year. For the first time since the girl showed up, it looked like Svetlana started measuring herself against this strange bird who had flown into our apartment—she looked like direct competition to my Russian roommate. She was tall and thin as a willow, and behind her puffed-up eyes and cheeks lay a beautiful, cast face that looked as though it belonged in a museum somewhere.

The girl finally stopped crying, for good this time. By that time Kylie had come back from the drugstore with fresh provisions of Metamucil, and the quiet Icelandic girl had finished her workout in the building's gym. There was something magnetic about her misery that we were all drawn to. Kylie fixed her another drink, and the girl, wiping away her tears, spoke to us. We all sat around her. This was her story.

HER NAME WAS LUCIA. She came from a tiny town in Slovakia, a town so small that it didn't appear on most maps, and even on those it did, you had to pull out a magnifying glass to make out its name.

She didn't mind, though. Living on a farm, she weathered the post–Berlin Wall years of want without too much struggle, at least relative to others—her father was a good farmer. The cows always seemed to have milk, the vegetable garden never seemed to fail, and the hens always gave enough eggs.

She'd spend her days running in the fields, making up stories about the farm's cows, about how X was angry with Y for looking at *her* husband, the big bull who snorted and kicked from the other side of the fence. She was happy.

Like so many other girls who ended up being models, her genetic blessings started out looking like faults—seemingly overnight she shot up to a full six feet, while everyone else stayed nice and short. She may as well have been a Martian walking down the dilapidated halls of her post-Communist school. As a couple years passed, though, people began to notice her astonishing beauty and recognize her as a homegrown Slovakian wildflower. The beat-up cars that belched blue exhaust would slow when they passed the farm as she hoed the vegetables in the garden behind her house, the grizzled men leering. Her father bought a shotgun—and *told* everyone how he bought a shotgun—to keep overeager boys at bay.

Lucia was the queen of the café in town when she visited, the people staying late, smoking filterless cigarettes and draining glass after glass of liquor as they told her stories of the old days, made jokes, and basically tried to win her over. She became something of a celebrity in her town without ever having done anything.

This part gets a little murky—she was so happy to talk about her hometown, her farm, all the old people, that every time she got to the part about how she became a model, she trailed off, as if it somehow was painful to her, and she just wanted to get through it. Somehow she ended up in Bratislava, the capital of Slovakia—or maybe it was Prague in the Czech Republic, I always forget. Some enterprising citizen of her town took her to see a friend of a cousin who was a photographer, wanting to share the country beauty with the big-city folks. She was sad to leave her home—this is what I basically understood through the sobs, which came in waves every time she got back around to her town—but was also excited to be seeing new things. She was around sixteen at this time.

Soon afterward, she was spirited away to Paris for the shows, walking the catwalk as gracefully as anyone ever could have, thrust suddenly into the spotlight to model clothes that were worth more than her family's annual income. But she stayed humble, or at least so she said, never forgetting about those damn cows and the café.

Lucia had been successful as a runway model—much, much more successful than any of us in the dorm. She'd modeled for such big names as John Galliano and Lanvin, that there had once upon a time been some rumblings about her being the Next Big Thing. Her mother agency gladly pimped her out to other agencies around Europe, and she strutted her way through job after job with a perfect body, complemented by a perfect face.

During a shoot in Paris, she met a fairly famous, British-born, black photographer who was based in New York. (And, I might mention, really hot. I saw him once at a party—without Lucia, thank god, she would have had a seizure of weeping—and I was stunned by how handsome he was, just oozing confidence and masculine sex appeal, definitely not one of those closeted fashion types. He was with his new model girlfriend, by the way.)

Lucia and the photographer hit it off right away. The night after she met him she convinced him to come stay with her at the lavish hotel suite the label had put her up at—she was just desperate for some company. It was like a weird little honeymoon, without the marriage, of course. The eighteen-year-old Slovak model and the twenty-something photographer turned the suite into a debauched sex palace, sticking their heads out, in between jobs and fucking, to get refills of cocaine and condoms. After so many lonely nights traveling around modeling, missing her family and farm, I'm sure Lucia was glad to have any form of companionship, and I'm sure the photographer was happy to get, well—you can figure that one out on your own.

The photographer had extended his little holiday for long enough, his business in Paris having been over for a while. It looked like both he and Lucia had to part ways. He left for New York but made her promise to be there within a month. With him. From what I've heard about him, he wasn't exactly a sentimentalist, but maybe his half-heart got the best of him, because it sounds like he truly wanted her to come to the States. Lucia used whatever clout she had at the time and angled to go to New York. With a bunch of leads, and a visa one of the photographer's lawyer friends helped secure for her, Lucia shipped off for the United States and her destiny.

After meeting with a series of people, Lucia decided to sign with the Agency, ready to make her mark in New York. And she did, at first. The success that she had found in Europe followed her to New York, and she booked a number of shows, grabbed an editorial here and there—but none of those big commercial jobs that could feather her financial nest for years to come. Prestige didn't always translate to cash, as all of us models would learn. She moved into the photographer's decent one-bedroom apartment in Brooklyn, accompanying him to all sorts of events. Everything was good. She still missed Slovakia, sending money back to her family, but life was all right.

And then the jobs started becoming less and less frequent. She was coming up on twenty-one, a time when most girls celebrate their journey into womanhood. For a model it was like a death sentence—at every casting you could see the older ones, their expi-

ration dates stamped in the corners of their eyes, the slightest wrinkle in their foreheads, the shifting of their bodies toward maybe
having a child. And the industry, being what it is—a business—
would toss out the expired fruit, as carelessly as you clean out a re-
frigerator with leftovers that are still *probably* good to eat. You just
don't want to risk it. Why would you? You can go down to the store
and get some fresh food.

With jobs drying up, Lucia spent more and more time in the
apartment, contemplating, well, what exactly, I couldn't say. The
photographer would urge her to go to more and more castings, hoping she still had it. But eventually he started becoming more distant.
And then he would disappear some nights, no excuse, really, except
that he had to discuss "projects" with an editor or some designer.

Scrolling through his phone one day while he was in the
shower, Lucia found out what this "project" was called: Geneva.
Through some elementary detective work, she found out Geneva
didn't have to do with that sober mountainous land of Switzerland
at all, nor any conventions, but was the name of an eighteen-year-
old model at one of the competing agencies. But Lucia, not prone to
a fiery temperament, kept her lips shut. She just hoped this Geneva
would pass. But she didn't. And then the photographer suggested
that maybe—just maybe—he and Lucia were spending too much
time together, that he was getting distracted from his work. That
maybe she should find her own place. "Finding her own place"
turned into "taking a break," and then "taking a break" turned into
"let's see other people." Lucia was stricken. She didn't *want* to see
other people; the photographer had wooed her there. She hadn't
even really had time to create her own support network, and with
her jobs disappearing as fast as age was appearing on her still-young
face, she didn't have too much money left over.

To give the photographer *some* credit, he wasn't dumb or the absolute cruelest person in the world: He knew the Agency had an apartment where they put girls who needed a place to stay. This also let him pull the trigger a bit earlier than Lucia had planned—maybe Geneva was whining outside, her bags in hand, waiting to rotate into the photographer's apartment.

And that's how Lucia ended up ringing our doorbell to stop my near-confession, tears brimming in her eyes, far, far away from her farm in Slovakia with her beloved home and hearth.

By the end of this tale of misfortune, we all were a bit misty-eyed—even Svetlana—and Kylie reached for one of the last remaining tissues to wipe the salty tears from her eyes.

"Fucking men," she said, and we all nodded. Those two words seemed to capture the sentiment of all of us.

The Icelandic girl felt compelled to run over to the computer and write an e-mail to her family, telling them how much she missed them. And we all shared a couple drinks in silence. Lucia's attack of weeping had pretty much subsided. I tried to welcome her as well as I could.

"It's not exactly the Gansevoort Hotel here, but I guess it's okay. I mean, we're all here for one another," I said, not mentioning the specter of eviction that hung over us all.

Lucia's eyes drank in the dismal decor but after having gone through the final month or two of his coldness, she seemed happy to be around people who could understand her situation. Well, as happy as she could be.

I spent the evening with her while the others went about their business. Svetlana braved the snow to go meet a promoter and dance at some club that was probably half-empty due to the storm. The Icelandic girl left to hang out with an Estonian friend of hers who was with Ford. Even Kylie disappeared—maybe her affair with the man had fired up again.

Talking with Lucia, just being around her, brought home the bitter reality of our situation for maybe the first time—here she was, far more successful than any of us had *ever* been. She'd had it all on the runways in Milan, Paris, New York (not that those paid a lot, but they were the dream jobs), and now she was weeping over a broken heart on a lumpy couch in the model dorm, already starting to be put out to pasture at age twenty-one. The whole thing just seemed *cruel*. Even if you *did* begin to make it, that was no guarantee. Faster than you could say "next top model," you could be yesterday's news, used goods. But what else was there? We had to keep chasing the dream, or there was no chance of ever getting it. No one ever made it as a model by being a loan adjuster in Dayton, Ohio. You had to go for it, all out. That's what I told myself.

My thoughts drifted inevitably toward Robert and the gigantic possibility my relationship with him presented. Lucia's photographer had obviously been a modelizer who'd traded up to a new model after a couple years of having her around. But Robert wasn't like that, I could tell. You can just . . . sense these things by the way a person behaves. With Svetlana safely out of the dorm, I brought the flowers in from the kitchen and really looked at them for the first time. I thought maybe they would cheer Lucia up, but mainly I just wanted to enjoy them without the Russian's eagle gaze.

It was beautiful, an elegant arrangement. Their fragrance was a welcome addition to the living room, which still hadn't shaken its odor. It was like a burst of joy had come in from the wintry outside world. I was afraid Lucia wouldn't find them so happy, that they'd remind her of her lost love, but I just wanted to see them, to touch them, to think about what they may or may not represent with Robert.

Lucia looked at them and pointed with a questioning look on her face.

"Sorry," I said, a bit embarrassed by my lack of self-control with this poor girl who'd just had her heart stomped on. "They're from a . . . man."

"That's good," she said. I thought maybe she was going to lose it, but she managed to stifle a sob and keep sitting upright on the couch.

The fact that the Slovak had just poured her heart out to us made me feel like I could trust her. If she had interrupted my near-confession to Svetlana about Robert, maybe she could take it in the Russian's place.

"Lucia," I said tentatively. I hadn't even told my *mom* about this. "Yes?"

"Listen, you know how I said these were from a . . . man," I said. "Well, I'm sort of in a *situation*."

"Situation?" she asked. She drew herself up a bit on the couch to listen.

"I mean, what would you do . . . if, well, one of your friends was in love with somebody, but you know it's silly and they shouldn't be, but they still don't care, but you think you may be starting to fall for the same guy. And he actually *likes* you?"

"A friend?" she asked. "How close?"

Should I tell her it was Svetlana? I chickened out.

"Oh, not, umm, too close a friend I guess . . ." I said.

"Well, I had situation with girl from Agency who wanted to get with—with—with—" As she reached the name of her ex-boyfriend, she couldn't take it, and it was willy-nilly with the tears all over again.

Great move, Heather, I told myself, mechanically handing her another tissue. Real solid confidante to choose. We ran out of tissues, and I had to grab a roll of toilet paper from the bathroom—the Icelandic girl, apparently trying to win us over, had gone on a shopping spree and stocked us with quilted T.P.

I avoided bringing up any more painful topics and moved the flowers back to the kitchen, on top of the fridge, where they'd be a little less conspicuous.

The snow outside wasn't stopping anytime soon, and I turned on the TV, anything to distract Lucia from her woe and me from my problem. An old black-and-white movie was on one of the classic movie channels. Lucia recognized it from her childhood, when she'd seen it dubbed. It was a romantic comedy. I went to the deli downstairs and even bought a pint of ice cream for us, knowing I'd be crippled with guilt the next day. I didn't care. The movie calmed Lucia, and I just relaxed, letting the witty banter and old-time accents of the actors take me to another place and time, where Hollywood ensured that the deserving girls got their man—and a fortune. We weren't two models worried about slugging it out with the competition in New York, obsessing over weight. We were just a couple of girls, one who'd had a good cry, watching a movie, indulging in a little sin of ice cream.

Svetlana came home a little earlier than usual that night, the cold and snow discouraging even *her* from partying until 4:30 A.M.

It somehow totally slipped my mind to bring up Robert again.

12

CHRISTMAS CAME, but there were no surprise gifts of modeling jobs for any of us in the apartment—no magazine editors were going to play Santa Claus and give us what we *really* wanted this year. The Icelandic girl rotated out, going back to her Icelandic land, leaving Kylie, Svetlana, Lucia, and me behind to carry on the struggle in New York.

Castings had become a bit more quiet, everyone in the industry getting wasted at holiday parties each night and looking forward to seeing their loved ones (or *not* seeing their loved ones and going to sun themselves in the blistering Rio sun). And I only had to go into the gallery a few times before I left for Christmas. I was sort of glad. Robert's warning about Willem had thoroughly confused me. Although I loved being in the art world—even if it was just sitting at the gallery, soaking in the pieces—I had become wary of the art dealer.

My last day at the gallery before the holidays, Willem gave me a gift, wrapped in novelty Jackson Pollock paper.

"I hope you like it," he said. "I thought you would but, then again, you never know."

I carefully unwrapped it: It was a thick catalog of American art since 1950.

He looked at me with eager eyes. The book was perfect, something for me to pore over during the boring nights at the model dorm when everyone else was watching reruns of *Will and Grace.* But I was paranoid about seeming *too* grateful, wondering if he'd take it the wrong way. I also checked to make sure there wasn't any secret mistletoe dangling anywhere.

"Thanks, Willem, it's really, really great," I said, somewhat flatly.

"Is everything okay?" he asked, sensing a bit of weirdness in the air.

"Yeah, everything's great, I'm just a little tired, you know," I said. He was willing to buy that, or at least pretend he bought it.

"The reproductions in there are the most outstanding I have come across. It is a totally new book, fresh from the ground up, not merely an updated edition of an older volume," he said proudly. "An advance copy, not even out yet—an editor colleague of mine got it for me."

I opened the book, and inside was a message: *To Heather: May your life always be a work of art as beautiful as you are. Best wishes for the holidays—Willem.*

My newfound prejudice against the Belgian began to crack a bit. . . .

"Oh . . . it's great, Willem," I said sincerely. "Thank you so much."

"See, I knew Daniel was wrong. *He* said you wouldn't like it!"

•   •   •

ROBERT AND I SAW EACH OTHER once before I went home for Christmas, and this date—while maybe not matching the first night at Bungalow, when I'd been fairly swept away—went a lot better than the second. (And, I should note, remained Svetlana-less.) I'd lost the courage that led me to the verge of confessing to Svetlana Monsieur du Croix's interest in me and had been content to keep things on *"le down-low,"* as the French, in their weird way of picking up American phrases, might say.

The Frenchman had been busy running around in preparation for the new club, getting permits for the New York Shiva Bar, holding meetings all the time about everything from the tile in the bathroom to the angle the DJ booth should sit at. But he asked me to meet him for drinks at the Soho Grand to toast the holidays.

The day of my night out with Robert, I decided to drag myself from the apartment into the cold, to finally make it up to the MoMA, since there were no castings—it had only taken me nearly four months to get up to the museum, when I'd at first thought I'd be there on a weekly basis. I comforted myself with the fact that I'd been working at the gallery a lot, so I'd been able to cultivate my interest in art—but the Clijsters Gallery was no MoMA, which was stocked with the world's best collection of modern art, even if, as Willem argued, its contemporary holdings were laughably weak.

On the way to the museum I passed by Rockefeller Center, which bustled with hordes of shoppers looking for that perfect gift. Others visited the city just to see the towering Christmas tree and watch the skaters at the rink stumble around, rosy-cheeked. I also passed by Saks, with its elaborate holiday window displays. I walked quickly by the department store, painfully aware of all the cute dresses, stunning shoes, and sleek handbags I *wouldn't* be buying. I imagined Jeanette browsing there with her mother, picking out expensive clothes with money from the campaign she'd gotten. I wasn't in midtown to shop, anyway, I tried to console myself. I was there to see art.

The new sleek MoMA space by the Japanese architect Yoshio Taniguchi was almost overwhelming, and I felt I was entering a temple as I ascended the escalators into the museum. The experience was blissful, and as I passed along the suspended walkways, I felt lighter and, well, more relaxed than I had since I'd first stepped foot in Manhattan. My measurements at the Agency—let's just say progress had come to a grinding halt—had started freaking me out again, and I was constantly under the gun of Luke's little book and his tape. But I felt none of that stress, moving in and out of the galleries, soaking in the beautiful pieces that people had dedicated their lives to creating.

I ended my visit by wandering into the photography wing. A few photos from the tragic photographer Diane Arbus were hanging there. Far from spending her life photographing the beautiful, the thin, the glamorous, the highest of high society that all of us models were trying to become, she had focused on the freaks, those left out by society, the people riddled by problems. There was a picture of an old woman wearing a rose hat and old-school, rimmed glasses. Her face had been ravaged by time. Arbus had been able to capture a deeply moving look in her eyes that seemed to be a time-worn, hard-bitten warning against vanity. Her skin sagged with years.

A tear rolled down my cheek, then another one. I couldn't tell you why. It was just moving—I wasn't necessarily sad. The particular unflinching beauty of the old woman's eyes had maybe lasted a moment and was now captured forever by Arbus's lens, on display in a museum. My thoughts ran, unwanted, once again back to the photographer I'd dealt with on the shoot—*"We just need you to look beautiful."*

At drinks with Robert, the Arbus photo stuck with me, bouncing around my head as we were surrounded by all the beautiful people. I had begun the night a bit more sedate than usual, the museum having had an almost overpowering effect, but after consuming a few drinks, I was bubbly enough. Robert, having gotten a lot of work done before going back to Paris for Christmas, was relaxed and charming again. Tourists and New Yorkers alike were getting into the spirit of holiday cheer at the hotel bar, which had been a stalwart of the "scene" for years now.

Robert apologized for being grumpy the last time we'd seen each other, and then commenced to flatter me by saying how beautiful I was, how it was a mystery I already wasn't gracing the cover of every major fashion magazine. His flattery was becoming a bit much, but I figured that was just in his French genes. I was willing to overlook it, especially since after my fourth cocktail I was a lot more interested in what he had in his jeans rather than his genes. I began looking at him all moony-eyed, just enjoying the moment. I made sure to avoid the following topics, just to preempt any problems like last time: Willem, Chelsea galleries, womanizing, woman-nabbing, dirty deeds, Stella Artois, and anything else even remotely Belgian.

The night was winding down, and Robert had to catch a flight the next day. We were gathering our things, when he stopped short, giving me a quick grin that showed he was up to something.

"Oh, I almost forgot!" he said. He hailed a cocktail waitress and whispered something in her ear. She looked at me, grinned, and went behind the bar. She emerged a few seconds later with a box wrapped in shiny silver paper, topped with a delicate bow. She gave it to Robert.

"Joyeux Noel," he said, handing me the gift with a smile.

"But I didn't . . ." I protested, not having gotten him anything.

"*Shh,* it's my pleasure," he said, touching my hand.

I unwrapped the box to reveal a pair of stunning Dior heels.

"Robert, you shouldn't have. I mean, these must have cost you . . ." I looked and realized they would fit me perfectly. "They're my size! How did you know?"

"A man knows these things," he said in that smoky French accent.

Outside, I wondered if it was going to be a kiss on the forehead or cheek this time, not wanting to get my hopes up after the disappointment of the last two dates. While I was feeling sorry for myself in advance, however, he pulled me in close and pressed his lips to mine. I swore I felt an electric charge pass between us. I pulled in a quick breath and let him hold me close, as we even—yes, I'm sure you're wondering—Frenched a little bit. It was, well, wonderful.

He pulled back. "I wish I didn't have to leave so early in the morning, otherwise I'd invite you back to my place for a nightcap," he said apologetically. Taking in his masculine frame and chiseled cheekbones, I was sorry, too, but I didn't want to start playing the desperate card.

"Next time," I said. "But I guess we won't be seeing each other until after the holidays," I said.

"No, I'm afraid not. I'll be in Paris through New Year's Eve," he said. "But you'll have a great time seeing your family, I trust?"

I nodded, even though I was dreading going back to see everyone with only one shoot under my belt in such a long time, after I'd landed a number of small jobs in Miami.

"Well, we'll definitely see each other after that, then," Robert said, opening the door to the sedan. "Let's be in touch." He kissed me one last time before I got in the cab. Since I was standing on the street and Robert on the curb, I leaned up on my tippy-toes, just like in the movies, to allow his lips to reach mine.

I stepped into the cab, dizzied, and he closed the door.

Inside the taxi, I examined the fabulous Dior heels he had gotten me. Just as I'd said the flowers were from my "parents," this pair of shoes would have to magically appear after my visit home for Christmas. Svetlana would be impressed by the good taste of my mother and father.

So, if Rudolph and company didn't drop any well-paid modeling jobs in my lap, (nor did I get a little action, in the holiday spirit), I did receive a pair of great shoes. Along with the advance copy of the art book Willem had gotten for me. *Willem.* I tried not to think about the huge conflict I was courting by working for the apparent enemy of the man I was seeing and who had such great taste in footwear.

Just before I went home to visit my family in Virginia, the Agency had its annual holiday fête at Hiro this year. A small affair, it was limited to bookers at the Agency, casting people, photographers, a handful of their friends and family, and, of course, us girls (we weren't allowed to bring anybody, however—keeping the bar tab down, I suppose. I had a weird feeling that maybe they'd be dividing the bill of the party and charging each of our accounts just a little bit to defray the costs, but I couldn't imagine Rachel would be *that* mercenary. But you never know). I hadn't seen everyone assembled at once, and all the girls in one place reminded me of a cattle call. Even though this was supposed to be a time to relax and celebrate, all the models eyed one another warily, taking mental note of what each was wearing, or if somebody looked like she was slipping.

Jeanette was there, all smiles and bubbling over. She, naturally, looked incredible. Starting to run on about her apartment, she told us how she'd gotten another job for a cosmetics campaign, and how she'd found this *really neat* investment banker who was from Salt

Lake, also a Mormon, and yaddayaddayadda. I just wanted her to shut up, to tell you the truth. I ended the conversation with some weak promise to stop by her place for tea.

A busboy came out to collect the first round of empty glasses, and he nearly fell over when he entered the back room—he was maybe five-five and was met with a forest of lithe tall models that he had to move in between, careful not to bump his nose into anyone's breasts.

It probably goes down in the books as the least fun party I've ever been to.

Svetlana and Yelena spent most of their time at a table in the corner, whispering to each other, every so often pointing and giggling. Kylie was off to the side, talking to an Argentine she'd been at a casting with the week before—neither had gotten the job. She looked like she was just drinking water, but every so often she'd disappear somewhere and come back a little wobblier each time. She probably had a baby flask she was taking nips from. That way she didn't appear a total drunk in front of the Agency people. Lucia, who'd been at the Agency for a couple years now, talked to some of the girls she knew who were still around. They consoled her, careful not to bring up Geneva from the other agency. Surprisingly, the Slovak shed no tears.

All the other girls knew I lived in the Agency's apartment. More than a few of the more successful models paused to innocently ask me how everything was, sidling up to me in their fabulous holiday dresses either their rich boyfriends or well-paying jobs had gotten them.

A French model I recognized from a billboard on the corner of Lafayette and Houston, on the border of Soho, even took time out of her busy mingling schedule to talk to me. "You leev in model apart-a-mont, no?" she asked, grinning like a bitch the whole time. Her accent was like a parody of what the French sound like, something like Pepe le Pew. Nothing like Robert's, which was polished and refined.

I gave shit right back to her. "I'm sorry, I couldn't understand? Could you repeat? Your accent's so—*thick*," I said. It was the only "thick" part of the sapling-thin French girl.

"Ze apart-a-mont of ze Agency, you leev there, no?" she said, unruffled.

"Oh, yes. Why do you ask?" I said, not blinking.

"Just wond-er-ing," she said. "Long time, you have been, I hear. I have not been. Nice?" She knew full well it wasn't nice.

"Nice enough," I said, tight-lipped. "If you'll excuse me, I need to use the restroom." I left the French bitch to find another girl to victimize.

Rachel was there, of course, looking fabulous down to every last inch. Her legs, freshly waxed, were still to die for, and she knew it. She was friends with the PR people for Calvin Klein and was wearing one of his most prized dresses, a gorgeous Zac Posen number that lit up the runway last season. Her husband was with her, and I saw the rumors had been true—he was the guitarist of a late-eighties/early-nineties hair band that had disbanded soon after the advent of grunge. In their heyday they'd been at the top of the charts, trotting around the globe with codpieces shoved down their spandex pants to accentuate their dick size, cranking out outrageous guitar solos that were complemented by fancy pyrotechnics. Apparently they met while he was on tour. She had also been pretty famous at the time, not technically a *super*model, but still a nice catch.

I wasn't sure exactly what he did these days, but the long hair was gone—he'd kept his wiry physique, and he still looked good for his age. But of course he did. I imagined Rachel kept him on some sort of regimen, if the way she treated us girls was any indication of how she went about her own life. It was strange: She spoiled her children and, from what I'd heard, was a kind loving mother. With everyone else—even her husband—she didn't give an inch. He sat quietly to the left of her, ogling the herds of beautiful girls.

The venue the Agency had chosen to have the party turned out to be unfortunate. Well, at least for *one* person. A couple weeks prior, Rachel had decided to drop a girl from the Agency after a long period in which she hadn't gotten any jobs. The girl, probably around twenty, had been devastated—just like most of us, she'd moved to New York to model, and being dropped was close to a death sentence. Kylie had been at the office when it happened, and apparently the girl had been begging them to keep her. But Rachel didn't budge.

"Listen, I hope you're done whining—I have to see my trainer in thirty minutes. Something maybe *you* should have thought about doing," Rachel had apparently said.

The pretty would-be model didn't have any trouble finding a job—tall beautiful girls rarely do. Only the job wasn't being pho- tographed for the pages of *Vogue*. She'd gotten a job as a cocktail waitress, not quite as glamorous, but I'm sure far more lucrative than any modeling job I'd gotten so far. And as the twisting of fate would have it, it happened to be the very same place the Agency was to have its holiday party. But instead of taking a stand, saying, "Hell, no! Put me on a different section; I'm not going to serve that bitch!" thus saving some sort of dignity, the girl had the genius idea that she'd be able to win back Rachel and the bookers by the speed and deftness in which she served hors d'oeuvres and drinks.

Rachel recognized her immediately and rolled her eyes con- temptuously when the girl first arrived.

"Can I get you anything, Rachel?" The girl attempted to suck up.

"*Anything* at all, just let me know, I can get it in two seconds, no problem."

"I think we're just fine, thank you," Rachel told her, giving her a "shut the fuck up" smile. The girl, not the brightest, didn't get the hint and kept bringing "special dishes" from the kitchen, along with more and more cocktails, until Rachel's table groaned under the weight of all the dishes and drinks.

Maybe most depressing was the fact that the poor girl moved around the room, serving the other models who had been her peers just weeks before. She tried to talk to them, but they blatantly ignored her, except to ask for a freshening up of their drinks—it was like she had suddenly come down with leprosy now that she'd fallen out of the Agency. She was done. Over. Finished.

The manager came over to Rachel to make sure everything was going fine. I saw Rachel whisper something in the man's ear, then point over to where the ex-model was busy scurrying around. He nodded in comprehension, walked over, and pulled the girl off the floor. She wasn't going to be serving *us* anymore.

A couple minutes later I went to use the bathroom and make sure my makeup was still in order. While touching up my mascara, I heard a whimper come from one of the stalls. I furtively looked under the stall door and saw the glittery black BCBG heels the waitress had been wearing. She cried some more. I decided to leave well enough alone and rejoin the party.

Rachel didn't give any speeches that night, telling us how grateful she was to have us with the Agency. Nothing like that. Not even a little anecdote to keep us all fearful: "Do you think I made it by trying to kiss ass while being a *waitress?*" The atmosphere—at least for me—had been sufficiently chilled by her rough treatment of the girl who had been excommunicated from the Agency. It seemed to say, once again: "You're a model, or you're *nothing.*" As if the night hadn't already been annoying enough as it was, I was now really on edge. I wondered how long Rachel would let me stay in the dorm without getting any jobs before she decided to start taking a close look at how I was doing. I stuck to one side salad and sparkling water all night, keeping an eye over my shoulder.

As the party wound down, Luke approached me, smiley as ever. He took a quick look at my half-eaten salad and glass of Pellegrino and nodded in approval.

"Hey, Heather, happy holidays!" *Kiss-kiss.* "Listen, when you get back, we should all have a talk, just to see where we're at, okay?"

A *talk?*

"Oh, okay," I said. He could see I was tentative.

"Don't *worry!* Just a checkup. You know, we can go over some goals, things like that. Totally good!" He was so damn cheerful, when I knew this "talk" couldn't be good. A stroke of panic ran through me, and I thought of the waitress, weeping alone in the bathroom. I wondered if the stall next to her was still open.

"Sure, Luke, I, umm, would love to come in," I said.

"Great! Happy holidays!" he said, disappearing into the crowd.

Happy holidays, indeed.

Maybe Kylie had had the right idea, after all. . . . I went looking for her, hoping she had a bit of artificial cheer left in her flask.

13

CHRISTMAS ARRIVED, cloaking the Eastern seaboard in a gray blanket. I took the train down to Virginia, my portfolio packed in my luggage, so I'd have at least *something* to show for the months I'd spent in New York. The monochromatic landscape blurred by the windows, frost dangling in the air. No amount of Christmas lights could cheer me up, shake the fact that I felt like things weren't happening quickly enough. And with Luke's "talk" awaiting me . . . That was going to be really delightful. I knew these things required patience, but I wondered how *long*.

The family gathered at my grandmother's home, and I was shocked by how normal everything was. Here I'd been in Manhattan, whisked around in town cars, dealing with photographers, castings, the New York art world, surrounded by girls who made the contestants on *America's Next Top Model* look like frumpy rejects. And everything was just the same back home. It was comforting but also scary at the same time—would this be what happened if I stumbled in my career in New York, would I just end up back here, where things rarely changed, forced to give up everything, even if "everything" wasn't even that much yet?

I truly felt like I hadn't accomplished anything up north, and I was embarrassed by how eager everyone was to learn about all that I was up to. I showed friends and family my portfolio, and there was plenty of oohing and aahing at the photos, like I was already on the level of Kate Moss. The photos for the Vena Cava look book had turned out pretty good, I must admit. But still, that was my *only* job so far. No matter: Everyone was convinced how fabulous I was and how everything was going *so* well.

I didn't go out of my way to try to change their opinion, launch into how nobody at the apartment had cleaned the shower in three months and there was mold growing in the corners, how we didn't even really have a closet, since they blocked the door with one of the bunks to fit in an extra two beds, how many hours we fabulous models spent just sitting around in faded sweats long overdue for the laundry, watching bad TV shows. Nor did I let them know that my basic source of income was from working as a receptionist at the gallery and not as a superglamorous high-paid model.

My parents were more astute than my extended family, however. They could tell things maybe weren't going as well as everyone else thought they were.

On the train ride back to New York, after a subdued New Year's celebration where some old friends from high school got really drunk on Jägermeister and stomach-churning champagne, I opened up my suitcase to find a magazine I'd bought. A thick booklet tumbled onto the floor: My parents had secretly put a catalog for the local community college in my luggage. A Post-it note with *"Think about it"* scrawled in my mother's handwriting was stuck to the cover. When I got into New York, I threw it out in one of the big garbage bins at Penn Station.

I was going to take the GED, which I'd scheduled online at the gallery after I first started work with Willem. But things were going to be on *my* terms. Besides, what kind of job could I get with a GED? And how would that compare to the money that would come with a big campaign?

Back at the apartment, a mini-disaster reigned. Svetlana was nowhere to be seen, but the stench of stale cigarette smoke hung in the air. Kylie had bought a miniature Christmas tree off the street a couple weeks before. It had turned definitively brown with neglect, the needles scattered on the floor beneath it. In the middle of the tiny bedroom was a huge pile of clothes she had haphazardly tossed there.

I opened the window in the living room to let in some fresh air and tossed out the soggy take-out containers that sat on the kitchen table, stacked on a copy of the December issue of *Vogue*. It was good to be home.

EVERYTHING SLOWLY TICKED BACK TO NORMAL after New Year's, the city shaking off its collective hangover after the orgiastic holidays, during which everyone overindulged in *everything*. I'd carefully watched what I ate, and if I was to believe the scale (the bathroom one, not the one in the bedroom—that was the *fat* one, or so we said, since it added a couple pounds), I'd kept a holding pattern on my weight, no small feat when surrounded by a constant stream of fudge, eggnog, and other holiday treats that were a model's worst enemy.

Robert was still in Paris, spending time with his mother, he said.

It shouldn't be too surprising that I could hardly wait for him to return after the last promises of a "nightcap" at his apartment. I also was able to wear the heels he'd given me without fear of Svetlana giving me twenty questions about where they'd come from—I'd gotten them from my parents, of course.

Things were more or less normal at the gallery when I returned; Willem never suspected that I was still keeping a close eye on what he did. He was preparing for a big Basquiat show and didn't have as much time to worry about me, anyway. We'd still have talks about art, though, him asking me what I'd looked at in the book he gave me, and then going off with a thousand little personal stories he knew about whatever artist it was. Even Daniel was starting to warm to me properly now, and when Willem was away we'd trade banter to keep ourselves occupied if there wasn't too much traffic in the gallery.

Maybe Luke had been drunk at the party, or he just forgot, but I wasn't called in for any special "talk" at the Agency. Not yet, at least. Perhaps they'd changed their minds—I didn't need some chastising and a session to set "goals." The thought of the community college catalog ran through my head more than once, and my New Year's resolution became that I was *going* to start making it. No way was I going to head back to Virginia in defeat. I wasn't going to be the next to be evicted. I vowed to take better care of myself, no more going out five nights a week! This was a new year, a new beginning! (Of course, you know how long New Year's resolutions last.)

Svetlana, even though she hadn't found out about me and Robert yet, knew that the club manager was in France, so I had at least a little while without fearing a straight-up Slavic explosion. Kylie, who'd actually gone home to Australia for the holidays, came back, full of resolve that she wasn't going to drink so much. She marched around the dorm unloading her bags, saying loudly this-

and-that about how she was going to be healthier—maybe her mom had given her a talking-to back in Perth. But by that night she was already half-lidded in her de facto throne, on the wrong end of four Metamucil martinis. Old habits die hard.

Lucia, meanwhile, had slipped into her own routine at the model dorm. She had allowed her melancholic nature to take over, and she moped around, cooking boiled potatoes with a dollop of butter—it was the only thing I ever saw her eat. Maybe it was the only thing she allowed herself. Butter, and all those carbs.

Even though she'd managed to snap up a new pseudo-boyfriend one night out at the Pink Elephant with Svetlana, she still pined over her lost photographer lover. Her heart wasn't in it. The new boyfriend was in his mid-thirties—and married, of course. His wife was about the same age, and an ex-model herself. I hoped Lucia wasn't planning on taking him away from his wife. I couldn't help seeing the irony in the whole thing: Lucia herself had lost out to a younger model with the photographer. But I didn't say anything and allowed her to go about her business.

The Slovak developed a pattern of nightly dejection. You see, while she was living with the photographer, they'd visited her hometown. Her ex-boyfriend had brought a video camera and shot footage of everything they came across. He'd edited the raw footage together and made a DVD as a twenty-first birthday present for Lucia. She had been ecstatic. Now this love letter to her home, from her former lover, was a bitter pill she took.

Practically every night the homesick Lucia would pop the DVD into our player and force us to watch it. I have to admit, the first time we did, it was interesting—the photographer had obviously shot it well, and there was a beauty in it that you pretty much never see in home movies. They'd visited everything important to Lucia, and the DVD had her running around the farm, in the small town, talking to people, her family. She was almost unrecognizable. She actually seemed, well, *happy*.

"Lucia show you Slovakia," she'd say, sliding the DVD into the player. Being around Svetlana had made her start referring to herself in the third person, too, as if that was the "it" thing for Eastern European models this season. The TV would go black as the DVD started up, and Kylie would groan but put up with it. She didn't have anything better to do.

Even after the twelfth time we had seen it, Lucia insisted on pointing out every detail as the DVD played out.

"Our cows!" she would say, pointing insistently at the beasts on the TV. They mooed nonchalantly at the camera. On-screen, the bubbly Lucia stroked their snouts as they munched on straw. The action moved to the town, and the photographer had an establishing shot of the café—I think he probably had some aspirations of being a movie director or something.

"Lucia's café!" our Slovak would remind us, pointing again.

"Reeealllly?" Kylie would ask sarcastically, sinking deeper into her seat. I'd shush her, letting Lucia have her moment.

Inside the windows of the café, a group of twenty-something Slovak men peered out, puzzled to see the gorgeous Lucia prancing around, laughing, being filmed by a black man dressed in de rigueur downtown hipster clothes from New York.

The climax of the DVD was a large dinner at Lucia's home. The whole family was there, feasting on pork sausages, Slovak goulash, and all other manner of dishes. Their modest home glowed with warmth, and I'd even let myself become a little homesick. Just a little. The DVD ended with Lucia sitting next to her father, a proud old man. He and Lucia each had a small glass of liquor. They toasted the camera and tossed the drink back, Lucia snorting a bit as the strong alcohol burned down her chest. Then she'd laugh and throw her arms around her papa's neck. The photographer had made it so the image froze, then slowly faded out.

Lucia, who would be enjoying the whole show up to that point, would then become somber.

"Here we go . . ." Kylie would mutter under her breath.

Lucia's married boyfriend, as a present to her, had bought her one of those iPod speaker docks, as if to say, "Well, dear, I know I'm married, so I can't really be *with* you. But here are some white speakers. Cheers!" She'd ceremoniously plug the iPod into the socket, then start blasting this Evanescence song, a song I learned quickly to loathe. The warbling voice would come over the speakers, and Lucia would throw herself down on the couch tragically.

"Now you know how Lucia feel!"

Then the tears would come, as usual, and I'd sit there and tell her everything would be all right. The whole thing had the tinge of the theatrical to it, and I couldn't help but imagine that Lucia vaguely *enjoyed* her ceremony of sadness, that it provided some structure for her.

After the song ended, she would pull herself up, dry her tears, disappear into the bedroom, and come out looking stunning, wearing a sexy slit skirt, or maybe sprayed-on jeans and a slouchy designer sweatshirt with an oversize collar worn as a top.

She was ready to go out and party, the tears and cows and disloyal photographer boyfriends apparently forgotten—or at least to be forgotten once the free drinks started coming. Svet and I generally joined her.

A COUPLE WEEKS INTO THE NEW YEAR, I had a promising lead: The publisher of a small but prestigious "art" fashion/photography magazine, *Velveteen,* had seen my comp card and requested me for some test shots that could lead to an editorial in the magazine—he was also a well-established photographer with a resume a mile long. As yet, it wasn't going to pay anything, and even if I *did* make it into the magazine, I'd probably earn very little. But, as Luke told me, the exposure would be priceless. Plus I'd get some good photos to freshen up my portfolio.

The week before, Svetlana had gotten a small editorial job that was going to appear in *Nylon* magazine. Little cash, but great exposure, too. We were moving forward. Baby steps. But forward, still. Maybe we weren't going to be stuck in model dorm purgatory forever. I made a mental note to keep any comments on art to myself—even though this was a high-minded magazine, I didn't want to go through another embarrassing episode where I would be told to shut up or ship out.

The offices of *Velveteen* were off Union Square and, as I found out, also served as the apartment of the editor, David Wilkins. He seemed friendly enough, giving me the *kiss-kiss* I was used to. Wilkins, probably in his late thirties, was short and had hairy forearms. He was putting the final touches on the setup for the shoot. The apartment extended deep into the building, the bedroom off to the side, separated by translucent walls. Winter sunlight streamed into the apartment, and he drew special shades to diffuse the light.

I thought it was odd that he didn't have at least one assistant to help him, but I supposed that since these were just test shots, and "artistic," he didn't need a large support staff. Or I guess *any* support staff. But I'd done other test shots for my portfolio (which the Agency had so kindly paid for in advance, then charged my account for), and there had been the photographer, two assistants, a stylist, makeup. . . . Here it was just him and me.

We were shooting in the main space. He tweaked the lights, creating a large contrast where I was to be posing on a couch, while I twiddled with my makeup. He came over and expertly helped put the final touches on. Off to the side was a rack of clothes, which he and I chose from. I changed into different looks behind a small Japanese screen, but it didn't really matter—he seemed gay, anyway. We moved through a couple outfits, and he was really pleased with how things were going, kept telling me how gorgeous I was.

The last shots were going to be in a black bikini—slipping into it behind the screen, I checked to make sure I wasn't looking flabby. Nope. Perfect.

He posed me on the couch, the lights shining brightly in my eyes. *Snap-snap-snap.* The camera whirred away. He stopped and came to switch my position. He came in close, so close I could feel his breath as he manipulated my arms and legs into a new pose. He was grinning. A chill ran down my back.

"Okay, now can you take your top off for me, Heather?" he asked, a bit nervous, but not nervous in a "I don't really want to ask you to do this" kind of way, but in a "am I going to be able to get away with this?" way. Creepy.

"Top?" I said. "Off?"

"Yes, yes, we *really* need a few of those shots, to show off how . . . hot you are," he said, grinning. The grin was . . . well, it didn't make me feel so comfortable. If Robert had warned me about Willem, what would he have said about *this* guy?

"Well . . ." I said. I'd had topless shots done—pretty much *every-body* did—but that was with a photographer and two assistants there at a studio, not in the apartment of some guy I'd just met. Alone. Suddenly he didn't seem so gay.

"C'mon, it'll be *fun,*" he said. I started feeling a bit nauseous, desperate for a way to get out. I looked at the clock on the wall above him. Time!

"Oh, I, I didn't tell you, I have an, umm, important doctor's appointment that I have to keep, and I, uh, didn't remember. . . . Sorry, that's going to have to be it." I dashed behind the screen and switched into my street clothes as quickly as possible, not caring about the possible fallout with the Agency for just bailing on a shoot. I didn't care—this guy was a *creep;* I could smell it on him now, was surprised I hadn't earlier.

"Doctor's appointment?" he said, knowing the jig was up. He suddenly started to get a bit panicky. I imagined he wasn't going to rat me out to the Agency for not getting naked in front of him, alone in his apartment, and that he'd want to cover his own tracks. Reputation or not, nobody likes a sleazy perv. "Listen, listen, Heather, don't get the wrong idea, I just thought those shots would be good for the tests, but if you have to go, that's fine, that's fine, everything's good, everything's fine."

I came out from behind the screen and looked at him.

"You better believe everything's fine," I said coolly, daring him to send a bad report to the Agency. His hairy arms made him look like a furry weasel. "Thanks for your time, David."

I walked out, mouthing "creep" under my breath, into the now-fading sunlight on the Manhattan streets. The residual effects of my visit made me want to take a shower.

When I got home, everyone was sitting in the living room, bored, glumly watching TV.

"Where you been, Heather?" Kylie asked.

"I just had this sorta weird shoot at this guy's apartment that was like his studio, too," I said, unsure of what to reveal to them, if they'd just laugh at me for running. Had I just been imagining things? But, reviewing events in my mind, I *knew* I hadn't just been making it up. There was something weird. "Test shots for this magazine."

"Which magazine?" Kylie asked. I had told her the night before, but we'd all had a bit too much to drink at Guesthouse, and she had apparently forgotten, or hadn't heard over the din of the crowd.

"Umm, *Velveteen,*" I said. At that word, all three of my room-mates sat up, at attention. "What?" I asked them.

"With the publisher, David Wilkins, that photographer who's also done all those editorials for *Italian Vogue?*" Kylie asked.

"Yesssss," I said, unsure of where this was going. Apparently they knew him.

"Did Heather . . . ?" Svetlana asked, daring me to fill in the blanks.

"I just did the shoot, but there was no assistant there. He wanted me to take off my top, and I got a really bad feeling about the whole thing," I said. "Why, what do you guys know about him?"

"Oh, nothing," Kylie said. She, Svetlana, and Lucia smiled at one another in a devilish way. "From what I hear, he's got quite a sur-prise."

"Surprise?" I asked.

They all burst out laughing—even Lucia!—and I decided to drop the whole thing and take that shower I'd been thinking about. I didn't even want to know if they'd dealt with him personally or just heard about other girls at the Agency who had.

I'd like to say that my men problems ended with Wilkins and that Robert came back and started to sweep me off my feet again, but I'd be lying. Robert told me his mother had taken ill, and he was forced to stay in Paris longer than he'd imagined. I'd gotten a long e-mail from him, though. He said he missed our dinners, that I was a "clever girl." I told him I missed him, too.

January continued its frigid ways, making inmates of us at the apartment—December and January were two of the slowest months of the year for models, and if earlier I'd been going to at least two castings a day, now, after New Year's, I was lucky if I got three a *week.* Boredom settled in, and Lucia's viewing of her DVD became even more compulsive, trying even my patience. And I had more sympathy for her than either Kylie or Svetlana. Kylie tolerated her, but Svetlana viewed her with suspicion, knowing full well that Fashion Week was coming down the pike and that they'd likely be up for the same jobs. They both fit the same profile, but Lucia's experience far outweighed the younger Svetlana's. My Russian friend tried to keep her distance from Lucia but didn't attack, as I'd seen her do to others. Perhaps Lucia was already too beaten down for even Svetlana to start throwing jabs at her.

At least I had the part-time gallery work to get me out of the house every now and then. One weekend, with gentle prodding by my mother and Willem, I took the GED and sailed through it—I was certain I'd passed but didn't know what that really got me. I sure wasn't going to use it to go back to Virginia and community college. It was going to be good to have, I told myself. Although at the time I couldn't really see how—waving a GED around at a casting definitely wasn't going to fast-track me to model stardom. They wouldn't have cared if I'd flunked out of kindergarten, just as long as I was pretty enough.

The other girls had nothing to do. We all started to get a bit of cabin fever in the apartment, living on top of one another. Of course we'd been in tight quarters the whole time, but earlier everyone had been in and out all the time, running to castings, just spending time outside even if we weren't trying to get work. Now we fought about what TV shows to watch (Kylie preferred reality shows; Lucia always wanted to watch old movies), and I'd even started to snipe to Svetlana about all the time she spent on the computer.

"But Svetlana *bored,*" she'd complain when I tried to get her out of her chat rooms.

"I'm bored, too, just get off, okay?"

Kylie even got in on the action, yelling at me about how I never cleaned up, although she was a close second with Svetlana in terms of sheer dirtiness, leaving glasses around until they grew a thick scum of mold on top. I knew we were all probably going a bit stir-crazy, so I just kept my mouth shut, not wanting a knock-down, drag-out war over who'd left a plate of food on the table. But we had nothing else to really keep us occupied.

At least until one cold afternoon when Kylie had gone down for fresh provisions.

Her trip was taking longer than usual—as I found out later, the closest liquor store had run fresh out of the type of Stoli the Aussie was favoring those days for her cocktails. Cursing under her breath, she'd wandered off in the general direction of where she hoped she'd find another store. I imagine she has some type of sixth sense for those sorts of things, because she eventually found another one in the neighborhood and bought two bottles of vodka, just for insurance. On her way back, the streets downtown were empty and dark, most of the bankers having already fled for the warm hearths of their Westchester, Jersey, or Connecticut homes. Taking a short-cut through a side alley, Kylie had come across something shivering in the dark. She'd screamed—she thought it was an oversize rat, since the streetlight was flickering on and off. She readied a bottle to smash it . . . and then saw it was a puppy!

The poor dog was shivering, trying to find somewhere to warm itself, pressing against an exhaust duct that was exhaling steam from a restaurant. It had looked healthy, not like some alley cur. It had no collar on, nor any other identification—apparently it'd been abandoned. Kylie crouched down and picked up the poor dog, which barked in gratitude as she pushed it against her warm coat. She spent a while walking around, seeing if anyone was looking for it, but to no avail. Not knowing what to do, she decided to bring him

back to the model dorm, naturally. Even though there was a strict
"no pets" policy, she imagined it wouldn't be a big deal for a day or
two, since there was also a "no men" policy and a "no smoking" policy, rules that had already been broken on more than one occasion.

"Look what I found!" she said in delight when she returned. As
if on cue, the puppy stuck its nose out of her jacket. It squirmed
from her arms and began prancing around the apartment, like it already owned the place.

"Oh my God, so cute!" Lucia said, snapping out of her normal
woe-is-me mood, reaching down to sweep the small dog off the
floor.

"Ummm, are we supposed to have dogs?" I asked, but no one
seemed to hear me. In about two seconds it had been decided that
we were going to keep it around. Svetlana was already doting over
the cute dog.

"Svetlana buy sweater and boots for doggie!" she said, already
imagining how she could accessorize him to go along with her outfits, apparently. I'm sure she saw herself just like the Donovan
heiress, bringing the pup around as a fabulously cute accessory at
the clubs.

"Hey, I found him; let me play with him!" Kylie said, tugging on
the poor dog's hind leg, while Lucia coddled it and Svetlana mentally started taking its size.

It was a definitive mutt, and even though it was young, it was
not a puppy, just a small dog. It had bristly brown hair and a black
button nose. If the men of Manhattan had seen it just then, being
fawned over by a roomful of models, half of them probably would
have given a year's salary to switch places with it!

The pup wriggled out of Lucia's grasp and took to sniffing
around the place.

"Is cute, yes!?" Svetlana said to me, all grins.

"Yeah, he's cute, but we aren't going to keep him, are we?" I said, trying to be at least somewhat sensible. "I mean, it's sort of against the rules, and who's going to take care of him?" I pictured the undone dishes, the old garbage that rotted under the kitchen sink . . . I mean, we could barely take care of *ourselves*.

"Come on, Heather, since when have we cared about the bloody *rules?*" Kylie said. Lucia and Svetlana nodded eagerly, trying to win me over.

"Lucia will take care!" the Slovak offered.

"Svetlana, too!" the Russian added.

"*I'll* make sure she's all right, don't worry!" Kylie said.

"Okay . . . but what if he has fleas or something?" I said.

"Look at her, healthiest dog I've ever seen, definitely no fleas, I'll *bet* you," Kylie said, desperate to make her case. We had all been so ground down under the monotony of the past weeks that this dog represented some excitement in the apartment—and, unlike other new roommates, he wasn't about to take any of our jobs.

"He does look all right," I said. The pup came trotting up to me and whimpered to be picked up. I did, and he gave me a little lick on the cheek.

"See, she like Heather!" Svetlana exclaimed.

With that lick, any reservations I had about keeping the dog around were washed away.

"All right, all right, but still, we should give it a bath; who knows what it's been rolling around in."

I don't think the other girls could have been more excited at the prospect of bathtime for the cute little dog if I had announced we had all just landed campaigns for Prada.

"Svetlana get bubbles!" Of course it had to have a bubble bath.

In the tub, the little dog shivered as we took turns sudsing it up.

"What should we call her?" Kylie asked.

"Oksana," Svetlana offered. "Like my favorite figure skater."

I had a strong suspicion the dog was a boy, and a quick inspection confirmed it.

"We can't call it Oksana, Svetlana," I said.

"Why no Oksana?" She looked at me with pouty eyes.

"Because it's a male. We can't have a boy dog running around with a girl's name," I said. "He's not a drag queen."

"How Heather know it man?" Svetlana asked.

"How?" Did Svetlana really not know? I pulled the pooch out of the bubbles and showed her his male apparatus.

She didn't get it. "How Heather know?"

I thought that Svetlana had had enough human penises flapping in front of her nose to know one in the animal kingdom.

"Look." I pointed to his equipment. "Lucia, you're from a farm; you know what I'm talking about."

"Definitely boy," she said.

"Oh."

Kylie had been thinking hard about something the whole time, then burst out, in a moment of inspiration: "Let's call him Tom Ford!"

The pup yipped happily at this, splashing around the bubbles, and so it was settled: The newest occupant of the model dorm would be a cute little dog named Tom Ford.

14

FASHION WEEK! The Holy Grail of the fashion industry crept closer and closer, where we'd go from lazing around all day to running to close to ten castings a day, fighting tooth and nail with other girls for a fifteen-minute turn in the spotlight on the runway. It could turn an unknown into a potential supermodel overnight if you got a big show. When I'd first arrived at the dorm, the Agency had sent me to a few of the castings, for very small shows, since my portfolio hadn't really been up to standard yet. But the Agency was ready to send me fully out there now that I had a book of fetching shots from the tests I'd done, along with the look book shoot (the newest were the test shots for *Velveteen* that sleazy Wilkins had provided—he hadn't breathed a word about my leaving, as I predicted).

I breathlessly looked forward to Fashion Week. Not only because of the career opportunity, even though I wasn't a classic run-way model, but also because Robert had said he would hopefully be coming back for the shows.

Having Tom Ford around helped us calm our nerves and focus on something else as the magical week in February approached, the fashion press already starting to salivate over what gems the designers were going to unveil to the public under the tents at Bryant Park. The little dog became a staple of our going out, as we took him everywhere. Svetlana particularly loved having him around, pretending that having Tom Ford as an accessory made her twice as glamorous. She'd brought him along shopping two days after Kylie had found him, and she'd convinced her wealthy "boyfriend" to shell out for a luxury leash and collar, along with a few outfits for the already-spoiled dog. Svetlana must have really had that mystery man (it wasn't the guy we'd met at the dinner club, but some new victim) wrapped around her finger to get him to buy things for her dog! Before going out with Tom Ford, she'd put gel in the tuft of hair on top of his head, styling it just right, depending on what party we were going to. He didn't seem to mind.

At first we'd all been pretty conscious about taking care of Tom Ford, making sure he got his walks, that his water bowl was fresh, etc., etc. Kylie had even crafted a makeshift schedule that she put on the fridge. It detailed who was supposed to do what and when. But every once in a while my roommates started missing their appointed shifts, too busy getting ready to go out to Marquee, or caught up in something on TV. I have to admit even I skipped one or two walks during that time. Tom Ford didn't seem to mind too much, though. He was so small that the apartment was big enough for him to roam around in—every so often he'd disappear, and we'd find him bur-rowing in a pile of bras and panties that had been kicked under the bed. We were proud of him—he was going to be a ladies' man.

As Fashion Week got closer, we were expecting at least one new roommate to be brought in by the Agency to see if she could cut it during show season in New York, and we weren't disappointed. About ten days before the shows were to start, I came home following an afternoon of poking around a couple art galleries in Chelsea to find an unfamiliar girl lounging on our couch, watching TV. She looked *young*. And wholesome, freckles dotting her fresh face. Uh-oh. Another Jeanette, I thought. Her bags still sat in the living room.

"Hey, I'm Christiane," she said, getting up. "I think your little doggie shit somewhere, because it sure does smell. I didn't check it out, though."

Tom Ford guiltily sulked around, and I found the offending pile.

"*Bad* Tom Ford!" I yelled at him. He flattened his ears against his head, full of shame. "No poopie!" I realized I sounded an awful lot like Svetlana when I talked to our dog. And I couldn't really be mad. It wasn't his fault that—let me check the schedule—Svetlana hadn't taken him out in the morning. I picked up the turd with a paper towel and flushed it.

"His name's Tom Ford?" Christiane asked. "That's sooo cute!"

"Did you check out the place? Well, I guess there's not too much to see except the bedroom," I said.

"I poked my head in there—some girl was snoring, so I thought I'd just let her be," she said. "I can't believe we have bunks like in a dorm—it's like college already!"

College already?

"How old are you?" I asked. She was by herself. I'd heard of high school girls coming with their parents but hadn't seen anybody alone yet.

"Just turned sixteen. My mom was afraid of me coming to New York, terrorists or something like that, but I told her I'd be all right on my own," she said. "New York's not too scary, just a lot bigger than Jackson Hole."

"Jackson Hole?"

"Yeah, Wyoming. I'm from there."

"That's, umm, near Utah, right?" I asked. Fears of Jeanette Part II danced in my head.

"Yeah, but that's where all those Mormons are," the sixteen-year-old said. "Wyoming's a lot cooler."

"Oh."

"Whatever," she said. "So can I go in there, or is that girl going to bite my head off?"

"We can go in. It's almost six P.M., anyway," I said, opening the door to the bedroom.

Christiane hoisted her bags up and walked in. I was already starting to form an opinion of her—at sixteen she was brash and brazen, and at least *acted* like she knew what was going on. The way she moved her tall frame reminded me a little of Jeanette. It seemed like she knew how to work it, her tiny hips moving sexily even as she dragged her bags in the tiny room.

Inside, Svetlana lay, a pillow over her head. She moaned in Russian.

"Go 'way!" she said, her head probably still spinning from the eight ball of coke she'd split with Yelena and a group of guys from some third-rate acting agency the night before. Tom Ford, who had followed us in, leaped onto the bed and burrowed himself under the pillow to lick her face.

"Svetlana, it's dark outside already," I said.

I was just met with a groan as she rolled over. I pointed Christiane to a lower bunk.

"I guess you can sleep under Lucia. She's from Slovakia."

"Uh-huh," Christiane said, not even really paying attention. She sat down on the bed, then jumped up and down a bit to test its firmness. It squeaked. She crinkled her petite nose at this and scooted a foot over, bouncing up and down on the mattress a few times again. It didn't squeak so much this time. Looking up at me, she smiled a not-so-innocent sixteen-year-old smile.

"So where do we go to meet hot guys?"

THAT NIGHT OUR NEW ROOMMATE came home later than all of us. We'd taken her to an open-bar event for *Surface* magazine at a secret club that, of course, Svetlana knew about. Before we piled into the cab, the high school girl looked at us seriously.

"I'm eighteen if anyone asks, okay?" she'd said. I found out soon that "anyone" meant "men."

We were all pretty wasted as the evening wore down, and we left Christiane in the care of a mid-twenties male model who had done some work for American Eagle the year before. I think she maybe even recognized him from the mall displays. She thought it was hot. Model-on-model make-out session.

I was fighting off the spins, lying in bed still awake, when Christiane came waltzing in. With the male model.

Light flooded in the room for a second.

"*Quick!* Shut the door," she commanded urgently. It was pitch-black again.

In the dark, I could hear their heavy breathing, then the sounds of them making out. Then: *Zip. Clunk. Rustle.* They were definitely throwing their clothes off at a rapid rate.

"*Mmmm . . .*" Christiane intoned as I heard smooching sounds.

The room spun around for me as I lay on my back, and I tried to focus on not throwing up. Svetlana snored below me, oblivious—along with Tom Ford, who had had a long night out with us girls.

Lucia's married boyfriend had canceled their date for the night, most likely to spend some QT with his wife, and the alcohol at the club had only made her more depressed. She'd been sniffling miserably up on the top bunk for about twenty minutes now.

The bottom bed creaked as Christiane and her catch lay down on it, naked as the day they were born. They settled in, then:

"Ow, *careful!*" Christiane said.

"Sorry," the dude said.

"It's okay, baby. No, a little—*unnnh*—up a bit. *Slow, SLOW!* You're so *big*, you have to go slow!" the sixteen-year-old commanded. "No, no, left. . . . Yeah, *yeah!*"

The man's breath caught sharply as she said this. Houston, we've penetrated the atmosphere.

They began going at it, Christiane apparently forgetting just exactly where the squeaky spot on the mattress was, because the bed was making a hell of a lot of racket. I pulled the pillow over my head in a vodka-cranberry-induced haze, half awake, half passed out. I closed my eyes and tried not to think about all the sex I *hadn't* been having since I got here, but instead imagined Christiane's eighty-three-inch-long, high school legs wrapped around the hot male model. (At least that way they didn't hang over the edge of the bunk. . . .)

"Oh, God, *gimmeitgimmeitgimmeit*," Christiane said, quietly as she could. How big *was* he? The bed creaked a bit more, shaking Lucia.

"Yeah, yeah, yeah, oh, *fuck*, that's good," he said.

"*Sh-sh-shhhh*—*ooooohhh*—you're—*unnn*—going to wake up my room—*unnnn*—mates," she said. I heard the clap of a hand over a mouth, then the man's muffled groans. He'd put his hand over her mouth, too, because her cries were dulled as well. I kind of wished the lights were on so I could see the comical sight, the two in a full-on carnal moment, each covering the other's mouth.

The bed still squeaked and creaked, however, and when their moans quieted, I could hear that Lucia was still up, victim to their lovemaking on the bottom bunk. The Slovak was tossed to and fro like a storm-lashed ship. She was still crying a bit, and as I finally passed out, the strangely alternating sound of Lucia's meek weeping and the sharp *squeak* of the cheap bunk bed as Christiane rode her American Eagle to orgasmic heights echoed into my dreams.

WITHIN ABOUT THREE DAYS, I knew the sixteen-year-old from Wyoming with the cute freckles was indeed a complete nymphomaniac. Every night she'd come back, spouting another tale of sexual abandon with an unsuspecting man who thought her to be of age—although thankfully after that first night she hadn't brought any of them back to the apartment again. And her mom had been concerned about *terrorists!* The high-school-age girl made Svetlana look as if she were ready to take vows and join a nunnery. But I didn't have time to ponder Christiane's bid for a gold medal in the year's sexual Olympics, nor did anyone else, either—Fashion Week was just days away.

Deep in my heart of hearts, I knew that this was going to be a watershed moment for me as a model. If I couldn't get any of the shows, I may as well just stamp a big scarlet L for "LOSER" on my forehead and go back to Virginia, enrolling in community college to wear clunky shoes all my life and have bad skin. I desperately wanted to get cast for a show, even though I knew I was better suited to commercial work and wasn't really a runway model.

I'd talked to Willem about it, and he basically told me I didn't have to come in to work at the gallery for the week before Fashion Week and then the week of shows themselves. My schedule was going to be packed with castings (and parties, of course).

The whole fashion sector was bubbling with energy. Stylists across the city compulsively gnawed their fingernails until they had to make emergency visits to the manicurist, models snacked on a half peanut every other day to maintain fighting weight for castings, the editorial assistants at the fashion magazines chattered incessantly about who was going to be a "breakout" this season, whether a certain designer would remain "edgy." To be fully under the spell of the glamour, lights, and nonstop parties of Fashion Week in New York is to firmly believe in the very pit of your soul that the line of dresses Caroline Herrera will reveal on the runway may be the most important thing to change the course of human history at least since the advent of the atomic bomb.

I have to admit I was swept away in the excitement of the whole build-up, wondering what castings I'd be sent to, if I'd get a request, if overnight I'd be splashed across fashion Web sites the world over for modeling on the runway. The offers for campaigns would then roll in, the next top model to make it into the elite circle. The dream never seemed so close to grasp—just one lucky break!—and my two sour experiences with the photographers vanished from my thoughts. This was the big time.

Like I mentioned before, models often fall into the two different camps of "editorial" and "commercial," with the angular, sometimes even bizarre-looking girls like Svetlana and Lucia falling into the former camp, the more "conventional" ones like me falling into the latter. Runway work leaned to girls who had a more interesting look, but the Agency was pulling out all the stops this season. Rachel was preparing to send her legion of girls out into the fray, hopefully returning with the glory of a high-profile runway job. It was going to be bloody.

My final measurements before Fashion Week hadn't gone so well. "You need to lose five," Rachel had said to me. "By Friday." She hadn't blinked. Her tone made her hidden message clear: "Eating is what *other* people do. Not models." Starvation, a small price to pay for fame, right?

Maybe I was getting delirious from only consuming what seemed like 2.8 calories a day to try to meet Rachel's impossible demand, but the time leading up to the crush of castings was filled with a sense of limitless possibility.

Robert had e-mailed to say he was coming back to New York for Fashion Week, and that doubtless contributed to my giddiness as well. I missed him, the only man I'd been seeing in New York since I arrived here. Don't get me wrong, I wasn't sad about that: Instead of bedding down with cheesy investment bankers and vain male models, I'd been going out with the most mature and damn sexiest Frenchman around, who knew how to treat a lady, who cared for his sick mother and wouldn't fall prey to the easy pleasures of a Svetlana. All right, all right, maybe I hadn't really landed him yet, but we had been seeing each other, and it seemed full to the brim with promise. (And I *do* have to own up: Christiane's sexplosions had only whet my appetite for having a man around, and my excitement about Robert's return wasn't all about good conversation, tasteful dinners, and his sexy accent.) It'd been over a month since I'd seen him.

The castings for Fashion Week came. One day we were just sitting around, poking at Tom Ford, bickering among ourselves, complaining about how cold it was outside, Christiane whining about some guy's small dick. The next we were bouncing like yo-yos across the city, running to castings in Midtown, Chelsea, Soho, *everywhere*. Early arrivers from out of town were starting to filter in, and Manhattan was suddenly occupied by an entire army of chic women and sharp men. It was as if the Third Expeditionary Fashion Force had parachuted in thousands of young models and designers, along with the writers and editors who covered the whole thing.

Although I'd been around during September's Fashion Week, I had still been getting my bearings and didn't appreciate the madness that came with it. I was going to at least six castings a day, sometimes as many as ten. Some, for bigger labels, were held in stylish studios on the West Side, others in cramped boutiques downtown, where we'd have to try on pieces and walk around the clothes racks in the showroom.

After a few days of this chaos and no big victories, I was beginning to wonder if any of us at the model dorm would get cast for a show. We all had our near-misses: Lucia was sent to the Calvin Klein general casting. Floating her way to the top of the competition due to her previous reputation. She was requested to come and walk, which was the step before actually getting fitted with Calvin, where he'd decide if you had what it took. The Slovak was probably the happiest I'd seen her and went to the request buoyant with energy. She came back in tears, heartbroken. There had been another girl who looked a lot like her and was from Russia. But she was a lot younger. It was a replay of her being replaced in the photographer's bed by the young Geneva. Y—3 and Derek Lam were close-but-no-cigars as well.

Kylie was also doing her best, but nothing was coming through. The people at Anna Sui had seemed to take an interest in her, yet even that fizzled. She doubled her nightly intake of Metamucil martinis to wash away her bitter disappointment. Svetlana had been requested for a big designer's show but, from what I could understand, one man there had taken a particular dislike to her. Svetlana walked for them, and the man had rolled his eyes as she finished, whispered something in one of his colleague's ear. All pearly whites—a Simon Cowell for the fashion world—he said thanks through gritted teeth and dismissed her.

The nympho Christiane didn't have much better luck, until she was cast for a smaller show that was going to be held at the Puck Building, not under the tents at Bryant Park. As often happened with small designers, she wasn't even going to get paid—they were just going to give her some free clothes.

Two days before Fashion Week was to begin, everyone except Christiane was starting to panic—were we not going to get invitations to walk for *anything?* Tom Ford sensed our anxiety and trotted around the apartment trying to give us comforting licks. But even his cute doggy ways couldn't hide the fact that the week had begun with a limitless horizon and now we were back just where we began: sitting in our apartment, not working. Slipping into self-pity, I realized I also hadn't heard a word from Robert. Willem called from the gallery to ask how everything was going, and I was curt with him on the phone, projecting my disappointment and bitter feelings. I had descended so deep into the mania of Fashion Week and the whole aura around it that I even felt a bit resentful about the time I'd been "wasting" at the gallery, when I should have been getting ready for this. Here I was, not even sure I'd passed the GED, having changed my whole life to be a model, and I couldn't even get a job during Fashion Week. The big time was slipping away again.

Then, when all seemed lost, fate intervened.

Svetlana and I were both sent to the same casting, for a hip Japanese label called United Bamboo. I hadn't been in direct competition with her before, and at the casting she was eyeing me warily, like just another girl who was going to take a job away from her. All bets were off outside the dorm—every girl for herself.

To my astonishment, she even tried to shake me before I walked for the people at the label. Nodding to the sheer white dress I was going to put on, she whispered to me, "Heather have body type for that dress?" Was she saying I was *fat?* Every fiber in my body wanted to slap her across her delicate Russian face, but I just smiled and replied, "Oh, I think it's just fine." I felt a little nauseous: Even though we weren't exactly best friends forever, it was still unnerving that Svetlana would use her verbal knives on *me* though. I guess it shouldn't be so surprising she took a sharp turn against me. Her comment had the unintended effect of motivating me, and I walked like I'd never walked before. My hips moved back and forth as I put one foot in front of the other as if I'd come out of the womb wearing couture. I'd show *her.*

It turned out her attempts to throw me off were a waste of her Russian breath—we were *both* booked for the show. As soon as she knew I wasn't going to be a threat to her, she threw her arms around me. "Svetlana and Heather have so much *fun!*" She had apparently forgotten all about the fact that she'd tried to sabotage me. I was thrilled to get the show but, just like with the look book shoot and the encounter with the *Velveteen* publisher, I felt, well, *not myself.* Was this what the world was like, where someone you think is your "friend" would throw you to the wolves to gain the slightest advantage? With other girls, yeah, I could see that, but wasn't there *some* sort of loyalty? But I guess I *had* been seeing her crush on the side. Oopsy. I pushed all these thoughts away, though: The show was in three days. Lucia and Kylie were left to sit on the sidelines.

.

THERE'S REALLY NO WAY to precisely describe Fashion Week under the tents at Bryant Park. It comes and goes like a whirlwind, leaving crumpled copies of *The Daily* on the curb of Forty-second Street as the only proof that it hadn't been one long fabulous dream. For a period, the eyes of the entire fashion world turn to a normal city park transformed into a showcase for the most luxurious and glamorous clothes money can buy (and prestige you *can't* buy). The tents blanket the park, with different shows running at all times in different sections, photographers dashing around, elbowing one another to get pictures of celebrities in town for the shows, candid shots of designers, and anything that will let the rest of the world know how fabulous Fashion Week in New York City is. Behind the scenes, in the trenches—while all the spectators gossip, settle into their seats, have their photos taken—are troops of models, designers, stylists, and makeup people, rushing around like their lives depended on it as the minutes tick down to showtime.

That's where Svetlana and I found ourselves on the day of the United Bamboo show, stuck in the middle of a buzzing hive of frenetic activity, *everyone* freaking out, making last-minute changes to our makeup, hair, deciding which outfit wasn't going to fit right with which model. Outside, where the runway was, I could hear the crowd murmuring as everyone settled into their seats on the bleachers that wouldn't have been out of place at a high school football game. This was a smaller show, but that almost made it more important for the people working to make a good impression on the fickle crowd outside.

This was *it*. I'd made it to the runway. What would come after this? With all the energy building, I couldn't help feeling that this was the beginning of something big.

At the fittings, when the stylists were deciding which pieces to use for the looks we were going to be walking in, both Svetlana and I had been eyeing the outrageous showpiece dress that I could just tell was going to be one of the hits of the show. It would look perfect on me. Unfortunately, Svetlana had the same idea about how it would look on her, too.

"Svetlana want dress, bad on Heather," she said, trying to get one of the stylists to hear her and, of course, agree.

"No, Svetlana, *I'm* getting the dress. You'd look horrible in it— it's totally out of proportion for you," I said, slipping into girl survival mode. I suddenly *needed* the dress as part of one of my looks. We both moved closer to it, claiming our territory. Just as we got ready to stake out the dress, one of the people working for the label walked right between us and pulled the dress off the rack.

"Excuse me, girls, this is for *her,"* the woman said, pointing at a famous sixteen-year-old model from Brazil who had been tagged by the press as the Next Big Thing. She brought it over to the girl. I could have sworn the little bitch stuck her tongue out at us, but I was probably just imagining things.

"In person she not so pretty," Svetlana whispered to me, back on my side now that we both had been foiled.

As the curtain time for the show crept closer and closer, everyone started to get nervous, battling to keep their nerves from getting the best of them. There were stations set up for each model, with support staff at each spot. For this show, each girl had three looks that had been chosen, and all the clothes for each look were ready at the stations for when they returned from their trips down the runway. One of the girls at my station, who looked like she was still probably in high school, glanced out at the unseen audience, unconsciously biting her fingernails. It was go time. I was ready in my first look, a blue plaid camisole with matching pants. I glanced at Svetlana and even gave her a small smile of encouragement, despite our spat earlier.

Three—two—one . . . The music outside on the runway kicked in, and before I knew it, I was being hurried out, toward the awaiting crowd. Adrenaline coursed through my veins, and my feet instinctively started kicking forward in that sassy manner only models can seem to pull off. Svetlana was two models behind me. I walked forward, almost there. Onto the runway . . .

The glare of the lights struck me full-on, and I was blinded with a thousand flashbulbs. I took it all in stride, never blinking for a moment. I started walking down the runway, focusing on one thing and one thing only: NOT FALLING. The whole thing seemed unreal, the faceless crowd, the music, the lights that fell on *me*. My expression totally straight, I walked the length of the runway and paused. *SNAP, SNAP, SNAP, SNAP, SNAP*—how many photographers *were* there? The crowd clapped. Were they clapping for the piece *I* was wearing? For someone else's, maybe Svetlana's? I couldn't know, as I mechanically spun around and made the return trip backstage, where my station and next look awaited. Dreams are made of such stuff.

Strutting back down the runway, I caught something in the front row out of the corner of my eye. Was that *Robert?* With some blond girl who had her hand on his thigh? I nearly stumbled. But there wasn't time to take another look—I had to keep my stride and make it back for round two.

If it had been frenetic backstage before, now it was downright chaos. Naked models were everywhere, throwing off clothes, putting on new ones, as assistants screamed to other assistants things like "I NEED TAPE NOW!" I didn't have time to think about the fact that Robert was maybe in the audience with some other woman, as the girls at my station started pulling at me in all directions, getting me out of the camisole and putting me in my second look. As they fiddled with the zipper, Svetlana came in off the runway to get changed.

She looked at me and confirmed my fears: "Robert in front row with blond bitch!" she yelled to me as the people at her station stripped her down.

"What are you talking about? Get in the skirt!" a male stylist shouted to her, sweat pouring profusely from his forehead.

Before I knew it, I was ready to go out again and was sent onto the runway to be met with another round of "oohs" and a blitzkrieg of flashes from the photographers. This time I'm pretty sure the claps were for me—well, for the chic piece that I was showcasing— but I didn't relish them. Making my turn, I came back and, breaking a cardinal rule, stopped staring straight ahead for a millisecond, glancing down at Robert. Our eyes met, and he looked stricken. But there was no hand on the thigh—had I just imagined that? Out of my peripheral vision, I saw him whisper something to the blond. He hadn't even called me, and now he was here with some other girl?

Backstage all the clothes came off again. This time when Svetlana came back, I yelled over to her station. We were both in the same Robert boat, as it were. "Who *is* that?!" I shouted to her.

"Quit moving!" one of the dressers said, trying to do some last-second adjustments to the strappy heels that weren't quite fitting on my feet.

"Robert blond look trash!" Svetlana said to me as the assistant attempted to stop her wriggling. At least we were on the same page.

My final turn on the runway, I looked imperiously ahead, not wanting Robert to think it bothered *me* that he was there with some-one else who may or may not be cuddling up next to him. My icy glare apparently worked with the pieces I was wearing, as I got the biggest round of applause yet.

Off the runway, backstage, people were hugging one another as the show came to a close, congratulating themselves that no disaster had occurred on their watch.

And then it was all over.

All the preparation, manic dashing around, anxiety—it had been distilled into eight minutes of calculated chicness, the photographers getting every second of it. But now, outside, the audience dispersed, talking to one another about the pieces, thinking about the next show they were to go to. The photographers quickly packed up their gear, stashed away their flashes, checking their list to see which designer they were to immortalize next. Everything in the tent would empty out, and then a bit later, the madness would fire up again, just with a different designer and another group of models who were hoping that *this* show would fast-track their careers to the top.

I was exhausted. But I'd done it.

THE DESIGNER HAD A BIG DOWNTOWN following, so they had their afterparty at the Tribeca Grand. Svetlana and I were, of course, going to be there. Even though walking on the runway seemed like it sapped every last bit of energy from me, I still wanted to go—plus I wondered if Robert would show up, with or without his blond companion. Had I just been imagining she was that close to him? Svetlana hadn't seen her hand on his thigh, but she still was convinced the blond was "trash." I didn't know what to think and hoped he would be there so I could find out the truth.

The Rapture were giving a live performance, and Justine D. and James F!@#$%^ Friedman were DJing, so naturally a line of downtown scenesters was formed outside the entrance to the hotel—not that *we* had to wait. Spiky Phil and Thomas were manning the guest list and ushered us inside, keeping the corny hedge fund bros at bay. Inside we were met with Tommy Saleh, the manager of the Tribeca. He was wearing a crisp white linen suit and a fantastic white straw fedora, looking cooler than anybody in the place—and he didn't even *work* in fashion. Tommy paused his conversation with some hipster type and handed us a fistful of drink tickets.

"You ladies look great tonight. Enjoy the party." Always a gentleman.

We walked down to the sunken main part of the bar, which glit-
tered with the fashion world's finest. The show had been a success. I
wanted to enjoy myself—I'd just been on the runway!—but instead
I was peering around, trying to catch sight of Robert. I knew it was
irrational, but now that I'd seen him with the other woman at the
show, I *needed* to talk to him. I'd already started rationalizing what
I'd seen. Maybe I hadn't really seen her hand on his thigh, maybe he
was just so busy he hadn't had a chance to call me. Self-deception is
a wonderful thing. (You, dear reader, know how it is.)

Svetlana scanned the room like a Russian hawk, doing the same
exact thing I was, except she didn't bother trying to hide what she
was looking for: "Heather see Robert? Robert here?"

I realized that I was turning into Svetlana in my relationship to
the Frenchman but, against common sense, I didn't care. I still
looked around for him, among the glitterati—just like I'd wanted
that showpiece dress, now I wanted to get my hands on Robert.

We were interrupted from our masochistic search by another girl
from the Agency. She hadn't been part of the show but had still come
to party—she was a bit shorter than us but was getting some really
big deals with makeup and hair companies. I'd seen her face on the
subway the week before, plastered across every inch of the car. She
was Bulgarian.

"Hi, guys. I heard you were in the show—congratulations!" she
said. Her English was a lot better than Svetlana's or Lucia's, due to
the fact that she'd moved here with her family in high school and
was now in college, trying to balance castings and classes.

"This is Tim," she said, practically beaming. She motioned to the
guy who was with her. He seemed like an unlikely choice: Even
though he looked like he was only in his mid-twenties, he was al-

ready almost entirely bald, something his shortly cropped hair couldn't hide. He looked like he hadn't shaved in a couple weeks, and he wore a pair of old jeans that were fraying at the bottom, completed with a dirty pair of Chuck Taylor All-Stars. He had on a smart three-button blazer, but the white shirt underneath was rumpled and in disarray.

"Nice to meet you," he said, winking as he came in to give me a kiss on both cheeks. I swore his hand glided against my ass. He did the same with Svetlana.

The Bulgarian started talking shop with me and Svetlana, and he looked around, yawning.

"Excuse me," he said. "I think I recognize somebody." He left us.

"Tim's a grad student at Columbia in English," the Bulgarian said to us, all excited. Well, I guess *every* model wasn't just looking for money. And he certainly wasn't a male model. "He taught my Lacan class, really opened my eyes to the erotic Other. He's like a genius or something. I think we're about to get serious!" she gushed.

"Uh-huh," I said, noticing that he was already talking to an Italian girl whose inviting breasts were spilling out of her low-cut shirt. And he was talking to her *in* Italian. "Well, good luck with that!" I said to the Bulgarian, going off in search of Robert again. After a few more minutes, I could see he definitely wasn't there and reconciled myself to it. At least I didn't start calling him like some crazy person (even though I secretly wanted to).

I fell into conversation with a South African model named Diaunna who had been part of the show. She had the deepest green eyes, and in the midst of all the Fashion Week flurry and posturing, seemed genuine and caring as we chatted about our families back home, friends we missed, and our dreams for the future. She'd modeled in Cape Town for some time and was starting to get some big jobs in New York. But, unlike so many of the other models I'd met, she seemed down-to-earth. Talking to her calmed me a bit after I'd come in with the vain hope that Robert was going to be there.

A tall guy came up to the table Diaunna and I were sitting at. He looked sort of like a mid-twenties Johnny Depp with a dash of Orlando Bloom thrown in. I thought he was going to hit on us, and I wasn't in the mood.

"Oh, Heather, this is my brother, Lee," she said in her beautiful South African accent, introducing me to him. "He's a professional surfer."

"Well, I don't know how professional anymore—being here in New York, there aren't exactly a lot of opportunities. Nice to meet you, Heather," he said, sitting down with us.

Lee was really nice (and *really* cute), and any other night I probably would've been excited to talk to him. Even though I wasn't being especially receptive, Lee kept the conversation going, a good sport, asking me questions about myself, telling me about how he was directing music videos.

He had to leave to go to another party, and his sister escorted him out.

"Lee really liked talking to you," she said when she returned. "What'd you think of him?"

"I already have a, uh . . . boyfriend." I don't know why I lied.

"Oh," she said. "Well, if you want to talk to him or whatever, I promised I'd give you his number. He's a good guy." She handed me a scrap of paper with the digits written on it.

"Okay, thanks," I said, stuffing the scrap in my bag. He had been a nice guy, I guess, and I didn't want to offend his sister.

I began to feel woozy, and the lights of the Tribeca started spinning across my eyes. The whole day's events suddenly fell on me, the stress of the runway job, the weird interaction with Svetlana, my strange obsession about Robert, how I'd just totally blown off a very cute guy, who, although he didn't seem to be loaded with cash, was a lot nicer than anybody I'd met in a while. Barely eating at all for the past couple weeks probably didn't help.

"Are you all right, Heather?" Diaunna asked, worried. "Do you want me to get you some water?"

"No, no, I'm okay, it's just . . . been a long day. I should probably go home," I said, steadying myself by gripping the table. Diaunna looked at me with concern.

"Let's get you in a cab, then," she said, helping me from my chair.

I said good-bye to Svetlana, who was just starting to get amped up for the night, which promised to go into the wee hours of the morning, judging by how wired she already seemed. It was only maybe eleven, but I just felt so fatigued.

Back at the model dorm, I walked straight past Kylie and into the bedroom. I threw myself on the bunk. Tom Ford whined below, and I brought him up, the two of us falling quickly asleep, leg in arm.

AROUND THREE A.M., Tom Ford decided he wanted down. He licked my face until I woke and brought him off the bunk, opening the door to let him into the living room. I'd fallen asleep in my clothes and stripped down before going back to sleep. Nobody else was home yet, of course. Right before getting back to bed, I heard my phone beep from my bag. I had a new text message. I was ready to just forget about it, but the beep was insistent. Probably Svetlana, wondering if I was going out more.

I checked it. It was from Robert, received a few hours ago. The phone must have been beeping a while and I'd just slept through it. Half asleep still, I read the message: *u looked great today! been busy, lets dine next week.—r.*

My head was blank: What could this mean? Did I *care* what it meant anymore? The whole thing seemed, for lack of a more polite word, *fucked*. If he *had* been with the woman, would he have texted me at all, having gotten caught, as it were? Probably not. But then again, maybe he was trying to pretend that it wasn't a big deal, that way he'd be able to just laugh it off, when in fact he had been with her. The whole thing revolved around the hand on the thigh. The lights were bright. Had my eyes been playing tricks on me?

"Goddammit!" I yelled to the empty apartment.

I was tired of thinking, tired of a lot of things. I didn't answer the message and just lay back down to get the sleep I needed. I had to start thinking about myself. I felt sapped, drained. And with Robert, as my grandfather would have said, it was time to fish or cut bait.

FASHION WEEK CAME TO A CLOSE, shivering in a final paroxysm of glamour, indulgence, and self-importance. The fashion industry across the city went into hiding to detox with seaweed wraps and all-juice regimens after a week of nonstop hectic shows and all the parties that went along with them. The normal postmortems, in which a couple of writers predictably declared fashion was dead, appeared in the newspapers. All was right with the world.

I started up again working at the Clijsters Gallery now that the insanity had subsided. I had made up my mind that no matter what Robert had said, I had to trust Willem—he had given me no sign to suspect him of anything. If he was going to pull some shady thing, let him try. I wasn't so naive as to fall into something just like that.

My first day back at the Clijsters Gallery, I even made a point to talk to Willem about how I'd been acting. "Hey, Willem?" I said.

"Yes?" he said, turning from going through a spreadsheet on his PowerBook.

"Listen, I just wanted to say, um, I guess, how much I appreciate working here at the gallery," I said. "I know I may have been acting strange lately."

"Strange, no, not at all," Willem said kindly, even though I knew he had suspected something. "I imagine you were just tired from working so hard. But know that we are appreciative of having you here, too."

And he hadn't once told me I needed to shed fifteen pounds.

My faintness after the United Bamboo show had been a wakeup call. It's true, I had gotten my first runway work, but I'd spent that night frazzled and malnourished, obsessing over Robert like a Svetlana Jr. in training, nearly passing out from the accumulated anxiety and fatigue from all the castings and constant uncertainty that had led up to Fashion Week. Willem and the gallery, on the other hand, provided the only stability—financial or otherwise—in my life.

Especially financial.

Now that the high fashion and chic fever had subsided from Manhattan, I realized that although the show had been glamorous, the check *hadn't* been: I earned around $600, which, of course, I didn't see any of, since I owed so much on my account with the Agency. How long would they let *that* ride?

The runway job had proven to the Agency that both Svetlana and I could get work, but it was peanuts compared to what a girl like Jeanette had done. And with both Kylie and Lucia striking out during the castings for Fashion Week, I felt that the eviction ax was going to be falling on one of us soon to clear the way for the next girls the Agency could lure in. The only question was who it would be.

In the mail, I received my GED results—I'd passed, as expected. It seemed like cold comfort, though. I didn't see how it was going to help me avoid being dropped from the Agency or aid me when I had to face my next measurements. I guess my parents would be happy.

Right after starting work at the gallery, a catalog for the University of New York had come, addressed to some girl who had probably moved out of the model dorm two years ago. Kylie was getting ready to toss it, but I'd saved it from the trash—I looked at the art history offerings, which piqued my interest. I had even mentioned to Willem that after getting my GED I was thinking about picking up some classes in art history, just to keep my mind occupied while I pursued my career as a model. He thought it was an excellent idea. But that was when I thought that by now I'd already have a few high-paid modeling jobs under my belt, and I'd have the money to pay for the classes. That hadn't happened—I was barely surviving on the part-time job at the gallery, and modeling hadn't gotten me a cent yet. How was I going to pay for the expensive courses when I couldn't even afford to move out of the model dorm?

I stuffed the GED certificate into my already-full drawer in the dresser and promptly forgot about it.

I'D TALKED TO ROBERT ON THE PHONE the day after the show. I was still unsure of him, but his voice seemed totally normal, not nervous at all. Maybe I had just been stricken with a case of paranoia?

"Heather, you looked beautiful, definitely the standout model of the show. Congratulations!" he said.

"Thanks. I thought I maybe saw you there," I said, leading him to try to explain the blond. He didn't flinch.

"Ah, yes, I was hoping you did—I definitely would not miss that show; the label is very hot," he said, as if he had gone alone. "I wish I had called you when I arrived in the morning"—he arrived that morning?—"so I would have known you were going to be in it. But it was a lovely surprise after not having seen you for such a long time."

We'd made plans to see each other the following week for dinner and drinks. He'd said his schedule was "very busy," and I'd said mine was as well, even going so far as to suggest Thursday when he originally planned on Tuesday. Tuesday was "all tied up" for me, even though I didn't have anything scheduled at all. I didn't want to seem overeager.

Besides, I still was feeling ambivalent—the upsurge of my jealousy and then desperation at the Tribeca had frightened me, and I wanted a little more time to sort them out before seeing him again. All I knew was that when I went out with Robert again, it was do or die. I was getting sick of having to wonder what was going on, along with the low-level drama it caused in my life due to living with Svetlana. Now that he was back in New York, she started up again, begging me—or anyone else around—to go out with her in the hopes of finding him, even resorting to tears on a few occasions. This concerned Tom Ford to no end, as he'd whine at her feet when she'd start crying.

I was getting tired of going out to the model parties, and instead was looking forward to going out with Willem and his friends more. Instead of talking about who got which campaign, or what celebrity might happen to be there, we'd talk about the art world, which contemporary artists might be making the next breakthrough, who their influences were. One thing I wanted to overcome was the fact that some of Willem's friends still sometimes looked at me as nothing more than a walking clothes hanger that happened to work at the gallery.

So instead of me, Svet often went out with Christiane. The Wyoming girl's compulsive need to get laid was starting to get more and more ridiculous. It was around this time that I walked in on her screwing the Brazilian male model (while wearing my Dior heels, thank you very much). I was starting to get tired of her constant antics. When was the sixteen-year-old going to get enough, or at least come down with a case of the clap to slow down her sex life?

Her promiscuity *did* manage to shed some light on one minor mystery, however. She'd been asked to go into the *Velveteen* "offices"— but it wasn't through the Agency. She'd met the famous photographer-turned-publisher out one night during Fashion Week, and Wilkins was enamored. They'd apparently made out at the club. Ewww.

Christiane's tastes were omnisexual, I guess—young, old, tall, short, cute, um, not-so-cute. I was going to tell her what had happened with Wilkins, but she was so damn excited about the prospect of getting photographed by *the* David Wilkins that I thought it better just to bite my tongue. She said it was going to be a "special" shoot. (And, need I mention, the whole time the publisher definitely thought she was eighteen.)

She came back after her "shoot" at the apartment of sleazy Wilkins but was glum, something I certainly hadn't expected.

"What's wrong, Christiane," I asked, all ears, "didn't the shoot go well?"

"Oh, hey, Heather," she said. "Oh, no, the shoot was great—the pictures are going to be amazing. He even had some chains. . . . I can't wait to get the photos for my 'private' book I can show to boys."

Chains? Wow, he had been prepared for some weird shit.

"Well, what's wrong, then?" I asked.

"The shoot was, like, cool, but it was afterward that was really . . . lame."

"Lame?"

"Yeah, it's like, we started to make out or whatever, and I reached down, and I couldn't feel . . . it," she said.

"It?" I asked.

"Yeah, you know, it's like *it* wasn't there. I think they call it micropenis or something?" she said. "Anyway, I'd gotten pretty excited with the pictures and then *pppbbbbb*. . . ." She held her thumb and forefinger apart only a couple inches, to show me how big he'd been. "And he definitely had it up. So I made him go down on me," she said matter-of-factly, before going to take a shower.

So *that's* why everyone had been smirking after I went to the test shots with Wilkins—apparently Christiane and I were the only people who hadn't known that the publisher of *Velveteen* was equipped with the smallest penis this side of Hoboken.

I chuckled about this, unaware that I was going to be faced with my own penis problem in little more than twenty-four hours.

15

"HAVE I TOLD YOU HOW BEAUTIFUL you looked on the runway?"

"Yes, a couple of times already," I said. Robert had his hand on mine. We had already downed a bottle of champagne at Soho House. (The Frenchman had a membership there, of course.) We had ended up there after a dinner at Indochine, where we'd had a meal with his colleague Mikael and his model catch of the day.

"Well, it's true, you were beautiful. You cannot stop a man from telling the truth," he said, squeezing my hand.

Dinner had gone fine. Halfway through our appetizers, I had asked Robert, straightforward, who the blond with him at the show had been. It had been bothering me.

"Oh, *her.* That was just an old friend from Paris. She was in town for the, ah, shows," he'd said. "Her boyfriend's just left her, and she is terribly upset about it. She wanted me to keep her company. She's a model, just like you. I should introduce you to each other."

I needed to believe him. And I did.

Where were things going with this? I'd come into the night determined, as I said, to either move forward or cut things off but, as usual, my resolve withered under his good looks and predilection for ordering the most expensive wines on the menu. Did things have to be so cut-and-dry? I mean, what if I scared him off? Every bit of advice my mother had given me about men eroded with each squeeze of his firm hand.

I finished my glass of champagne and dramatically put it down on the table. I flipped my hair and gave him a smile.

"Should we go?" he said. I nodded.

There were no separate cabs this time, dear reader.

Taking the elevator up to his apartment, I was almost giddy, having been such a nun for so long, while everyone else in the model dorm was having their fun. As the elevator rose to his floor, he pressed me against the brushed steel of its wall and dramatically kissed my neck. I closed my eyes and sighed.

Outside the door to his apartment, Robert stopped.

"Just want to say, this apartment is not totally to my liking yet; it is still in a state of flux since I have yet to move here permanently," he said with false modesty.

Just as Robert's clothes were always impeccably stylish, his apartment radiated good taste, from the furniture to the lighting—it was bachelor minimalist chic, with sleek black leather furniture and modern lamps. The living room had floor-to-ceiling windows with an unobstructed view of the Empire State Building. I knew Robert was rich, but I didn't know he was *this* rich. Certainly Shiva Bar couldn't be providing such luxury. . . . But, as is so often with the rich, it's better if you don't ask where the money comes from and just enjoy the benefits.

"It looks great, Robert, and I have to say that it's a lot cleaner than where I live," I said, thinking about the trash that was towering out of the kitchen garbage can, neglected by all of us.

"Well, I can't take credit for that—the cleaning lady came yesterday, and now it's spotless," he said.

Robert fixed us two vodka tonics, but we barely sipped them before starting to make out on the couch in the living room. All the passion I'd stored up let itself go, and I didn't care about anything, about that blond, whether he'd been lying, none of it mattered anymore. There was just the *now* of it, and the now was that I was hooking up with a man whose every atom screamed *sexy*. We'd ended up lying on the couch, and Robert suggested we go to the bedroom. I followed him, floating on a sea of hormones.

On the bed, we continued our foreplay. He took off my shirt, and I unbuttoned his. Everything was going perfectly. My hand ran across his smooth chest, down his toned abdomen. I unbuckled his pants and reached down. . . . It was finally going to happen—we were going to make it happen!

Uh-oh. Well, now, what was *this?* My Harlequin romance fantasy had run straight into a *soft* wall. I kissed him a bit more, trying to get him excited, but nothing was happening. Hadn't he said I was beautiful?

Robert laid back, sighing in despair. "I'm sorry, I just, you have to understand . . ." Robert said. "It's not you. You're very sexy, trust me—I just have a *problem*. Often." But he wasn't even trying to get it to, um, "work"—was there no hope, was this something that happened all the time?

"Oh, don't worry, Robert, it's okay," I said, playing the part of the understanding girl. BUT IT WASN'T OKAY! I was ready to go, had been waiting for this *forever,* and now HE COULDN'T GET IT UP? It was like some cruel joke from the cosmos.

"I need to go to the bathroom," I said, more wanting to process what had just happened and to cool down a bit.

It seemed so ironic—the sexy Frenchman who graced the pages of magazines, the man whom girls like Svetlana (who could get almost any man) was stalking, the handsome, dashing, devil-may-care rich playboy . . . couldn't . . . get . . . it . . . up. I realized that he was definitely middle-aged. I guess these things happened. Maybe a few minutes and I could change his little friend's mind.

The toilet wouldn't flush—it was a gleaming black bowl that looked like it had come from a spaceship. Apparently form had won over function in this case. The light bouncing off it was near-blinding, like it had been spit-shined. I stood up and jiggled the handle. I took my sexual frustration out on it. Dammit! Work! While messing with the handle, I had a view right behind the toilet and saw something that caught my eye. What was that?

"Heather?" Robert called from the bedroom.

"Just a second, Robert, washing my hands!" I turned on the sink but went back to peering behind the toilet. What was that? It looked like a pair of panties. Ripping off some squares of toilet paper, I reached back and pulled the evidence out. It was a sexy black thong from La Perla. There *was* another girl!

I looked around and saw how shiny everything was in the bathroom, and remembered Robert said that the cleaning lady had come the day before! There was *no way* the cleaning lady could have missed something like a thong on the floor—the base of the toilet was thoroughly scrubbed. That meant that not only was there another woman, but she had probably been in the bathroom that very morning. Did he just have a rotating cast of girls to bring back here to show them his impotency? I inspected the sink, and sure enough,

Exhibit B was waiting for me: A few strands of long blond hair were on the sink. They measured about the length of the hair of the model "friend" Robert had been sitting with at the show. The housekeeper would have certainly wiped them away.

I kicked the thong back behind the toilet and washed my hands. I walked out and smiled. I didn't have any intention of some dramatic showdown, nor did I want him to even know what I discovered. I just needed to leave.

"Hi, Robert," I said in a saccharine voice.

"Heather, I think things may start working down there," he said, looking at me hopefully. I put on my shirt and shoes quickly, then turned to give him a kill-him-with-kindness grin.

"Sorry, I just remembered I need to walk Tom Ford."

I slammed the door when I left. Well, just a bit, for dramatic effect.

IT WAS LATE WHEN I GOT BACK to the apartment, just closing time for the bars and clubs. I had to hail a cab but walked a couple blocks away from Robert's apartment just to avoid any curbside dramatics if he tried to come down and talk to me about why I'd just left with no explanation. My phone rang while I waited for a cab: "Incoming Call: ROW-BEAR." I shut it off, glad I was taking control of *something* in my life.

In the cab, I tried to squelch my indignation about the way things had ended up with Robert. It wasn't that he was seeing other women—it's not like we were seriously going out or something, and I'm not some crazy Puritan—it was that he'd straight-up *lied* and been totally shady about it. *Plus* it was another model, *and* she'd been there that very morning. I wickedly thought that it seemed like a man with Robert's "performance problems" might want to slow the pace of things down a bit, take some time to smell the roses, instead of embarrassing himself like that in the bedroom. I have to admit that I was also pretty disappointed with not even getting to any fireworks in bed—if he was going to disappear for weeks at a time, then lie about what he was up to, at least he could have made the evening memorable!

I thought back to how he hadn't even called me to let me know he was back in New York, and then, after seeing me on the runway, he was all hot to trot on getting together, telling me how beautiful I was. Was I just going to be another notch on his model belt? Was he one of those guys who didn't have enough faith in his own judgment about whether a girl he was with was attractive? Did he need some outside jury to tell him she was beautiful before he'd be interested?

I smiled, taking small solace in the fact that he probably thought I'd run out because he couldn't rise to the occasion, as it were. Good. Let him squirm.

For once I got back to the model dorm after everyone else, even Christiane. When I opened the door, I was met with her and some guy making out on the couch. Christiane pulled away from the guy when I walked in. His hand had been hiking up her skirt, far enough that I could see she was wearing thigh-highs.

"Oh, hey, Heather," she said, as if it were totally okay at all times to use every square inch of the apartment to satisfy her libido. "This is Danny. His mom's visiting from out of town and staying at his apartment, so we thought we'd hang out here."

Danny was in his late twenties, the kind of guy who looked like he'd jumped straight from his frat house at the University of Virginia to some analyst job at one of the nameless firms on Wall Street. He was wearing a bad button-up shirt and had spiky hair. Like I said, Christiane's tastes ran the gamut. I didn't know if I bought the excuse—this kind of guy had a girlfriend already stowed away, ready for marriage.

"Hi, Danny," I said, going to the bedroom, where my other roommates were already sleeping. Tom Ford was waiting at the door to get out, and I let him into the living room so I didn't have to bother with him whining while I tried to sleep. The little pup trotted out to the kitchen to get some water and food. I closed the door and tried to sleep.

I was starting to nod off when the sound of Tom Ford yipping pulled me back awake. *Yip! Yip!* What could he possibly be barking at? He *never* barked.

Ohhhh . . . I heard a distinctive Christiane moan, then some panting—that came from Danny, *not* Tom Ford. Our dog continued barking. I tried to put the pillow over my head to block out the sound, but the barking was insistent, and the sounds of Danny and Christiane became louder and louder. Apparently the banker didn't have Robert's problem.

Svetlana was fast asleep still, but I could tell from Lucia's breathing she had been woken up. Kylie, too.

"Shut up! Shut UP!" Kylie said, quiet at first, then louder. They obviously couldn't hear her, between Tom Ford's yapping and their own sounds as they went at it. "Heather, you awake?" she whispered.

"Yeah."

"Go out there and tell that slut to stop making so much damn noise," she said in hushed tones.

"Why do *I* have to do it?" I asked.

"Christiane slut," Svetlana said, having woken up and added her two cents. "Svetlana have casting, want sleep."

"You or Svetlana should do it," I said to Kylie.

"No way am I going to interrupt," Kylie said. "You've already seen her fanny, anyway. Just go out there so we can all get back to sleep."

"Tell me I'm the best!" Christiane shouted from the living room. All right, enough was enough. I guess it was going to be up to me. These sort of shenanigans had to stop right now.

I opened the door, not really too concerned with what I'd find at this point. We were all just tired, and it'd been an emotional evening for me. She needed to shut up.

I'd imagined they'd just be on the couch, the back shielding my view of the action a little bit. I saw with a shock that I couldn't have been more wrong—Danny had Christiane bent over the back of the couch, in full view. His pants were down around his ankles, and he had her skirt hiked up.

Christiane was shouting now. "Who's hot? I AM! Who's hot? I AM!" Tom Ford was yipping, jumping up and down at Danny's leg, probably convinced the guy was attacking our roommate. They were so into it, they didn't even hear the door open. My cheeks burned red—should I just walk up to Danny and tap him on the shoulder: "Excuse me, sir, but I'd be much obliged if ye'd quit doing me roommate? We're all trying to get a nip of sleep, you see. Much obliged." That wouldn't do.

I cleared my throat. "Christiane." Louder. *"Christiane!"* Tom Ford stopped barking and looked at me, and then both Danny and my roommate turned their heads, caught in the act. "You can't do that here, okay? We're trying to sleep," I said, turning quickly around to go back to bed. They hadn't said a word.

I crawled back into the bunk. About a minute passed, and I heard the front door close. Christiane didn't come back in the bedroom. I didn't care where they'd gone. I just wanted to get some sleep—with everything that happened with Robert, the last thing I needed to worry about was my nymphomaniac roommate. All I know is that when I woke up at noon the next day, she was sleeping like a stone in the lower bunk, a rosy glow on her freckled face, like an innocent babe.

ONE DAY LATER CHRISTIANE just disappeared. No note, no good-byes, nothing. I just came back from a day working at Willem's, and she wasn't there, all her bags gone. It wouldn't have been *too* strange—girls would leave all the time—but the beautiful, tall model from Wyoming seemed like she was in it for the long haul, especially after having gotten booked for the show during Fashion Week. I had no clue she'd been evicted.

I wasn't thinking about it too much, just flipping through the book Willem had given me, checking out some Chuck Close paintings, when Kylie came in.

"You won't *believe* what happened with Christiane," she said, bursting with the information. She'd heard it "straight" from the source, i.e., a friend of hers at the Agency who wasn't at the dorm. This other girl was really friendly with Luke, and he'd let her in on the unbelievable details of what happened.

Turned out that after I came out and interrupted Christiane's tryst, she and Dannyboy had left the apartment, looking for a place to continue. They took the elevator to the top floor, then went into the stairwell, walking up to the very top, stopping just before the emergency exit door that led to the roof. No one would bother them there. Little did they know that the building had a security camera installed to monitor the comings and goings of those who went to the roof, since over the summer some drunken idiots had tossed a couple of lawn chairs off it onto the building next door.

The doorman had been looking over the security monitors when he saw the two having sex in the stairwell. It was Christiane's dumb luck that she happened to be facing the camera, so the doorman saw clearly who it was. And he knew her name. She'd demanded he bring up a couple packages that had come for her earlier that week.

He let them finish their business—he at least owed them that— and waited until the morning to phone the Agency. Even though she was apparently able to fool scores of other men out at the club, the doorman had seen her without makeup and knew she was *young*. According to Luke, Rachel had been furious and desperate to keep everything quiet, since there was a minor involved. She called Christiane's mother back in Wyoming, taking care to say how painstakingly the Agency tried to protect their girls, but they couldn't watch them *all* the time, weren't liable, etc., etc. Luke secretly listened in on the call.

Christiane's mom nearly had an aneurysm when she got the news.

"I knew it! *I knew it!*" What she knew was unclear—that Christiane was a nympho, or that she just knew something generally bad was going to happen, even if it didn't have to do with terrorists. "Don't tell her anything!" her mother commanded Rachel. "Don't tell her a goddamn thing. I'm catching the next flight out to New York to get her. If you tell her, she'll run. I'll use chloroform to get her to come back if I have to!"

We'd never know if she had to pull out the chloroform or not— all we knew was that her mom had gotten a last-minute flight to New York and spirited Christiane back home.

We never heard from her again.

ROBERT LEFT ONE MESSAGE. Then another. Maybe a week later, another. And then that was it. I didn't listen to any, just deleted them. I sent him a short text: *"Very busy, talk 2 u soon."* Anyway, I'm sure he had his model "friend" to keep him company and console him about his erectile dysfunction.

After deciding to cut things off with the Frenchman, I figured at last I could learn what had happened between Willem and du Croix—what had caused Robert to warn me away from the Belgian?

Willem was inspecting a Chuck Close he'd just purchased, making sure it was pristine after being shipped to the gallery.

"Terrific, isn't it?" he asked me. "A real find. I mean, it's not on the level of his Philip Glass portrait, but what is these days? I've already phoned Mr. Smith about it."

I agreed—it was a great piece. But I had more than art on my mind just then.

"Hey, Willem, remember how I mentioned Robert du Croix?" I asked innocently.

He pulled away from the canvas, looking at me gravely. "Yes . . ." he said.

"Oh, don't worry, I don't . . . I mean, he's nothing to me now," I said. "He just . . . mentioned some things about *you,* and I was wondering how you guys knew each other."

"I'm very glad to hear that you are not seeing that man anymore," he said. "I restrained myself from saying anything earlier, in the hopes that he had mended his . . . ways. I did not want to spoil anything, or have you feel I was sabotaging your life."

He cleared his throat and continued. "Some time ago we knew each other in Paris. Even then, his taste for models had reached a fever pitch—he could not see enough of them, consuming them and then spitting them out in favor of the latest to arrive. He was very careful, though, and his good looks, charm, and money allowed him to run over these poor girls. He had a stable, as one says. There was one model from Belgium, a dear friend of mine. He had been seeing her only casually, keeping his other girls a secret, but she was already starting to fall perilously in love with the beast. One night at Shiva Bar, I had the unfortunate pleasure of sharing a table with du Croix, who was drunk. One of his friends asked him whom he was going to choose: a new eighteen-year-old Finnish model, or the twenty-three-year-old. I realized he was talking about my friend, who at that very moment was probably crying her eyes out over the fact that she could not see him that night.

"At the question, Robert smiled. As if he had been talking about the latest Porsches, and not human beings with feelings, he laughed and said, 'Well, both are stunning, but that one is eighteen . . . so I guess her!' The company chuckled, and I said nothing. 'But I'll keep the old hag around for a bit, just until I break in the Finn.'

"I excused myself from his company for the evening, citing a headache. I went to my friend and perhaps foolishly told her what I had heard. She was destroyed, irrationally blamed *me* for bringing her unhappiness, said she didn't care, she would have been with him even if there were others, as long as she had not known what he had said. She banished me, then went to Robert's, somehow getting in the building. There, in his apartment, she interrupted one of his 'breaking-in' sessions with the Finn. Robert lost both girls. He was convinced that I told my friend out of jealousy and not her best interest. I had no such aims with her, however—she herself fell into a depression, and the whole episode spoiled her modeling career. I also lost her as a friend, because of that man. And even though within a month he most likely had another beauty on his arm, his pettiness led him to blame me for his loss of her and the Finn. He would never have looked to his own philandering. Robert has been a bitter enemy ever since."

After reciting this history, Willem took a deep breath. The loss of the Belgian girl still pained him to this day.

"Wow . . ." I said, processing everything he had just revealed. "And you didn't tell me?"

"Heather, my dear," Willem said, smiling. "If I had told you these things, what good would have come? If you still wanted Robert, you would have surely thought I was trying to get between you and him. And I would have lost another friend. Which I cannot abide."

He placed his hand on my cheek. Breaking the moment, he turned back to the Close painting. "Now, let us take another look at this, make sure no brutes damaged my latest baby."

LUCIA WAS THE NEXT TO GO AT THE DORM. Her melancholy had only increased since not getting any shows during Fashion Week, and the Agency had stopped sending her to as many castings—always a bad sign. Afternoons she'd sit, vacant-eyed, Tom Ford licking at her hand, trying to cheer her up. I felt incredibly sorry for her, but I could tell Svetlana saw her slow burnout as a good thing—even though the Slovak hadn't come into conflict with her during show season, there was no telling when they might go into competition. But Lucia had really stopped caring, just ate her boiled potatoes and thought about the might-have-beens of her earlier career that had led her ultimately to the small apartment, stripped of her photographer boyfriend, victim to a fresher face, just as Robert had planned to leave Willem's Belgian in favor of the eighteen-year-old Finn.

Rachel had called Lucia into the office and unceremoniously told her that the Agency wouldn't be renewing her contract. That she'd lost her interest in the business—and that it probably would be best if she went home. Rachel and Luke somehow knew she was depressed. Although it wouldn't take a PhD in psychology to see that Lucia's mood was turning grayer every day, I once again wondered if there was a tattletale who had wanted to get the beautiful Slovak out of the way, even though she was already wounded and not much of a threat.

Being told she was being dropped, Lucia nodded silently and thanked Rachel for the time she'd been with the Agency. The Slovak had known her days were numbered as soon as she was sent to the model dorm after already peaking in her career, and the unblinking machine of the fashion industry had left her behind, another casualty. Old at age twenty-one. The eviction was probably the gentlest any girl had gotten, though. Rachel, even though she could be ruthless, and encouraged it among the girls, didn't bother chastising Lucia about how she was a failure or anything like that. Even *she* knew it was probably best if Lucia returned to her native Slovakia.

We had a small going-away party to send her off, putting up streamers in the color of the Slovak flag in honor of her home. I'd taken some of the money I was making from the gallery and bought a few bottles of champagne, and Kylie made a vague attempt to clean up the place. She Febrezed every inch of the carpet in the living room to mask what was now a permanent odor. Svetlana dressed up Tom Ford for the occasion, and he wore a doggy party hat. He trotted around happily, unaware that his friend was going to be leaving him. A couple other girls from the Agency Lucia had been friends with deigned to visit the model dorm, bringing bottles of liquor and cards that wished her well. Yelena and Svetlana chattered a mile a minute to each other in Russian.

Even though the party should have had a solemn side—Lucia *was* getting sent home, after all—it was a happy occasion. After leaving Slovakia years ago, she had spent a lot of her time alone, going from hotel to hotel, show to show. And then being left by the photographer. There were not enough cameras and runway shows in the world to fill the hole she felt in her heart. She was now going back to her family, which was where she belonged.

We had a final viewing of the DVD, and Lucia pointed out all the details for the last time. Yes, she cried, but this time they were tears of joy. She'd talked to her mother and father. They were getting her room ready for her. She was going home. The cows were waiting.

LUCIA LEFT EARLY IN THE MORNING, and I groggily murmured a good-bye from my bed. After tearing down the streamers, cleaning up the empty bottles, and scooping up the little pile Tom Ford had made in the corner after everyone neglected to take him out, I sat down on the couch. After Lucia's case, I couldn't help but think about my own situation again. I had the feeling that the next time Rachel peered down at our comp cards in her office, wondering where to trim fat in the Agency, she'd come across mine, slash a big "X" across it in red marker, and then promptly evict me.

My measurements had become tired theater, in which Luke and I were like old bored actors reciting our lines for the thousandth time. He'd tell me I needed to lose weight, I'd nod and say I *definitely* would. We'd go our separate ways until the next time, when we'd go through the whole thing again. My weight wasn't budging, no matter how little I ate. How long would we go through this? Fatigue was settling into my body, fatigue from the castings that were always filled with new faces, fatigue from the anxiety of wondering if I'd ever get my break, fatigue from the pressure we felt living in the model dorm but didn't really acknowledge—we were all just a moment away from being evicted. The more time I spent around the whole industry, the more I was getting sick of it. The whisperings at castings, the secret maneuverings to get ahead, the potential to be stabbed in the back at any moment by a "friend," even if it was over just one shoot—or maybe a man.

But what option did I have but to stick it out? Was I anything more than just a pretty face? The only reason I was living in New

York at all was because the Agency had allowed me to stay in the model dorm. If they hadn't decided to give me a chance, I may have already returned from the small-time in Miami back to Virginia, living with my parents.

Maybe Lucia left a bit of herself behind, because the whole thing was just so *depressing.*

After taking a shower, I fished in my drawer for a pair of jeans I hadn't worn in a long time and came across the GED paperwork. I thought about the catalog for the University of New York with longing, thinking about how instead of constantly being filled with anxiety about succeeding at a casting, I could be sitting in a seminar on art history, learning, expanding my horizons. But what chance did I have of getting in, anyway? I hadn't even finished high school—the GED was a nice little piece of paper that probably wouldn't go far when I applied, I thought. And even if I *did* get in, where was I going to live if I wasn't working as a model and how would I afford the classes?

Either I'd succeed as a model and move out of the dorm or it was good-bye to the life I felt I'd only just started in New York. I felt it had just started, especially now since I'd shaken my attachment to Robert, whose handsome face and wealth had held me in a spell, even from a distance, for so many months.

I'm not ready yet! I wanted to yell to the modeling gods. *Don't take me away! I've still got things to do!*

16

ANOTHER GIRL ARRIVED AT THE MODEL DORM, this one named Margo, but I barely noticed. I was trying to spend as much time at the gallery as I could, picking up shifts here and there. The new models that came and went were becoming interchangeable. All I knew of Margo was that she was supposed to be an "All-American" girl from a trailer park in the Upper Peninsula of Michigan. Her mom, for her Sweet Sixteen, had maxed out her credit card to get her liposuction. With dollar signs in her eyes, she'd sent Margo to New York to model. Margo wasn't doing much modeling, though—she mostly ate bologna sandwiches slathered in mayo and watched *Judge Judy* during the day, going to maybe half the castings she was supposed to.

Svetlana loathed her, making fun of her clothes behind her back, turning her nose up at her when they shared the living room. She was "fat American cow," Svet said.

With Margo around, the apartment became even more disgusting, her half-chewed bologna sandwiches competing with Kylie's dirty glasses for space in the sink. And Margo was so lazy that even though she thought Tom Ford was the "cutest little thing," she would never even take him out. And through some bizarre logic, both Svetlana and Kylie thought that if *she* didn't have to walk him, *they* didn't have to take him out as often. It seemed like I was the only one who walked him, and I was constantly cleaning up messes Tom Ford had made. But I couldn't scold him—it's not as if he could let himself out of the apartment, hop in the elevator, push the button for the lobby, go do his business outside, and then come back!

His trips out with Svetlana were becoming less and less frequent, too. She'd gotten tired of Tom Ford, like he were last season's Marc Jacobs bag that everybody absolutely had to have, which now had become old news. I felt sorry for the pup and tried to pay him as much attention as my schedule would allow. But what had I expected? The attention span at the model dorm was about 2.4 seconds. Just as careless as they were about paying attention to messes or too lazy to even ask before pirating somebody else's wardrobe, Kylie, Svetlana, Margo, and whoever happened to be at the dorm preferred just to forget about him. He was starting to get a little skinny, too, from infrequent feeding.

And then one night it was the final straw. Literally.

Yelena was paying Svetlana a visit, and from the constant trips to the bathroom and their high-pitched stream of Russian, I knew they were keeping up their spirits with a bag of coke Yelena had probably brought over. Margo slumped down on the couch, watching *America's Next Top Model* and complaining about how the girls on it would *never* make it in the "real" world of modeling. I wanted to ask

Margo what *she* knew about it, since she barely left the apartment.

Margo sniffed the air. "Ewwwww. . . . Tom Ford shit again, Heather!" she called. I was in the bedroom, folding some laundry. I came out and saw that he'd left turds all over the place, like he'd just been fed a laxative. But we'd all been there; he was always a good dog and let us know when he had to go, especially number two.

I looked for him and expected him to be somewhat ashamed of himself, sulking as he usually did when he did a "no-no." But instead he had a strange, manic, "I can take on the world" look in his puppy eyes—where had I seen that before?

Before I could fully ponder this, Tom Ford began jetting around the apartment, yipping like a mad dog, jumping up and down on everyone's legs. He flew like a bullet, ricocheting off the walls.

"What wrong with dog, he go crazy living here?" Yelena asked. You could always count on her being bitchy.

Svetlana had gotten up to go to the bathroom amid the canine chaos.

"Uh-oh," she said from the bathroom.

"What?" I asked.

She leaned down to the floor and picked up a portion of a straw that Yelena had brought to snort lines with. It was gnarled, all chewed up. The Ukrainian model had carelessly left it on the back of the toilet bowl after graciously scooping a bit into her bag and preparing it for Svetlana's next bump. It had rolled off onto the floor, and Tom Ford had gotten ahold of it, gnawing on it like a little chew toy. Luckily he hadn't swallowed it, probably turned off by the bitter taste of the drug, but he'd gotten enough to be sufficiently coked up.

Ruff! Ruff! He barked at me, his jaws chomping, before racing off again, spinning around in circles.

"Tom Ford on coke!" Svetlana giggled.

I was sure he'd hate himself in the morning.

•   •   •

THE POOR DOG WAS A MESS the next day as I nursed him back to the land of the living, pouring some Vitamin Water in his doggy dish. He eagerly lapped it up and perked up a bit. I figured a long walk would do him some good. Spring wasn't yet here, but the temperature had warmed, giving everyone hope that the bitter winter would be gone soon enough.

Tom Ford walked along readily enough, but I could tell he wasn't himself. I felt it wasn't fair: We had chosen to live in the Crazy Pigsty Formerly Known as Apartment 1480. Tom Ford hadn't. He'd been brought there and had no say in things. And after the fiasco with the straw, I couldn't help but think that living around Svetlana was liable to give even a helpless *dog* a coke habit. If he'd been taken care of at first, now he was just neglected, forgotten by the other girls.

"Oh, your dog's so cute!" a woman said to me as I thought about all this, staring off into the distance. She was in her early thirties and had a small boy with her. "I used to have a puppy that looked just like him when I was a girl. He ran away when I was ten."

"His name's Tom Ford," I said. She pet him.

"Say hi to the doggy," she said to the little boy.

"Hi, doggy," he said, scratching Tom Ford between the ears. The dog returned the favor by licking his hand.

"Isn't he cute, Paul?" the woman said. "Okay, well, I guess we'll be going. Let the nice girl take her doggy." She grabbed his hand to walk away.

Inspiration struck me.

"Wait, wait!" I said. She turned back to me. "Do you want him? I mean, Tom Ford?" She looked at me quizzically. "He's a great dog, I can tell you, it's just that, well, I'm moving and I can't have dogs in my new place and I've just been going crazy trying to find a suitable home for him."

"You want me to take your dog?" the woman asked. I nodded and held the leash out to her. Little Paul ran to Tom Ford and threw his arms around the pup.

"I want doggy!" he said. The woman was tentative, didn't know what to think.

"Please, he needs a good home . . . better than we, I, can provide him," I said, starting to get a little emotional now that the weight of what I was doing fell on me. "You said you remembered a dog like him from when you were a girl—just . . . take him."

I handed the leash over to her, and she gently took it, still unsure, while Tom Ford happily licked Paul's face and the little boy giggled.

"Are you sure?" she asked. I nodded, starting to get a little teary-eyed.

"I mean, I should call my husband to see if . . . Well, he might say no. It would be better if I just brought him . . . hmmm . . . All right," she continued.

"You be a good doggy, Tom Ford. I'll miss you," I said to him, giving him a final kiss on the nose. I quickly walked off before the woman could change her mind, not looking back. Even though I was sad to let him go, I was happy he'd have a decent home. I was even sort of envious.

I was nervous walking back to the apartment without Tom Ford: What was I going to tell the others? I couldn't say I just gave him away without asking them, especially Kylie.

When I first walked in, the Aussie noticed I was dogless.

"Hey, where's Tom Ford?" she asked.

"Kylie, there's something I have to tell you. . . . I was walking him when he saw a squirrel. The leash slipped out of my hand and he ran off into the street." I said, as sadly as possible.

"You KILLED TOM FORD?" Kylie said, sobering up, and sitting up straight as an arrow.

"No, no, I mean he ran off across the street, and I lost sight of him, and by the time traffic cleared, I couldn't find him," I said. "I searched around forever, but he was gone."

I felt bad—I knew Kylie cared for him in her way, even though she hadn't actually been taking care of him. When Svetlana got home, Kylie told her all about how I had lost and/or killed Tom Ford. The two girls berated me about how irresponsible I was. I just took it, not revealing to them I'd given him to a better home, where he'd be taken care of. My roommates were up in arms, and there was even some talk of forming a search party. But it was nearing time to go out, and Svetlana was convinced she knew where Robert was going to be that night. And a new episode of *American Idol* was on for Kylie to watch. The search party got scratched.

After a couple days, I never heard Tom Ford's name spoken in the apartment again—well, at least not in reference to the *dog*.

I MENTIONED SVETLANA looking for Robert—yes, she *still* was in pursuit of the Frenchman, who more often than not eluded her, although she was getting closer. I'd gotten reports from nights out when she'd actually run into him, ambushing him from some banquette at whatever club they were at. He'd politely say hello before ignoring her. One of these times, he'd apparently asked about me before excusing himself from her company. Svetlana came back, filled with suspicion.

"Why Robert ask about *Heather*?" she asked. It was almost laughable that only now, after I'd decided not to see the modelizing du Croix, that Svetlana thought there was something between us.

"I dunno, Svet, he probably just has a good memory and re-members me from Marquee back in the day," I said. She stared at me for a moment, eagle-eyed, seeing if I'd give off any sign that I was lying. I didn't flinch. It didn't matter: From then on, the Russian watched my every move, and the distance began to grow between us. Even though she wasn't the sharpest tack in the drawer, her intu-ition rightly told her something was up. She just didn't know what. Too bad she was a couple months late.

"HEATHER, DO YOU MIND COMING in for a little chat?" Luke said on the phone, as sweetly as he could in such circumstances. "Rachel would like to talk to you."

My cell had rung, and my stomach sank when I saw the call was from the Agency. It was nearing mid-March, and I hadn't gotten any-thing since Fashion Week. I'd flown under the radar for long enough.

"Oh, no, not at all, Luke. Today? Like right now . . . ? Okay, I'll come over there, just let me get ready," I'd said.

Was this *it?* Was I going to be *evicted?* The blood drained from my face, my breath quickening. Hands shaking, I put on a pair of flats. What was I going to do if they gave me the boot? Where was I going to live—how was I going to survive? I knew that any day something like this could happen but had managed to push it out of my mind. But now dreaded reality was coming to bite me in the ass. Maybe. I tried to comfort myself with the fact that maybe it wasn't going to be as much of a bloodbath as I thought.

I walked quickly through the living room, and Kylie saw my pallid complexion, my face twisted in fear. Svetlana had gone out somewhere.

"What is it, Heather?" she asked.

"The Agency. They just called. Want to have a chat," I said, my words clipped.

"Oh, shit," she said. "Well . . . good luck, love, that's all I can say."

IN THE OFFICE, Luke dispensed with the normal humiliating measurements. There was no need. He brought me directly to Rachel.

"Take a seat," she said. Luke pulled out a chair for me. Did I look as terrified as I felt? Rachel had been filing her nails and hadn't even looked at me. She was cool, controlled, as if this were the most banal thing in the world, what she was about to say. Finishing her nails, she blew on them in a final dramatic flourish, just to show how little I meant to her. She crossed her legs and finally turned to me.

"Heather, questions have been brought up about your perform-ance," she said, staring me down. I tried not to quiver.

"Performance?" I said.

"Yes, we've given you all the advantages of the Agency, giving you access to all the best jobs the industry has to offer." She paused. "And I have to say, we're disappointed in how seriously you've been taking the opportunity we've put before you." She was using the royal "we." The nerve.

I started grasping for straws. "Well, I know I haven't gotten a lot, but I did get a show during Fashion Week and—"

She cut me off.

"That was thanks to my hard work, pulling strings for my girls. It had nothing to do with you," Rachel said to me. "I don't think you appreciate how we've sheltered you, let you stay in the model apart-ment while you try to start your career."

"Oh, no, I appreciate it, Rachel, I really do," I said. "I'm trying my best, I really am. I go to all the castings. . . ."

"Trying your best?" she asked, looking me straight in the eye. "Then why are you still five pounds over—why haven't you been working out?"

"Oh, no, I've been working out, I really have," I lied, just wanting to get out of there in one piece.

"Heather, we *know* you haven't been going to the gym, so cut the shit, okay?" she said. There was something about the way she said they knew I hadn't been working out. It wasn't like she could just tell from how I looked; it was as if she had a hidden camera outside the building's gym that recorded every time one of her girls went in. How would she have known?

"Maybe if you spent a little less time at your outside job, you could spend a little more time working toward something that's actually important."

She knew about the job at Willem's, too? The mole, after a few months' hiatus, seemed to have surfaced again, whispering poisonous things into Rachel's ear.

"Do you think I made it by just sitting around, waiting for success to roll in?! No, I was in the gym every morning at six A.M., working, sweating to make sure that *I* was going to get the next campaign, not some snot-nosed little bitch from Italy."

"I'm sorry, Rachel, I really am. I'm going to work twice as hard from now on," I said, once again realizing I had no contingency plan if she decided on a whim to evict me. I needed to be as servile as possible. "Thanks so much for your advice. You're really an inspiration. I'm going to make sure I stay in shape."

She nodded. *A victory,* she probably thought. She'd put the fear of Rachel into me.

"Consider yourself on final warning," she said before dismissing me.

Outside, it had begun raining. I'd forgotten my umbrella. Raindrops mingled with salty tears on my face.

It took me forever, but I finally caught a cab in Soho on this rainy afternoon—not before I was fairly soaked, though. The taxi dropped me off in front of the Clijsters Gallery. Final warning. Just what Laura had received before being evicted.

I walked into the space, soaked, pathetic, still sniffling a little bit. Willem took one look at me and knew something was terribly wrong.

"Daniel! DANIEL! We're going to need some tea for Heather!"

AFTER DRINKING THE TEA in the back office, I'd told Willem what had happened, how I'd been put on "final warning" by the Agency and was a hair's breadth away from getting kicked out of the model dorm and dropped as a model.

Willem thought for a moment, then excused himself to make a call. He was gone for about ten minutes while I sipped another green tea, warming up from the cold March rain.

"Good news—I think I may have something," he said when he got back, the concern that had furrowed his brow replaced by his traditional smile.

The previous week he'd happened to have lunch with an art critic friend of his who also taught classes at the University of New York. Willem remembered that I'd once mentioned taking classes there, and he'd asked the professor in passing about the program. He'd said it was excellent.

"I just called my critic friend, and he told me that the university is still accepting for the Fall term, if you like," he said. "Although I cannot guarantee you will be admitted—that will be up to the committee—my friend said if you would like, he can make sure your application does not get lost in the shuffle. It is past the date for priority candidates, but you can still squeeze in for late admission, if space is available."

"I don't know," I said, still feeling miserable about myself after being chewed up and spit out by Rachel. "What if I don't get in? I've only got a GED, and if I *do* get in, how would I pay for it, for books, for living? It's all so expensive."

"Heather," he said, earnestly looking at me in the eyes. "There are always ways—loans, things like that. If you *really* want something, you can always make it happen. You're a smart girl and would be a great student. I told this to the professor. I'll also write you a recommendation, although who knows how far my word will go. But you need to try if you think it's something you'd want. You deserve better than to be treated like shit."

Willem was right.

After I dried my tears, Willem helped me fill out the online application for the University of New York. In the "intended major" box I scrolled quickly past "Undeclared" and checked "Art History." I felt in control of something, for once.

We saved filling out the application until I had the rest of the materials. Over the next few days I wrote my application essay using the computers at the gallery. It was on Basquiat. I also wrote a supplementary essay they required for GED students who were applying. As promised, Willem sent in a letter of recommendation. He let me look it over—it was so glowing, it made me blush.

Everything collected in the application at the end of the week, I clicked on the ominous SUBMIT button, just a day before the deadline. It was now out of my hands.

17

AS IF BEING PUT ON FINAL WARNING with the Agency wasn't nerve-wracking enough, I now spent my days riddled with anxiety about what would happen with my application to the university—I knew I was going to be waiting for at least a little while, but every day I religiously checked our mailbox, hoping for the big envelope that welcomed me as a student.

I didn't tell Kylie or Svetlana that I'd been put on final warning, but it seemed they somehow knew. Svetlana had been acting very strangely around me lately, and more and more rarely asked me to go out with her—not that I'd really want to run into Robert, anyway. She viewed me with more suspicion, and her comments became more biting. I thought back to how Rachel had said they *knew* I wasn't working out. They'd also mentioned my job with Willem, which not a lot of the girls were aware of. Was *Svetlana* the mole? How could she be, though? She'd liked Laura, had tolerated Lucia, and I'd been with her for months now. Could she be *that* low to sabotage me?

One afternoon crystallized the whole thing, drawing back the curtain to reveal the villains of our little drama.

I was ambling around Soho after checking out the shiny Power-Books at the Apple store. They remained well out of my price range. It was one of the first warm days of the year, and the streets were clogged with foot traffic. I turned a corner onto one of the side streets, soaking in the warm sun that had been hidden for so long during the winter, when I passed by a café. I idly looked in through the window and almost fell over—there, sitting across a table from each other, were Svetlana and Rachel, chatting like old chums. I could tell from their body language that the conversation was friendly. . . . *What the hell?* Rachel was supposed to be the sworn enemy of all of us girls, the Queen Bitch, not our good pal.

I dodged behind a small tree. It obscured me while still letting me see what was happening. They kept talking, and although I'm no expert lip-reader, I could swear they both were saying one thing a lot: "MARGO." I thought of our lazy new roommate who was quickly gaining back all the weight she'd "lost" during the liposuction her mother had mortgaged the family future for.

Before being spotted, I ducked away and wandered around for a good hour, trying to understand what it all meant.

That night when Svetlana got back, I asked her where she'd been.

"Svetlana go castings all day," she said, not mentioning one word about meeting with Rachel.

"Oh, really . . . ?" I said.

"*Da,* Svetlana *tired,*" she said, shuffling into the bathroom.

The lying little minx.

Two days later produced the final proof that Svetlana had been the mole. Margo came back from a meeting at the Agency— she'd been excited, since Luke had "big news," just like he'd told Laura before they banished her. All of us happened to be there when she got back, and I was glad. I wanted Svetlana to see first-hand what her double-dealing caused. I expected Margo to come back a mess, in tears, crying about being evicted. But instead she was *happy!*

"Omigod, you guys, it's great!" she said, bubbly. I hadn't seen her that energetic since she walked in the front door of the apartment, just before sitting her ass down to watch TV for the next thousand hours.

"The Agency is sending me to Tokyo! They say there are lots of great opportunities out there, especially for a girl with my 'look'!" she said, beaming, almost boasting to us.

I looked at Kylie uncertainly: Should we tell her? Kylie understood my look and shook her head firmly, "no." So I didn't say anything, letting Margo gush about the "great opportunities" that were on the Pacific Rim.

Japan was where our Agency sent girls either to get experience or earn their money back, working them on backbreaking schedules, fourteen hours a day. And then when they return home they're just as often as not dropped, the Agency taking all the money from their work to pay back the money they "owed" on their accounts, in addition to taking a hefty commission: "Thanks for making money for us! No need for you now! Toodles!"

Svetlana had probably informed to Rachel about Margo's utter sloth. That had likely been the grain of sand that tipped the scales for the girl, who already wasn't going to the castings she should have and was gaining weight at a perilous rate. The Agency would farm her out as an "All-American" before she got any bigger and make back the money they'd already lost on her.

"Omigod," Margo said, breaking me from my thoughts. I wanted to tell her about why she was being sent off, but there was a chance that she could do really well out in Asia. Or at least I told myself that.

"What, Margo?" I asked.

"Will you guys teach me how to use chopsticks before I leave?"

A week later, Margo was on her way, all smiles and hugs. Soon she was yet another distant memory.

SVETLANA WAS PACKING HER BAGS, trying unsuccessfully to cram a pair of knee-high leather boots into her luggage. She grunted and pushed, her skinny hands not able to exert enough *oomph* to get them in that last centimeter.

I'd come in and Kylie didn't say anything, just nodding toward the bedroom, rolling her eyes. Svetlana had stopped fighting with the luggage when she saw me enter the bedroom.

"Heather! Svetlana have such good news!" she said, jumping up and down. "Svetlana get holds for *two* campaigns in PARIS! Svetlana go Paris! Paris!"

"That's great, Svetlana. Really. Great." I was cold.

I saw she'd been rewarded for all her informing to the Agency. I hoped she was happy with herself. She clearly had no clue I knew about her deception, and I had no intention of bringing it up—what good would it do? I looked at her, all smiles, and I felt sick: Her backstabbing had most likely gotten Laura evicted, Margo sent to Asia, the pregnant Keyshia kicked out, Lucia sent home. . . . *And* she'd probably brought me to the point of "final warning."

I knew why she was so happy to go to Paris, besides those supposed holds: The week before, even though I hadn't heard from him since storming out of his apartment, I received a text from Robert: *zoning problems with shiva bar ny. returning to paris in days, farewell.* The text was probably a ploy on his part to see if I'd meet up with him for a final fling before he left, where he could try to redeem his manhood. But I hadn't replied at all.

"Svetlana must hurry, flight leave soon! Svetlana so happy!" she said, scouring under the bunk beds to make sure there were no pairs of shoes she was leaving behind. I wondered if this was all part of her act, too, if she'd known about this for a couple of weeks, and was just using this to be all dramatic—of course they absolutely *needed* her tomorrow, she was in such demand—as if in Paris they'd demanded, "No, not the next day, dammit! Get her on the flight *tonight!*" That's what she wanted us to think, at least.

As she flitted around the apartment, I studied her, she who had seemed like a friend to me over the months. I wondered how many nights we'd spent out together, true pals at the club. I'd been dating her huge crush on and off for the past months, and she'd been ratting me out to the Agency. I realized I didn't even know her last name. Like I said, true pals.

She finished packing and had her bags assembled, ready to go for the car that was waiting downstairs to take her to the airport. Time for the good-byes.

Svetlana started her waterworks with what I could only imagine were manufactured tears.

"Svetlana miss you guys," she said.

She went to hug me, and I let her, just wanting to get the Russian's theatrics over with.

"Svetlana hope Heather can be as lucky one day," she said. Then she whispered in my ear, venomously, showing her true colors, "I say hi to Robert for you."

The doorman helped bring her bags down, and then, after a whole fountain of Slavic tears, she was gone, whisked away to whatever Fate would hold for her in France.

The door closed, the whirlwind subsided, Kylie fixed us extra-strong Metamucil martinis.

"Well, that was bloody weird," she said. All I could do was nod in agreement.

AS WAS BECOMING TRADITION with the girls who left the model dorm, we never heard from Svetlana again—apparently living in the outside world exposed just how tenuous our relationships had been.

I never saw her appear in any future campaigns—and I looked, trust me. Apparently when she'd been put on first option for whatever big campaigns she'd been promised, it hadn't worked out. I had no clue if she managed to track down Robert, was living happily in Paris, was getting smaller work, was maybe going to get some shows. I didn't care.

About nine months later, though, I received word of my former Russian roommate. I ran into one of the girls from the Agency on the street. She had gone to Moscow to work for a week or so. While there, she'd been taken out to one of the glitziest clubs in the city, which was packed wall to wall with rich Russian oligarchs. As is the case with so many places in Moscow, the club had to do with sex—it doubled as a high-roller strip club/brothel. Sipping her drink with whatever banker she happened to be with, the girl from the Agency swore she spotted Svetlana across the room, wearing lingerie. She couldn't tell for sure if it was her, though; the smoke swirling around, along with the frenetic lights, made it difficult for her to see. The model said that the girl who looked like Svetlana appeared to be having a great time, though, sitting on the lap of a middle-aged gentleman who was kissing her collarbone. The girl had gotten up to get a closer look, but just as she did, Svetlana (or the Svetlana look-alike) got up with the man and walked to one of the back "private" rooms.

I never heard anything more about this, so I don't know if it was all just a champagne- and coke-induced dream on the part of the model from the Agency. But, wherever you may be, Svetlana, I hold no ill will for you now. I wish you the best, if you're living the good life in Paris or working a sex club in Moscow. May you be kept in Dior, and may the men never run out!

18

A LITTLE OVER A MONTH after being put on "final warning," I'd survived and was still being sent on castings. And then I opened the mailbox and there it was: a big fat envelope from the University of New York, not one of those skinny rejection-letter ones. I whooped like I did when Luke told me I got my first job in New York. The doorman looked at me.

I opened the envelope, just to make sure. I read the cover sheet: *"It is with great pleasure that I offer you admission to the . . ."*

"I got in!" I said to him happily. Like he'd know what I was even talking about.

"Congratulations," he said, amused.

Upstairs, I tore fully into the packet and was doubly stunned—I found out why I'd had to write the extra essay for having a GED.

The letter from the dean of admissions told me that I had been accepted into the university *and* that I'd been selected as a finalist in a special scholarship competition for GED students!

The letter informed me there was a special panel interview for the scholarship scheduled two weeks away. *Two weeks!* It seemed like an eternity.

That night I went out with Willem and his friends. He was so proud of me, he said. He was bursting, like I was his own daughter! He kept telling everyone about how I was going to study at the university, how I was certainly going to win the scholarship, any fool could see that. He bought rounds of drinks for everyone in my honor. At last I felt like I wasn't viewed by his colleagues as just a model.

At the model dorm, Kylie and I, the final veterans, were suffering from some of the worst times yet as I waited impatiently for the day of my interview. It was so bad that I almost wished Christiane was back living with us, engaging in her sexual exploits. It would've been far better than what we were going through: It was high school spring break, and the dorm was filled with teenage girls *and* their mothers. You could barely breathe in the apartment, it was so filled with luggage and cots for the moms who refused to sleep in the bunks. The mothers were much more annoying than the would-be models themselves, each constantly dropping backbiting remarks about how *her* daughter had worked so hard and was *soooo* beautiful and was *definitely* going to get some jobs out of the go-sees she was being sent to. Oh, yeah, and the girls always got their stunning looks from their moms, that's another thing I learned.

The living conditions were intolerable, and Kylie and I shared more than one long knowing stare of sheer misery as the girls and their mothers blathered on about how exciting it was to be a model.

And in New York City! I tried to be in the dorm as little as possible, only to sleep, shower, and change clothes.

One morning I was in the bedroom, getting ready to go to a couple of castings. The apartment was blissfully empty, most of the girls having already fanned out into the city to seek their glory. I heard Kylie's phone ring. She answered it. It was a short call, and she didn't say much, just some "uh-huhs," and an "I understand."

She walked into the bedroom, stone-faced.

"What is it, Kylie?" I asked. She was silent for a moment.

"I just got a call from the Agency," she said. She was so still, I imagined that it must have been terrible news. Her eyes had a far-off look.

"Oh, God, what they'd say?" I said, expecting the worst.

"I . . ." She stuttered, "I . . . I got a campaign." She looked at me, and her eyes slowly focused. "I got . . . a campaign! Heather, I got a bloody campaign!!!"

"KYLIE!!!!" I shouted, shocked by the happy news. We jumped into each other's arms, given up to the pure joy of the moment. She'd done it, after all those nights, the self-pity, the questioning, the sullen TV watching. She'd DONE IT!

After we settled down I learned the details: The campaign was to be the face for—brace yourselves—a huge *vodka* company as they rebranded. The contract was for a year, and it was print *and* television! She was going to be making loads of money. They had to work out the details, but it looked like she was going to have to move to L.A. Kylie had hit the goldmine—and her face, fittingly, was going to be associated with vodka, her favorite.

That night when I came home, she was in her normal seat, watching TV. But what she had in her glass didn't look like a Metamucil martini. The liquid was clear. I knew she'd be celebrating, but I didn't think she'd go to the straight vodka.

"Hey, what are you drinking, Kylie?" I asked.

"Oh, this?" she asked. "Just some water. Have to keep fit and trim for the campaign. All that booze makes your face puffy, you know. I'd stay away from it, if I were you." I didn't see her drink a drop of liquor before she left for L.A.

And that's how getting a campaign *for* vodka broke Kylie's addiction *to* the stuff.

THE DATE FOR THE SCHOLARSHIP interview approached nearer and nearer, and I was becoming nervous, as if I'd been requested to walk at the Marc Jacobs show. Except instead of having to strut in the designer's clothes, I'd have to do something even more anxiety-inducing for me: answer any and all questions the panel might have about my academic and life qualifications for this scholarship.

I had mock interviews with Willem, where he'd play the part of the stern academic. Pacing back and forth in his office, he would ask me every question that could conceivably come up in my interview. Daniel would take notes. We'd finish, and Willem would break out of character.

"She did great, right, Daniel? Just great!" Willem would say. "Heather, you're going to knock their socks off, as they say."

THREE DAYS BEFORE THE INTERVIEW, I received a call. I read the caller ID: The Agency. I panicked, didn't want to answer it. So far I'd been able to squeak by on "final warning." I just needed a bit more time to settle things before leaving the model dorm.

But there was no use in avoiding the Agency. I had to face up to things.

"Hello?" I said, as nonchalantly as possible.

Rachel sounded like she was on speakerphone. Her voice was unmistakable, but her attitude wasn't.

"Hello, Heather dear, how *are* you?" She sounded like we had been bosom buddies since camp in middle school, not that she had threatened to throw me out on the street the last time we had spoken.

"Umm, good, Rachel . . . How are you?"

"Just fabulous, fabulous," she said. "Listen, Heather, I've got absolutely *unbelievable* news. Are you sitting down?"

"Yeah," I lied. I didn't know why I needed to sit down.

"*Günther Wohlheim* has requested you for an editorial—can you believe it? It's absolutely amazing!"

"Really?" I asked, in shock. Was she just trying to pull a fast one on me?

"Yes, really, it's incredible. The girl Günther originally wanted had to go to Paris for another shoot at the last minute, and they requested *you!* He's just in town for a few days to do this, and you're going to be part of it. Absolutely great."

I kinda sorta did need to sit down. Günther Wohlheim was one of the biggest photographers in the game, had photographed innumerable celebrities. His style was unmistakable, his taste unquestionable. And to get an editorial with him . . .

"The shoot's in three days. It's going to be all day upstate. We'll have you go up there the afternoon before," Rachel said, still gushing, all of a sudden my best friend, my biggest champion.

Three days? Uh-oh . . .

"Excuse me, you cut out there, Rachel, when did you say it was?"

"Three days from now. We'll go over all the details later," Rachel said.

"Oh, okay. . . ." Three days from now I was supposed to be sitting before the panel at the University of New York for the scholarship, not cavorting around in Balenciaga for Günther.

"All right, Heather, congratulations again! I knew you had it in you!" Rachel said. Yeah, *sure* she did, I thought. "Make sure you get some rest. . . . And try not to eat too much the next few days. Want you to look your best!"

Click. The line went dead.

I was stunned.

I ran back to the model dorm and found the number for the admissions office at the University of New York and dialed it quickly.

The secretary for the dean of admissions answered.

"Hi, this is Heather Johnston. I'm scheduled to interview for the Chancellor's GED Scholarship in three days," I said.

"Hello, Heather, what can I do for you?" she asked.

"Umm, yeah, I was just wondering—is that the only day I can interview? Is there no other time to come in?"

"Oh, certainly not, Ms. Johnston. The panel convenes on that day and that day only. Why, is there a problem?"

"No, no problem, I was just curious. I'll be there, trust me!"

I hung up. *Now* what was I going to do?

The editorial job was for *the* Günther. This was exactly what I'd dreamt of when stepping off that plane at JFK so many months ago with dreams of being a model carrying me to the dorm. Working with him could get me the exposure I needed to make it to the big time, finally take that next step in my career.

The prestige of the job was undeniable. But the pay, that was another issue. It was an editorial for a magazine, so the check wouldn't do anything to help my bank account. Though the exposure could lead to a campaign, if someone noticed me in it. That "if" was huge, hanging there in the air. What if nothing came after the editorial? I'd have some pretty pictures to show my grandkids. The scholarship was an "if" too, though. . . . If I was selected I'd be saved thousands of dollars in backbreaking student loan debt I'd otherwise have to take on, and I'd also have the prestige of simply having won the scholarship. And what would Willem think of me if I bailed out now?

I called the Agency.

"Hi . . . Rachel?" I said. "It's Heather."

"Oh, hey, Heather, what's up?" she said. I was obviously disturbing her, but now that she was convinced I was her number one girl, she suffered the interruption.

"Listen, is the shoot with Günther absolutely three days from now?" I asked, knowing it was silly to think that it could be changed for a no-name like me. "There's no way to . . . reschedule it, is there?"

There was a long silence on the phone line. Rachel was choking down her disbelief.

"*Günther* doesn't reschedule; *Günther* gets girls to fly halfway around the world for just fifteen minutes before his lens," she said.

"I'm sorry. . . . I . . . I can't do it," I said. I'd made my decision. "I have this scholarship interview, you see, and it's really important for my future, for you know, when I'm done with modeling—"

Her screaming broke off my sentence.

"When you're done with modeling?" she shrieked over the airwaves. "When you're done with modeling? I can make that happen sooner than you'd like, little girl. Your ass is going to be upstate at the shoot three days from now, do you understand?"

"I'm sorry, you can yell at me all you like, but I can't! I know it would be great for my career, and all, but—"

I could almost see Rachel's eyes bugging out of her skull with rage.

"You little bitch! What the *fuck* do you think we kept you around for all these months, your *brain???!*"

Rachel continued yelling. I held the phone away from my ear, letting her call me every word my mom had taught me never to use as a little girl. If I had been ambivalent at all before, *this* definitely let me know I'd made the right choice.

Rachel didn't even give me the courtesy of saying good-bye. She just hung up.

THE SCHOLARSHIP INTERVIEW was in a wood-paneled conference room at the university. Six people sat around the table as I talked about myself, my interest in art, what had led me to apply to the university. I explained how I'd had to leave high school (I didn't use the term "drop out") to pursue modeling, but now I was ready to get serious. I talked about how working at the Clijsters Gallery had given me experience that was as valuable, if not more valuable, than time in the classroom.

Surprisingly, I wasn't nervous—I guess going to a couple hundred-odd castings over the past months had made me used to walking into a room full of strangers to be judged. Those on the panel, a mix of admissions officers and professors, were kind. They asked me about myself. And not once did anyone ask me if I'd cut my hair and color it.

I shook all their hands and left the university building, stepping into the warm afternoon. It was May Day, and spring had finally come. I ended up poking around the Strand bookstore, then ambled next to the dog park at Union Square, wondering if I'd stumble across Tom Ford, whom I missed every now and then.

My phone rang. The caller ID showed a "212" area code. It was in Manhattan, but I didn't know the number. I normally screened my calls, but for some reason I decided to take this one.

It was a woman from the panel. I had been a very strong candidate before coming into the interview, and at the interview I'd convinced them of one thing—that they needed to award me the scholarship!

After giving her my thanks and telling her about twenty times to thank each and every person on the panel, I sat down on a bench, exhausted, a silly grin plastered on my face. The excitement I felt over getting the modeling gigs couldn't compare to the feeling of pride and worth over winning this scholarship. It was a new feeling, and one that I really liked.

The routine of all the others in the city washed around me, couples walking by, a businessman in a suit rushing off to an important meeting, a professional dog-walker zipping by with ten different pooches on his tangle of leashes.

They all passed, and no one seemed to notice that sitting there, right there on that bench in Union Square on that warm spring day, was the luckiest girl in the world.

19

AGAINST MY PREDICTIONS, I wasn't immediately evicted from the model dorm after turning down the prestigious Günther job. That would have been uneconomical for the Agency—they still thought they could get some money out of me.

Luke had called. Rachel was probably unable to even *think* about talking to me without descending into a shivering rage.

"Heather, you should come in, we've got some great opportunities for you . . . in Osaka!" Luke said. I remembered Margo's fate and said no thanks. Instead of being evicted, I decided to leave the model dorm of my own accord—it was just time to move on.

After Rachel's meltdown, I had been sure. I was going to get evicted from the model dorm, so I tried my best to find someplace else as soon as possible. Once again Willem came through for me. I guess I should probably be thankful to Robert and bless the day I met him—it was the Frenchman, after all, who brought me to Bungalow 8 on that fateful night, where I met my Belgian friend.

One of Willem's colleagues had a gallery in Williamsburg, Brooklyn, that had a room in the back—I could stay there in return for working reception just a couple days a week. It wasn't really a "room," per se, more like a cubbyhole with a bed in it, and with a full bathroom down the hall. But after eight months of living in the model dorm, I could put up with anything—even Brooklyn. Besides, it was just until I could get my bearings and find my own apartment, and I didn't mind so much at night, staring up at the Surface to Air and Kenzo Minami murals for inspiration. My parents, thrilled that I was going to be in college, had promised to help a bit as I started my new life as a student.

Taking an inventory of all my things as I started packing, I came across a slip of paper. It had LEE and a number scrawled on it. The brother of the beautiful South African model. He *had* been cute. I wondered if he'd remember me.

The night before I left, the new girls in the model dorm decided to send me off by taking me out for one last hurrah. They looked on me as the wise one, as I regaled them with tales of Tom Ford, Svetlana, Fashion Week, evictions. Our time at the model dorm was already becoming the stuff of legends. We went to the hot new club—one day it had simply materialized, butting up against the other clubs in West Chelsea. The girls, just arrived to the city, buzzed with excitement as they peered around, looking for celebrities and hot guys. One girl, a British model I could already peg as the Svetlana of the new generation, was working the room, trying to find some coke. She was soon sitting at a booth with two bottles and two good-looking men.

I went to the bathroom and when I returned, I just watched the group of them for some moments. They were unaware I was back. They stood clustered, a group of gorgeous tall models, the center of attention in the VIP room. And they knew it, tossing their hair back as if they didn't have a care in the world, sipping their vodka cranberries, whispering to one another about the male model they'd just seen go up to the bar. In their bodies, on their faces, I could see Laura, Lucia, Svetlana, Christiane, Kylie, Margo, even me. Flickering, the resemblances swelled and faded as the models moved within the candlelit shadows of the exclusive room. They were the new girls, the next to get their faces in magazines, all convinced you'd know them by only their first name in just a few months . . . the next top models.

I slipped out the back door of the VIP room, leaving the girls to have their fun. I wanted to get home. I had summer reading to do.

Acknowledgments

We would foremost like to thank our editor Suzanne O'Neill at Atria Books, as well as our agent Joe Veltre at Artists Literary Group for, you know, everything. We would also like to acknowledge Becki Heller for all her help with making this book happen. Also, we greatly appreciate the editorial contributions to *Secrets of the Model Dorm* made by Brian Perkins. Thanks to Lisa Mayock, Dana Loia, and Jordan Long too. Oh, and of course we'd like to say hi to all the girls who came in and out of the model dorm—the real heroes of the story. Thanks!

Amanda Kerlin wants to thank:

Thanks to my parents Ray and Trudy, whose constant love and support over the years will never be forgotten. To my family: the Kerlins, the Nowaks, the Groves, and the McEwens—I love you all. A special thanks to Rad Bratich, for always being there for me with support, and showing me what I am capable of. To Sara, Rich, Michael, Noelle, the Phoenix crew, and all the people who have made the last few years in New York unforgettable.

Phil Oh wants to thank:

I'd like to thank my parents, Timothy and Kyosik, for not pressuring me to be a doctor, lawyer, or pianist. Jane and Jim McCoy and my nieces, Catherine and Elizabeth. Also, a big thanks to Cat Hartwell and Andy Van Houten for everything they've done to convince me that this was a good idea. Oh, and my pals Ili, Jacky, Lucas, James, Jasmine, Jill, and Toni at I HEART, Maxt Shanktaneo at WOWCH, Matthew McClellan, Mike and Cromie at Popist, Lauren, Latif, DQ, Ralph, Regina and Chris, Grandin, and everyone on my MySpace friends list. Thanks guys.